D1522967

SoulSeeker

RISE TO CHAOS

ELLIOT GRAVES

Bloomington, IN Milton Keynes, UK

authorHOUSE®

AuthorHouse™
1663 Liberty Drive, Suite 200
Bloomington, IN 47403
www.authorhouse.com
Phone: 1-800-839-8640

AuthorHouse™ UK Ltd.
500 Avebury Boulevard
Central Milton Keynes, MK9 2BE
www.authorhouse.co.uk
Phone: 08001974150

First published by AuthorHouse 1/4/2007

ISBN: 978-1-4259-5917-3 (sc)

Printed in the United States of America
Bloomington, Indiana

This book is printed on acid-free paper.

A few other titles that Elliot keeps
buried in the Graveyard out back:

Rush the Wicked

Jasmine's Tears

The Redemption of Crestwood Heights

Big Thanx to the family and friends (including the good people at the Arkansas State Revenue Bldg) that have tolerated this waste of time of mine thus far. It'll most likely only get worse from here.

Write on.

Even Bigger Thanx to Brenda and Hugo...for obvious reasons.

– *Stanley*

A misspent youth still in progress...

1

The Wicker Basket had become her home away from home, or in this case her home away from the single bedroom dive embedded in the ten story pile of steel and bricks that wasn't worth the wrecking ball that it so desperately needed to put it out of its vermin infested misery that she called home. The bookstore had always had a warm and inviting feel to it ever since Jordan Carthright had first escorted her through its doors.

Jordan had always loved books just like his father who had been an English Lit. professor by trade. He'd passed his admiration for the written word down to his sole heir which would eventually lead to the opening of a depository deemed the Wicker Basket, a quaint corner of the retail market that derived its name from a receptacle that had once rested on the living room floor of the Carthright home next to the couch. It was known to house the senior Carthright's most sought after reading material whenever the idiot box; being navigated by someone other than himself, began, as he would put it, to insult his intelligence. The store was Jordan Carthright's testament to his father's never-ending quest for knowledge.

Jordan also owned the apartment that resided above the bookstore, and with this place being the closest thing that he knew of in the way of sanctuaries it wouldn't allow him to turn away the homeless amnesiac that he had found wandering the highway just outside of the very small town of Wilderbrook, Kansas when she pleaded with him for a job at his place of business.

Jordan had found this fetching young vagabond hoofing it along one of the back roads out of town after detouring through the minute settlement that was Wilderbrook when a severe traffic obstruction that the onboard tracking system he had rigged into the Mazda Miada he drove directed him off of the main path that he'd been traveling along. He had been on his way back home to Chicago from a book signing he had attended in Scottsburg, Kansas when the detour placed him directly in line with the route she'd been utilizing.

She wore a bright blue and white loose fitting flannel shirt that was draped over a white T-shirt and dangled untucked over a pair of stonewashed blue jeans. Looking up at the murky cloud cover overhead and fearing the worst, Jordan pulled over and slowed his automobile to match the pace of the stride that she refused to cease even as his passenger side window lowered.

He asked the dark haired young lady if she needed a ride. The conversation, once she had agreed to get in the car, left much to be desired. She mainly kept to her side of the vehicle, her limbs hardly ever breaching the barrier that the armrest between them seemed to serve as. Rarer still was it that he even received a fleeting glance from her. No. She just sat there staring out of the front windshield with a placid, content look on her face.

Her name was Katelyn Bree. Jordan had gotten that much out of her but any information beyond that was choppy at best. The woman who had appeared to be somewhere in the area of nineteen and twenty three years of age (Katelyn confessed to not knowing the exact number) knew where she was along with the location of the farm that she had started out from approximately ten miles away but had absolutely no memory of her life or anything else that had occurred prior to her waking up that morning. Jordan offered to drop her off at the nearest hospital but she refused. Katelyn felt fine and other than having no inkling of how she came to be in the town of Wilderbrook alone and confused she didn't think there was anything else wrong with her, especially nothing worthy of immediate medical attention.

Inquiring about where he was headed, Katelyn, figuring that Chicago was just as good a place as any, asked if she could tag along for the duration of his voyage. His indecisiveness apparent, Katelyn assured him of her passivity and swore that she wouldn't be a burden financial or otherwise but his hesitation endured. Playing on his sympathy and attempting to tug at the heartstrings of a man sensitive enough to the human condition and so taken in by the sight of a woman in peril that he would risk picking up a stranger on the side of the highway, mile by mile she managed to sway the pendulum of his trust in her direction until Jordan was absolutely convinced that what he was doing was nothing short of a good deed.

Katelyn had also triumphantly managed to dispel any conceptions that he was the one being taken for a ride, or being coerced into a situation that he would eventually regret upon conclusion. She had quickly ascertained from his composure, giving nature, quiet uncomfortable ways, and nervous tics that this man posed very little physical threat to her. Not that she feared as much. Katelyn felt more than confident that she would walk away from any physical confrontation that this man could initiate unscathed. Thankfully it didn't come to anything remotely resembling such an outcome, allowing her to peacefully remain Jordan Carthright's passenger all the way to Chicago, Illinois.

Unlocking the door to the Wicker Basket, Jordan stepped inside the darkened bookstore with his companion trailing closely behind. He'd spoken often and quite fondly of this place and upon entering she found it was all he had said it to be and more. Jordan hit the panel of switches on the wall next to the door and a shower of florescent brightness spilled down from the ceiling bringing to life a room filled with wooden stacks and shelving overflowing with literary works. The two of them proceeded down the aisle that was formed by the arrangement of the shoulder high row of stacks on either side of them as Jordan pointed in all directions while speaking, either to himself or her. The joyous tone in his voice made it hard to make a clear distinction.

The skylight above the center of the store glowed blue and ceiling fans everywhere spun as Jordan went about pointing out several sitting areas, coffee machines, and genre sections that were of particular interest to him. When Katelyn brought her eyes down from the ceiling Jordan had managed to place some considerable distance between the two of them. In fact, he was already halfway up the wooden staircase leading to the upper level of the store while she still remained on the main floor some twenty odd feet from the first stair step.

From where she stood she could see more sets of stacks beyond the railing above her. Continuing on his fevered rant, Jordan made it up a few more steps before turning and coming to the realization that he was alone in the store. He called her name a couple of times but came up dry. All is well that ends well, he supposed. He only hoped that he had done the young lady a favor by bringing her this far. She had never indicated any specific location in the city that she had desired to be dropped off in front of. Just as far as he was going was what she had said. With no memory, no contacts, place to stay, or even a change of clothes to speak of, Jordan hoped that this mysterious woman would somehow manage to safely find her way to wherever it was that she was headed.

Katelyn headed up the block as she continued to put distance between her and the bookstore. The kind gentleman had really been of subsequent use, cutting down on her travel time to a most pleasant degree. He liked his bookstore and Katelyn hoped that he'd be happy enough there to remain and not attempt to find her. As for her, well she too had to find a place of residence that she would feel comfortable occupying for the time being. Katelyn looked up at the sky. It would be getting dark soon and she was going to need a place to bed down. A reasonably secure roof over her head was going to require money; money she didn't have; money that she needed immediately. Acquiring the funds that she would need through legal channels would most assuredly expend time she didn't have. She was going to need an alternate mode of operation to accomplish her goals.

Katelyn had made it nearly six blocks away when she saw a corner grocery that sparked a particular interest inside of her. She found the patrons inside to be far and few between. The sole register in operation was being manned by a scruffy looking individual who eyed her with a lecherous gaze from the moment she stepped through the automatically parting doors. She held his gaze, those ever watchful eyes, with a reciprocating half smile as she passed in front of his counter at the front of the store and moved through the aisles. Katelyn looked up constantly as she perused over the groceries, checking to see if she still held the clerk's attention. She did and shooting him a few glances from across the market that displayed her interest in him allowed her to keep it. Soon she returned to the front of the store, her face all smiles, and leaned down on the counter next to his register.

Politely, and with as much flirtation as someone could put in a line like this, she asked if it was alright if she could use his restroom. Going along with whatever game the attractive brunette in front of him was trying to initiate, he replied with as much overt masculinity as he could muster, directing her to the back of the store. After a daintily spoken comment by Katelyn about how she hoped she didn't get lost back there laced with suggestion she headed on her way.

It didn't take long. Curious as to his missing temptress's whereabouts and with a minimal amount of heads bobbing through the aisles, the grocery store clerk abandoned his post behind the counter and headed through the doors at the back of the store marked **Employees Only** in search of the woman who had failed to return. Maybe she really had gotten lost.

Or...

Maybe she'd been back there waiting patiently for him to make the next move in their little game of seduction and seek her out in the store's more private areas so that they might consummate their obvious mutual attraction without an audience of prying eyes.

Katelyn Bree returned from the back of the store alone. She made her way directly to the front counter. Taking note of the patrons who continued about with their shopping, Katelyn opened the register and relieved it of all its paper currency before exiting the store, the patrons inside unaware of the robbery that had just taken place. She crossed the street and headed up the block making the first corner that she came to. Katelyn suspected that her gentleman caller was still wandering the shadowy depths of the back storeroom seeking out the sexual rendezvous that he was sure laid in wait for him. Katelyn, in the meantime, went in search of a newspaper box.

She spent that first night in town within the confines of a cheap motel that cared more for the money it was paid than the comings and goings of its clientele. She sat on the floor with her back against the bed and the television on the stand in front of her glowing bright. She flipped through the classifieds hoping to make her stay in this place as short as possible. Katelyn didn't like it there. It didn't feel right; her refuge being this closely surrounded by so many people, strange people that she didn't know, didn't trust; coming and going at all hours, listening through the walls, peeping through windows.

She needed her privacy and though this place provided lodging, seclusion was definitely in short supply.

The next morning Katelyn found herself in the building manager's office sitting across from the slumlord who ran the Cumberland Apt. building. He was contemplating whether or not to render the hollowed out confines of apt. 714 over to her. The apparition of two months' rent in cold hard cash helped sway his decision. Katelyn had her own place. True, it was reprehensible as far as dwellings went but it would provide her with a more reasonable amount of isolation when she needed it which is what mattered. Now all she had to do was chase off the dust bunnies, brush away the cobwebs, and furnish the place. To do that she would need more money. Her current supply dwindled but it was sure to get her through the next few days.

Too many repeat performances of how she acquired her initial funding would only bring more attention to her presence than was needed. Another option would be a legitimate source of income. Katelyn thought of the kind gentleman who had given her a ride into town and the bookstore that he owned and wondered if she had completely tapped the well of his generosity.

2

Katelyn Bree had been on the Wicker Basket payroll for the past four years. It wasn't much but it was enough for her to scrape out something that closely resembled a living. The lights were on in her completely furnished apartment. The refrigerator was stocked. As far as she was concerned Jordan Carthright had done alright by her.

It was just another day at the Wicker Basket. Customers coming and going; their needs being tended to by the courteous and always helpful staff. Katelyn had quite the reputation within the social circles that inhabited the bookstore. All the employees had been made aware of her amnestic affliction and were informed about the origins of her relationship with Jordan by the man himself. The rest she took care of all on her own.

Katelyn's strict work ethic raised an eyebrow in even the most loyal of the store's employees. When there were no customers to be helped she cleaned; vacuumed the carpet; polished the wooden stacks; dusted the books; even cleared away the cobwebs that formed in the less trafficked areas of the store.

When there were patrons that required her help Katelyn came to their aid equipped with a near infinite knowledge of whatever subject the customer happened to be interested in. Any staff member close enough to see her in action would assume it was attributed to the fact that on her down time (breaks, lunches, before her shifts, after her shifts) she could be found roaming the store speed reading every book she could get her hands on. Katelyn Bree. First one up. Last one down. She was Jordan Carthright's star. The store owner's pet.

In all the time she had been there working side by side with the rest of the staff she had yet to make a single friend or string more than a few words together in anyone's presence that wasn't work related. She had walked into the building; the break room; closed in on ongoing conversations and caused immediate silence on several occasions. Katelyn had always known she was different ever since her first interaction with Jordan which was the first instance of human interaction that she could remember. But the more people that she came into contact with the more she felt like an outsider and became that much more withdrawn.

Tripp Manning was propped up on his forearm and leaning to the side, his upper body slumped over the open book he had lying on the counter. Tripp was stationed at what had been jokingly dubbed **The Coffee House** by the employees and regulars who frequented the counter where various caffeinated drinks were sold. The lack of thirsty readers had afforded him the opportunity to lose himself in the pages in front of him. That is until Morgan Paleto walked up and patted out a quick drum solo on the counter next to his book with the palms of her hands. She had his attention.

"So," she said, leaning forward on both of her forearms. "What's the latest?"

"Latest?" Tripp hoisted himself up higher so that he could see over her brown head of hair. He spotted the raven beauty that was Katelyn Bree in one of the reading areas off to his right. She was clad in all black from the form fitting T-shirt she wore to the black steel toed boots, one of which was propped up on the small table in front of her. She rocked herself back and forth in the chair that she sat in as she flipped through the book she held at the rate of about one page per second. "By latest you mean my latest theory on the origins of our little space cadet?" Tripp leaned back down to her grinning face and took that as an affirmative. "That's just it. She's an alien. Left behind when the mothership had to double time it back to their home planet that was about to be engulfed by an intergalactic war."

"Where did you come up with that one?" Morgan said through her laughter.

"No. I'm serious this time. Her home planet, collateral damage. Now she's stuck here...with us...for the rest of her life."

Laughing harder at the fact that he was trying to be serious, Morgan attempted to speak. "I suppose that's about as plausible as anything else you've come up with." Her giggles continued.

A few other guesses by Tripp had included: escaped mental patient; the likes of which wasn't welcomed back into the asylum; pod person from the planet Pluto; Russian spy planted in the bookstore on a mission to steal information. Each one had succeeded in getting a slight chuckle out of Morgan and helped to pass the slow flowing hours in the store.

Zackery Collins, a regular, entered the store and immediately moved towards the muffled sounds of laughter he heard. "Aren't you two supposed to be working?" he asked, his emerald eyes accenting the smile he wore.

"We are working," the short brown haired young man behind the Coffee House counter said to him. "Keeping up with that head case is a full time job."

Zackery looked out across the bookstore toward the sitting area that Katelyn inhabited off in the distance. "What's my girl been up to today?"

"Why don't you go ask her?" Morgan said, daring him to make contact with the recluse. It was a sporadic pastime that the occupants of the Wicker Basket used to amuse themselves during particular dead stretches. It was always an amusement to pretend not to be watching when all you were really doing was watching after one individual had dared another to initiate a one on one interaction with the strange girl while others gawked at the awkward spectacle it would inevitably grow into.

Zack didn't mind much being the guinea pig at the butt of their little experiment. He'd taken the bait quite a few times and never regretted doing so. His audience of two watched as he walked over in her direction, once again taking them up on the dare, hoping they would get as much pleasure out of it as he did. When he made it over to the sitting area that Katelyn resided in he stepped down into the large depression in the floor and stopped, waiting to see if she would make even the slightest acknowledgement of his presence. She didn't, same as always. He continued to stand there for a moment watching her as she turned page after page before taking a few more steps.

"Stop," Katelyn commanded.

He halted his motion and stood in place. She continued moving through her book. "Stop what?" he asked. "I haven't done anything yet."

"No. Not yet. But you were about to offer me a mocha late, cappuccino, or coffee; ask me what book I'm reading; offer to take me out for a drink. Don't bother."

"For all you know I could have come over here with some all new material," he said, trying to keep the conversation going. He knew Tripp and Morgan were too far away to hear them clearly, if at all, but he knew they were watching and enjoying every minute of it just as he was. "You're not the only one into expanding their mind."

"What are you into?" she asked him, closing the book she held and giving him her eyes. "Why do you keep doing this? What do you want?" Zackery was flabbergasted. The most that he'd ever gotten out of her from these little exchanges were very embarrassing, sometimes extremely audible, declinations of whatever proposal he was attempting to make to her. "Everybody else that's done this to me has only tried it again once and occasionally someone goes for a third outing. This is number fourteen for you. Why do you keep bothering me?"

She had succeeded in reddening his cheeks once more. "You knew what we were doing this whole time?" He looked behind him over at Morgan and Tripp at the Coffee House counter. He couldn't hear them but he could see the giggles erupting from the pair. "Why didn't you say something?" he asked, turning back to Katelyn.

"You didn't answer my question."

"What? I was trying to get to know you. You got a problem with people talking to you or something?"

"I have a problem with people talking to me just to have an excuse to make fun of me some more."

"You should have said something," Zackery said in an attempt to defend his actions.

"I wasn't aware that that particular fact needed to be explained to you upon our initial meeting. Please leave now." Katelyn went back to her book.

"What's that you're reading?"

"You know, your new material has an odd familiarity to it."

Zackery grabbed a chair and pulled it up beside her. "You didn't answer my question."

When he sat down Katelyn looked up at him again. "I thought I asked you to leave? I'm sure Morgan and Tripp are eagerly awaiting your return."

"You asked. Doesn't mean I have to. And they can wait. I want to talk to you for a moment."

"What the hell is he doing?" Tripp said to Morgan. It was extremely rare that any humorous exchange that was perpetrated on Katelyn lasted this long and it was unheard of for anyone to settle in and make themselves as comfortable as Zackery seemed to be getting.

"Feel free to go over and find out."

"What do you want?" Katelyn asked.

"A chance to make it right. Make up for being such a shit to you."

"You can accomplish that by leaving."

"How about dinner? My treat."

"There's that or you could get up from that chair, turn around, and leave me the hell alone. The latter might be gentler on your wallet."

"You're not gonna budge, are you?"

She closed the book she held and stood up. "My break's over. I have to get back to work."

When she left Zackery made his way back to the counter where his two accomplices waited. They unleashed a floodgate of laughter upon his return.

"What happened?" Morgan asked him when her laughter subsided.

"Ask me again later," Zackery said, his eyes on Katelyn as she moved toward the nearest customer she could find.

Zackery hung around the Wicker Basket until Katelyn's shift was over. Then he followed her. Followed her down the block; around the corner; up the street. Intrigue had gotten the better of him. Who was she? Where was she going? What did she do with herself when she wasn't on the clock at the Wicker Basket? Just a few of the burning questions that he so dreadfully desired to have answered. What he did know for sure was that she definitely would have objected to the way he went about his fact finding mission.

The Chicago night had engulfed them but none the less he continued his pursuit. Katelyn turned into a bar. When Zack stepped inside he was immediately taken in by the seedy element that mingled all about the smoke filled interior of this place. He found Katelyn at the bar and quickly rushed to her side, instinctively wanting to huddle next to someone he knew for the safety that numbers might provide in this hostile environment. She, of course, was less than excited to see him.

"You come here often?" he said to her.

"Yes, as a matter of fact I do and I don't recall ever seeing you here before." She pulled a cigarette out of a pack lying on the bar. Placing it between her lips, Katelyn produced a wooden match. She struck it on the bar top and brought the flame up. "What happened, you go out for a stroll, see the decorative sign outside, and decide to pop in for a beer?"

He watched the smoke expel from her lips and nostrils in complete astonishment. "I didn't know you smoked."

"I don't see how you could've. Jordan doesn't allow it in the store and we've never interacted in any other venue." Katelyn finished her double shot of whiskey. "Until now."

"You're just full of surprises, aren't you?"

"And you're bothersome."

"Hey, I'm trying to make conversation. You get to know me and who knows. Your opinion of me might just change."

"I'd expect as much though I doubt it would be for the best." Katelyn ordered another drink.

She fended off, carefully evaded, and skillfully dodged his prying questions through the five doubles and six beers that she ordered while sitting through, for the most part, a one-sided conversation. She'd asked him to leave several times and through his cunning linguistic skills and pure stubbornness Zackery was able to talk his way around quite a few premature exits by offering to pay for her next drink, redirecting her request by instigating a conversation about various reasons why she would want him gone, among other riffraff. Katelyn could have forced the issue, seen to it that he departed her company, but there was something going on deep inside of her that wouldn't let her do it. Anyhow. It was time to go.

Katelyn tucked the unfinished pack of cigarettes into her pants pocket and stood up from her seat at the bar. "Thanks for the drink but I have to be getting home."

"Hold on a sec. I'll walk you."

"Don't worry about it. I can manage."

Katelyn left Zackery at the bar and continued down the street she had been on before making her pit stop. But something was different now. Different about her disposition now than when she had left the Wicker Basket earlier. Katelyn had a smile on her face. Not a big one. Not a bright toothy grin that spread from one cheek to the other but it was a smile. Lip corners cocked up at both ends. No matter how slight, there was no denying it. And then...it was gone.

She headed down a staircase toward the subway station that she was expecting to deliver her within two blocks from the place she called home. That's when it hit her; when she realized that something was wrong. The bowels of the subway station were virtually empty aside from a few wandering commuters but her worry increased all the same.

Zackery moved down the staircase into the subway station. He made it through the turnstile and hustled down to the nearest platform. The scatter of individuals leaning against the walls and wandering around the concrete pillars (mostly winos and an assortment of other unsavory characters) left no sign that Katelyn had come this way at all. He continued along the platform wanting to give the area one quick pass before admitting to himself that he'd lost her.

Other than the humiliation that would be his to bear, the bill for Zackery's unwanted act of chivalry was also going to include a more than thirty minute hike in the opposite direction of where he should have started for home along with the sure to be sore feet he would have to suffer when he finally did make it back to his apartment. Looking around he could see that Katelyn was nowhere in sight.

He, on the other hand, had unwittingly caught the eye of a few of the unsavory individuals upon stepping onto the platform. Individuals who lingered about and were currently peeling themselves off of the walls and moving in his direction. Zackery was ready to leave anyway and the fact that he wanted to avoid a trip to the emergency room being tallied to his bill hurried him along.

He didn't make it more than a few steps before witnessing the emergence of Katelyn from behind one of the stone pillars. "Why are you following me?" she asked as she approached him.

Zackery looked back over his shoulder at the oncoming trouble and then back at her. "I just wanted to see to it that you got home safe. Speaking of which..." He took another quick look over his shoulder. "Can we talk about this later? I think we should leave."

"Yes. Leave." Katelyn continued her march in his direction. "You're leaving this station and I'm going home...alone. Now."

"Sure you wouldn't like some company there, sweetheart?" a voice bellowed from behind Zack's back. His backdrop was soon engulfed by a small swarm of leather vested, tattooed, chain link pierced ruffians.

"Positive," Katelyn said, tilting her head to the side and addressing the one who'd spoken. Her head moved back to its original position. "Get out of here."

"You got it," Zack responded. "But I think we should leave together. You know. Just in case."

"Wait a minute. Nobody's going anywhere." Zack took a step toward her and felt a palm grip his shoulder, halting his movement. Katelyn let her eyes drift away from Zackery and move over to the fellow who was speaking. He began to close the distance between the two of them. "At least not until I say so. This party's just getting started. You wouldn't want to be rude; walk out before the first dance, would ya, sweetheart?"

Stopping directly in front of her, the pasty faced, shaggy haired individual took a quick peek back over his shoulder after hearing the sound of the young lady's companion trying to make a move toward them and being instantly restrained by the hoods all around him.

"Leave her alone!" Zack shouted, hoping at least to draw more attention to their situation. The winos looked on but didn't seem to mind what was happening.

"Is that what you want, babe?" the hooligan in front of her said, the piercings in his face glinting at her as he spoke. "For me to leave you alone?" He rubbed his hand up the bare skin of her arm. "Or maybe you'd be interested in something else."

Katelyn glared back at the lascivious look in his eyes and nonchalantly reached over with her right hand and took hold of his. Applying an ever increasing amount of pressure that resonated through every bone in his hand, Katelyn watched as salivation morphed into gritting distress; confidence into panic; the expectation of pleasure into the realization of extreme pain. When he dropped to his knees Katelyn watched the expressions on the faces of her victim's four cronies change in unison. His cries of anguish brought two of them in her direction.

Katelyn twisted swiftly, bringing her captive to his feet; feet that subsequently left the concrete floor beneath them as his body soared through the air towards the newspaper boxes that lined the wall approximately twenty-six feet away. The first one of his accomplices to reach her received a stomping kick to his solar plexus that sent him gliding back, first through the air then across the platform floor a few yards past Zack and the two hoods that continued to hold him hostage, the three of which now looking on in utter amazement as her third attacker got within inches of her.

He swung once with a left. Again with a right. Katelyn ducked them both, answering the second missed punch with an uppercut that slammed into his stomach with the impact of a swiftly swung sledgehammer, doubling him over. Katelyn pulled her deeply imprinted fist away from his body and let him fall to the ground clutching his abdomen.

She moved toward the remaining two on either side of Zack, watching them tremble at her approach. The desperate soul to his left made a run at her and Zackery blinked in disbelief as the bookstore clerk threw her hand out in a blur of motion and clasped her fingers around his neck before the fist that he had cocked back ever had the chance to come forward at her.

He clawed at her wrist with both hands as she squeezed his windpipe closed while slowly lifting him up from the ground. He gagged and wheezed his breaths in and out. His feet kicked and struggled to find their footing but eventually he was kicking at nothing but air. Katelyn's visage remained fluidly emotionless even as she pulled him into her and pushed him away with enough force to send him flying up over Zack and his fellow onlooker's head before he dropped down to the concrete several yards behind them.

Her continued approach sent the remaining member of the unruly rabble scrambling away for his life and left Zack wondering if any painful repercussions were about to be inflicted on his person. The sound of the oncoming subway train distracted her eyes from him. The flashing lights behind the rapidly passing subway car windows slowed into a dull glow and the car doors slid open.

"Go home," Katelyn uttered before turning, walking, and boarding the train.

Zackery couldn't heed her advice fast enough, moving cautiously past the bent and twisted bodies that lie in his path writhing on the floor and moaning in agony. He hurried up the steps hoping to make it to the streets above before the antagonizers that Katelyn and he, mostly Katelyn, had just faced got back up on their feet.

Too angered to sit, Katelyn remained standing, holding onto one of the metal handles above her the entire train ride back to her neighborhood. If she didn't mind wasting the money she might have considered taking a cab home tomorrow. The nerve of those guys, was all she could think. Bastards! And when those thoughts faded the images of the fight that had taken place played over in her head in vivid detail. People were watching. They had seen her. The way she dispatched of her numerous attackers, so quickly, so forcefully. Someone had to have noticed the abnormality of it all. The abilities she possessed; the ones she felt most assuredly labeled her as different; Katelyn had always done her best to mask, but as tonight clearly demonstrated some instances were more difficult to contain than others.

Katelyn departed the train and the station once she reached her stop. She moved through the night laid out before her with that much more caution. The Cumberland apartment building wasn't far. Katelyn picked up the pace. She was anxious to get home and get some rest. After all that had transpired she still had to be at work tomorrow morning.

3

Katelyn Bree walked into the Wicker Basket at fifteen 'til ten the next morning to the usual assortment of rudely staring eyes that always greeted her. She clocked in, donned the nametag that identified her as an employee of this establishment, and began attending the customers who had been filtering into the store ever since it opened two hours before her shift began.

Zackery's entrance coincided with that of Tripp Manning's who was in the process of taking more than a few peeks at his wristwatch (five til two) hoping that Zack's barely coherent babbling wouldn't slow his stride to the time clock.

"Who knows? Maybe she took kung fu in another life. What are you getting at? I'm gonna be late for work."

Zack couldn't believe what he was hearing. "You of all people don't think that it's just a little strange that the walking X-Files episode was somehow capable of taking out four psychopaths without barely batting an eyelash and still show up for work on time the next day?" Tripp had played at being a conspiracy theorist, quite an amusing one as far as the Wicker Basket employees were concerned, but the events of the previous night had transformed Zackery Collins into the real thing. Stories of alien invasions, cover up conspiracies, demonic possessions all polluted his mind to the point that he barely managed a couple of hours of sleep the previous night.

It was impossible, that encounter; the outcome of which and everything in between. No matter how many angles he looked at it from or how many ways he tried to rationalize the showcase he had witnessed the fiber of his being that screamed impossibility at every turn continued to vocalize its opinion until he had no choice but to listen.

Lunchtime.

Katelyn enjoyed her PB&J, orange soda, pork rinds, and apple half in the seclusion of the apartment above the bookstore. Jordan was present, of course, constantly moving from one end of the gadget littered apartment to the other. Paying little attention to her gracious host, she glanced over the kitchen counters, living room floor, the kitchen table that she sat behind, all cluttered with six-legged mechanical marvels, gyroscope burdened creations, program boards, and various other pieces of entangled wire and plastic that were visible along every line of sight. Projects begun and forgotten; incomplete works; creations in their final stage. They were everywhere. The place was a mess.

Jordan Carthright passed in front of her vision again. "Hey," she called to him.

Tapping a sauntering iron to a lime green program board, Jordan halted what he was doing and turned toward the kitchen table. "What?" he said as if she'd just startled him. "What is it?" His agitation at her interruption showed on his face along with the worry of whatever it was that was bothering her.

Katelyn understood that whatever it was that he was working on, no matter how trivial, meant a considerable amount to him and the fact that he would distract himself from his work to take heed to the disturbance that was her was a big thing as far as she was concerned. "Anybody say anything to you about me?"

"What is it, little lady? Those guys downstairs still giving you a hassle?"

Katelyn had never come to him about it but Jordan had been well aware of her reputation throughout the store along with the frequently lamented taunts that the personnel and occasional patron lavished upon her. She would never make much of it and shunned all senses of accomplishment whenever he made an attempt to come to the her defense or reprimand an employee for their behavior. Secretly she was flattered, however unnecessary she found it. Katelyn found it quite pleasing that Jordan Carthright saw fit to even make an attempt at defending her. Perhaps it could have been the fact that he was the only one to have done so that made him stand out so much in her mind and arouse such feelings.

Katelyn stood up from the table. "Guess not. I'm going to head back down and get to work. Thanks for your help."

Taking up for her the way he did, watching her exit his apartment after yet another odd encounter with her, even Jordan had to admit noticing the air of strangeness that seemed to follow her wherever she went.

She headed back down the stairs toward the bookstore below, confident that news of the spectacle Zackery had witnessed the previous night hadn't reached the ears of her employer and possibly jeopardized her employment at the Wicker Basket. Mr. Carthright remained unaware but that didn't necessarily mean that Zackery had kept his mouth shut. Reaching the guard rail, looking down at the stacks from the upper level, and seeing Zackery attached to the hip to Tripp Manning, talking his ear off, she was sure of it.

"Just make sure you call me before you punch out."

"Whatever," Tripp said, hoping to shoo him off with his response. It worked out in his favor and as he watched his friend's back putting some considerable distance between them Tripp caught sight of the sleek figured brunette out of the side of his eye. When he turned to get a better look he found that she had been taking in an eyeful of him. Shaking off the eerie feeling that shuddered through him, he immediately turned his attention back to the unopened boxes of creamer and sugar he had sitting on the Coffee House counter. He sliced the lids open down the center along the strip of tape that held the two identical sections of cardboard together.

"Aw come on, Zack! You can't be serious," Tripp complained as he came to a sudden halt on the sidewalk allowing Zackery to progress three steps in front of him before he too came to a stop and turned to find out what the problem was. "I mean look at this place," he said, his right hand motioning toward the beer logo embroidered tavern window. "If the girl's whacked out enough to spend her nights sucking in muffler exhaust and meth fumes then that's a little bit more about her personal life than I'd care to know about."

"Look, I'm going inside...and doing so under the pretense that you're the type of friend that wouldn't let another friend walk into a place like this alone." Zackery turned and continued on his way again.

"You've done it before and nothing happened."

Zackery stopped walking again but this time kept his back to him. "The first round's on me."

Tripp had regretted placing the phone call to Zackery ten seconds into it and that feeling had yet to leave him. Whatever mysteries this bar held, whatever wonders that Zackery was so eager to let him in on might have been worth the hours of nighttime T.V. he was forsaking along with the series of drinks he planned on siphoning out of his reckless companion.

"First two rounds," Tripp demanded and resumed his stride along with the friend in front of him. Zackery entered the smoggy atmosphere of the establishment followed by Tripp who was now wondering if the payment that he had settled for would even begin to be settlement enough.

Zackery scanned the area around the bar while Tripp tried his best not to make direct eye contact with any of the regulars. Zackery quickly found what he was looking for and signaled Tripp to follow him. She was seated at the far end of the bar where the counter made a corner, making it easy for her to spot their approach. Although there was nothing in her expression that said she was pleased to see him, Zackery helped himself to the seat next to her, dragging Tripp along for the ride.

"Katelyn," Tripp said, greeting her. "Funny meeting you here." When the bartender approached he ordered two beers.

"And then there were two," Katelyn said to herself, promptly finishing her tequila shot.

"Well seeing as how we had such a good time the other night I thought I should start frequenting this place a little more often."

"Is that what you thought?" she said to Zack, having to turn and give him her eyes.

"Yeah. And speaking of last night, do you mind telling me where you learned to handle yourself like that?"

Katelyn hopped down off the stool and took up her bottle of beer. The next thing Zackery knew her back was to him and she was slowly putting more and more distance between the two of them. Tripp had also turned to watch but unlike his friend he quickly lost interest. "Freak," he spoke softly into his bottle before turning it up. It wasn't until Zackery climbed out of his chair that his interest in anything other than his free beverages was sparked. "Hey, where are you going?"

Ignoring him completely, Zackery continued in his pursuit to close the distance between him and the fleeing femme. The thunderous roar that was the music that the band played began to grow louder in his ears as he approached the area of this establishment that housed a stage and spread out dance floor to cater to the band and the crowd they played for.

Katelyn slowed.

His approach remained steady.

Eventually his chest was against her back. Staring out at the writhing bodies that covered the varnished hardwood floor, she made no move to get away from him or did anything for that matter to express any discord for his current proximity. Having previously witnessed her ability to fend off any unwanted physical contact, it was with the sincerest caution that he went about his next course of action. Zackery slid his hand across her hip and as if the sensation of that wasn't enough, the feel of Katelyn's body leaning back into him, the soft, somber strands of hair brushing across his left cheek as she made herself comfortable on his shoulder nearly set his blood on fire.

When her body began to gently sway from side to side with the pulsating rhythm that filled the air all around them Zackery had no choice but to take her lead. He wondered if she had any idea of just how long he'd desired to touch her in such a way; to know the feel of her body pressed against his. He wondered if she had any inkling of what she was doing to him now.

Tripp sat at the bar taking in the bizarre episode that was unfurling some distance in front of him with no clue as to where this was all headed. Whatever those two were up to he just wanted it to succumb to whatever resolution lie in wait before one of the Neanderthals roaming the premises found probable cause to shatter one of the numerous beer bottles floating around and hold the jagged shards of the piece remaining in his or her grip to his throat.

As Katelyn slowly turned away from the grungy, festive scene that had once held her so captive Zackery continued to hold her body against his until he found himself holding this shadowy vision by the small of her back. He stared down into a sultry set of dark brown eyes and did his best to just hold her captivating gaze without pressing his luck to the utmost extreme by leaning in to place his lips against hers. On the surface he looked calm as ever, not showing the slightest hint of the storm raging its way through his body.

"You looking for a good time?" she said to him softly, leaning her lips in closer to his ear, making sure she'd be heard.

"I think I just found one," he said, breathing in the scent of her hair.

"Well...from now on..." Lowering her head, she breathed warm breath on the side of his neck. "Start looking for it someplace else. I'd really hate to have to leave Mr. Carthright short one loyal customer. Am I understood?"

She brushed the tip of her nose across his cheek as she turned her back to him once more. This time Zackery remained where he stood and watched her take her leave of him, turning up her bottle as she walked. He turned and headed back to the bar, retaking his place beside Tripp. "What the hell was that about?" Tripp asked him.

Zackery took hold of one of Tripp's bottles. "I think she's warming up to me," he said before taking a drink.

"If you ask me, that girl's a bad influence on you. You're almost as insane as she is."

Morgan Paleto was manning the counter at the Coffee House when Jordan Carthright came walking through the entrance of the Wicker Basket. He headed straight for her station awkwardly dodging the wandering customers along the way. When he finally reached the counter Tripp was in the process of joining Morgan at her post. "Oh, Tripp," Jordan said as if he were surprised to find him there.

"Yeah, Mr. Carthright. What can I do you for?"

"It seems we had a small delivery mix-up during the morning shift. I'm going to need you to take the van and make a quick pick up for me."

Tripp moved over to the cappuccino machine and slid a paper cup under one of the three spigots. He pressed the button labeled *Almond.* "Can it wait, Mr. Carthright? I just clocked out for break."

Jordan turned his eyes up and occupied himself with his thoughts for a moment. "Actually no. Not really. It can't. Is Craig still here?"

"Clocked out for lunch ten minutes ago," Tripp informed him.

Disappointed once more, Jordan turned his eyes pleadingly toward Morgan. "Do you mind?" he asked her.

Morgan smiled pleasingly. "No problem, Mr. Carthright. Nobody except Tripp is drinking right now anyways."

"Thanks," he said and started on his way. "I'll be right back with the address," he called back to her. "Oh, and take Katelyn along. I want her to start getting out more and familiarizing herself with some of our outside clientele."

Every ounce of cheer that she possessed suddenly began to drain from her face at the mere mention of that dreaded name. Noticing her apparent tension, Tripp predictably fell into chuckles. "Looks like you've got a problem now," he said to her.

Morgan was seated behind the steering wheel guiding the white Wicker Basket company van with the name embroidered on both sides in all capital light brown lettering to a coffee shop across town that was currently heavy two cases of books that were earmarked for an entirely different destination. They made the pick up and were on their way to make the drop off.

Katelyn hadn't said so much as one word to her for the entire duration of the trip. Morgan had even been so bold as to try and strike up a conversation with her over such asinine topics as whether or not she wanted to change the radio station or if she preferred to leave it where it was. Whenever she didn't outright ignore her completely she would only answer with a hunch of her shoulders or a wave of her hand. Engrossed in a state of utter silence and sightseeing, Katelyn just kept to her open black khaki shirt over a white T-shirt, black slacks, and black and white low top Converse wearing self. Leaning back in her seat with one foot pressed against the dashboard, it took nothing but the view outside of her window to keep her amused.

With the second half of their delivery done Katelyn was left with the duty of securing the rear doors of the van while Morgan climbed back into the driver's seat preparing to take them back to the Wicker Basket. It was all Morgan could do to mask her eagerness to finally get this social experience over with.

Katelyn finished securing the dolly in the back of the van and hopped out to the ground below. She closed one door, went to close the other, and froze. Katelyn could tell that he wasn't paying very close attention. With the cell phone pressed against the side of his head, the man behind the wheel of the automobile went on with his conversation with little regard for the environment outside of his car.

Unfortunately the small child who appeared to be four or five years of age didn't seem to be paying much attention either as he ran after the fleeing red ball that bounced away from him across the supermarket parking lot. His mother busied herself with the grocery bags that she clumsily tried to shove into the backseat of her car. She called out to the child constantly in a sweet motherly manner, but with her head tucked inside the car she remained unaware of the impending danger that lie in wait.

But Katelyn was. She was aware of the incident set to transpire off in the distance in front of the van far from where Morgan had parked the Wicker Basket transport, and now she found herself stuck with the dilemma of what to do with that knowledge. Intervention could mean exposure. The incident was set to take place some three hundred and ninety four feet away from her within the next thirteen seconds.

Chances were good that her preventative measures would be effective, but the option to simply close the door and climb into the van with Morgan was still on the table. She had nothing to gain with either choice. The only question Katelyn struggled with now was whether or not this kid's life was worth the trouble that saving it could possibly bring down on her. In the end it came down to the realization that she was more than adequately equipped to deal with whatever situation arose after the fact. This child, however, was at the mercy of his situation, a situation that he was presently unaware of, the outcome of which was sure to be dire indeed.

Morgan sat behind the steering wheel waiting to hear the slamming sound of the second rear door. She grew that much more agitated with each passing second that she was deprived of the sound that would signal the end of this excursion and the eminent termination of this cruel coupling. Morgan finally turned to see what was keeping Katelyn and found nothing but an open door behind her. She faced front just in time to catch sight of her would-be passenger moving off in front of the van and breaking out into a sprint as she made it to the street just beyond the coffee shop parking lot. "Great," Morgan said. "Now what?"

Ignoring the honking horns of the vehicles that were forced to screech to a halt to avoid colliding with the body that sped across the pavement in front of them, Katelyn pumped her arms and legs at an increasingly furious pace, the bouncing red ball, approaching distracted driver, and oblivious child, all in her sights. Not even this mad woman very audibly disturbing the flow of traffic had been enough to distract this motorist from his phone call or turn this eager youth's attention from his pursuit. Katelyn's rate of speed increased to a point that she subconsciously knew would seem freakish to any onlooker present. But what other choice did she have if she was to prevent the incident that most assuredly lingered on the horizon.

The bouncing red ball hopped off of the sidewalk and landed on the street. The cell phone maintained its siren call. The child laughingly continued its pursuit. Katelyn dug deeper and ran faster. She saw his eyelids spread wide open and the phone drop from his fingers as he clutched two fists around the steering wheel. The kid was inches away from the front bumper and the screaming brakes that closed in on him. A great swell of astonishment and shock engulf his tiny face. It would take that to get his attention, Katelyn thought as she stretched out her arms and reached her hands down to scoop him up.

Diving back to the sidewalk, she barely managed to dodge the promising damage of the barreling automobile herself as she took care to try and shelter the child as she fell onto the pavement and rolled across the sidewalk. The noise of all the excitement had alerted the mother to the commotion involving her offspring, subsequently prompting the startled woman to rush headlong and irrationally panicked in Katelyn's direction. Katelyn released the kid resting quietly on top of her body. Ignoring the screaming rants of the woman that hurriedly approached them, Katelyn focused her eyes and mind on the automobile that had swerved just in time to avoid colliding with both her body and that of the youngster that she took up in her arms. Too bad his reflexes weren't quick enough to miss the red ball that was able to accomplish a single touchdown on its hood before the momentum of the vehicle veered off on a new path.

Katelyn violently urged the infantile body off of hers as she witnessed both oncoming and rear traffic recklessly adjusting themselves to make way for this out of control automobile. *Just my luck*, Katelyn thought as she made it to her feet. The discombobulated pilot *would* make the snap judgment to steer the car towards the gas station across the street. Stopping the car from slamming into a set of pumps right side first was unavoidable.

It was the fire that had been sparked by the colliding machinery over the gasoline drenched ground that prompted another explosive burst of motion from Katelyn. The once distracted driver who had nearly run down a small child was in the process of reprising his roll, only now it was the after effects of the collision that kept him too preoccupied to notice the scene taking place outside of his car.

The flames that had sprang up around the vehicle prevented Katelyn from gaining access to the bloody faced man through the driver's side door. Maneuvering around to the other side, Katelyn took hold of the door handle and the frame. With one sharp tug she pulled the hunk of metal open and threw her upper body into the car. She snatched away the safety belt holding this disoriented mass in place. Katelyn crumpled up the lapels of his suit jacket in her fists and jerked his limp and battered body out of the car.

The blaze grew brighter and the flames grew hotter as the fire all about sought to swallow the automobile whole. Dragging her parcel away from the car in one hand, Katelyn twisted her body and hurled the man through the glass window of the gas station just before the car's fuel tank exploded. The force of the blast sent Katelyn's body rocketing after the one she'd just tossed. A shelf of single serving cookies and potato chips made an attempt to help cushion her crash landing but did little to soften the blow. Aggravated and annoyed with the outcome of this fiasco, Katelyn turned to get a look at the moaning heap that was the previous operator of the flaming auto outside and guessed that between the two of them she had definitely fared the better.

Morgan's face was still locked in a state of shock even though the fire department had long since extinguished the roaring blaze and the medical personnel on site were already tending to the very much alive, barely injured participants of this accident scene that they had been summoned to. One of which happened to be none other than Katelyn Bree. She sat in the back of one of the ambulances present; the back doors open and her legs dangling in front of the back bumper, having her wounds, which consisted of only a few cuts and scrapes, tended to and bandaged up by a pair of gentlemen who simultaneous congratulated her bravery while scolding her brash behavior.

It wasn't until the suggestion was brought up that she accompany them back to the hospital for a more thorough check-up that Katelyn began to display a more resistant demeanor with regard to their studious attention to her wellbeing. Katelyn hopped out of the ambulance, planting her feet down firmly on the concrete below. "Look, fellas," she said, spinning around and raising her palms up in the air beside her as she backed away from them. She lowered them again. "I appreciate the concern, but as far as the hospital is concerned I can assure that it's not necessary." As far as she was concerned she'd received more than enough attention and a far too overtly thorough examination of both her physical and mental being than she felt comfortable allotting to these people. Katelyn continued to remain weary of any further inspection of her by these people.

"Ma'am, our follow up examination will be as noninvasive as deemed necessary. We just want to make sure that you're not suffering from any complications that might be more easily detected back at the emergency room."

"I'm fine," she said. "I've got to get back to work."

Katelyn turned and started on her way away from the two overly concerned caretakers only to run smack into Morgan Paleto. "Katelyn, What's wrong with you? Go with them," Morgan said in a tone that was almost demanding, making Katelyn feel that much more uncomfortable about hurrying off in such a rush. "Don't worry about Carthright. I'll go back and tell him what happened. I'm pretty sure he'll find it in him to forgive your absence just this once."

Now she was just being snide, Katelyn thought, but in a way she could see the logic in what everyone around her was proposing, despite the needlessness of such a thing. She definitely didn't like the spotlight. Maybe playing along and going through the motions for just a while longer would bring about a counteractive result. "Fine," Katelyn sighed, turning and heading back to the ambulance.

Katelyn leaned back and hoisted herself up on the sterilized paper covered hospital bed. She listened to the hustle and bustle of the to and fro traffic sweeping through the emergency room. Thankfully the doctor didn't keep her waiting long. "Well hello now," the kindly gentleman greeted her after pulling aside one of the curtains shielding her small confinement from the patient's accommodations next to hers. "I hear we had ourselves quite the adventure today." The near fortyish features of his brown haired mustache, short beard covered face fashioned themselves into a bright smiling fixture as he approached her.

"I really don't think it was that serious," Katelyn replied.

"Is that so?" he said, removing the bandage covering her left elbow. "The way I hear it you're all lucky to be alive." He held up her arm and inspected the injury. "Huh?" he uttered curiously.

"What is it?" she asked him.

Failing to answer her, the doctor immediately went for her right arm and peeled away one of the bandages there. "Were these wounds sustained prior to the accident?" he asked her, squinting his eyes behind the round frames of the spectacles that covered them.

"No," Katelyn said, suddenly put off by this man's now meticulous inspection of her. "I got them after the explosion. Why?"

He let loose with a strange and unnerving chuckle. "I'll tell you why. Because given the accounts of your proximity to the explosion it's surprising enough that this was all the damage you suffered, but..." Katelyn waited in suspenseful agony as this strange man continued to let his eyes crawl all over her while selfishly neglecting to reveal his findings. So she wasn't battered to a pulp. Would he have been more pleased had she been? "... they're nearly completely healed over."

After peeling back one more bandage he turned away from her and went over to a nearby counter. He started removing all sorts of instruments from the drawers beneath the basin . "First off I'm going to need a blood sample," he said, turning, needle in hand, only to find that he was all alone in the small cordoned off space. The instruments he held were quickly placed down on the counter before he darted through the curtain and moved out into the emergency room traffic. There was no sign of the mystery woman that he so desperately sought among the many faces that were present. He looked to his left; to his right; turning his body around a full three hundred and sixty degrees.

Nothing.

She was gone.

Confused and with a mind swimming with questions that he yearned to have answered, the doctor made his way back through the curtain and turned his eyes to the blood soaked discarded patches of gauze lying on the padded table that the raven haired young lady had once occupied.

Morgan walked up to the front counter of the Coffee House inside the confines of the Wicker Basket bookstore. Tripp was currently manning the post there. "Where's your co-pilot," Tripp teased as Morgan made her way behind the counter. He slid the customer in front of him his cup of Joe and collected the fee that was laid down on the counter. "Did you girls use that time to bond?" After handing his customer the change due and wishing him well as he made off into the depths of the bookstore, Tripp turned a devilishly smiling visage to his co-worker.

"You are not going to believe this," Morgan said, speaking with her eyelids closed and her right palm held up next to her down turned face.

"I might."

Morgan opened her eyes and turned her head just in time to see Zackery Collins approaching the counter. "Try me."

Morgan spilled her guts to the both of them about the extravagant events of the past hour involving none other than the seriously quirky, scarily enigmatic, Katelyn Bree. Morgan spared no detail in reciting the ridiculous scene that she had previously witnessed, the contents of which left Zackery feeling that much more justified in his suspicions, and Tripp, ironically, much more critical of the supernatural wonderment with which his two companions were currently regarding this woman.

"I'm telling you, I've never seen anything like it in my life," Morgan said to them, once again raising her right hand and swearing to her word. "If you had seen this girl run..."

"Run?" Zack said. "Try watching her scrap it out with a gang hopped up lunatics." He turned his eyes to Tripp and stared across the counter at him. "Did I or did I not tell you that there was something very, very Twilight Zonish up with that girl?"

"Like that's news," Tripp said, waving a dismissive hand at both Zack and Morgan's stunned demeanor. "News flash. The chick's a freak show. Tell me something I don't know."

After hearing his name being barked out by the same voice once more as he moved down the hospital hallway, Dr. Harper finally turned to get a look at the individual feverishly attempting to address him. "Is there something I can help you with?" the doctor said, addressing the subordinate nurse who chased him down.

The young lady handed him a large envelope. "Just got the results back on that blood work you ordered from those bandages you removed from your TA patient earlier today."

"And?" he asked, opening the envelope.

"I have to tell you, the boys down in the lab sure didn't appreciate your sense of humor."

"What are you talking about?" he said, still flipping through the paperwork he held.

"Nothing," she replied. "I was just wondering how long you thought it would take them to figure out that wasn't blood on those bandages."

4

"I'm very busy right now, Captain, so unless you've got something of the utmost importance to discuss with me I suggest you return to whatever task was previously occupying you."

Captain Blair ignored the sternness of tone that had accompanied the man walking next to him for as long as he'd known him. Colonel Tobias McPhearson and his fierce rigidness retained a presence that resonated throughout the corridors of this facility and maintained a certain chill in the air no matter the temperature of the room he just so happened to be occupying at any given time. This brown eyed soldier with hair as black as the mood he was typically known to be found in carried with him an air of uneasiness that was felt by anyone unfortunate enough to find themselves in his immediate presence.

His boots were shined to a mirror polish. The creases in the gray, white, and black camouflage pants that he wore could slice paper. The black short sleeved shirt he wore was tucked tightly into his pants and molded itself to the slim muscular frame of his torso. McPhearson had perfected intolerance, impatience, and stubborn indifference down to an art form. It was the credo by which he lived his life and governed his subordinates. Already well versed in the nature of such things, it was with the sincerest reluctance that Captain Blair approached the aloof Colonel with his recent findings.

Blair extended the hand to him that had a clipboard attached to it and the Colonel snatched it away from him. He let his eyes run furiously over the man walking next to him with the short brown hair who, aside from the camouflage jacket he wore, was dressed in an identical, though not as meticulously cared for, uniform before letting his eyes drop down to inspect the information he'd just been handed.

"Sir, I think we have a hit."

"I couldn't care less about what you think, Captain. All I want you to do is tell me what exactly it is I'm supposed to be looking at before I have you busted down to guard duty for wasting my time."

Knowing that this man was definitely serious about what he was threatening him with, Blair sucked in a chest full of air and said, "Our guys down in Tech. came across a medical file regarding a blood test performed on a Caucasian female approximately twenty three years in age..."

"Approximately?" McPhearson said to him.

"Yes, sir. She confessed to the officers that arrived on the scene of the automobile accident that she was discovered at that the bout of amnesia that she was currently suffering from prevented her from giving them an exact age. In any case, I imagined that those facts along with a subsequent blood test revealing a zero count of erythrocytes, leukocytes, or plasma warranted bringing this to your attention...sir."

McPhearson flipped from one page to the next, giving each sheet of paper only a mere second's worth of a glance before moving on to the next one underneath. "Given this impressive show of intelligence gathering I can only assume that you have a location."

"Chicago, Illinois, sir," Captain Blair replied.

The numerous pages slipped from his fingers and Colonel McPhearson slapped the back of the clipboard against Captain Blair's chest. He instantly relieved the ranking officer of the burden of its extremely light weight. "I want every ground troop in uniform and every tact vehicle this base has available enroute to her position. You have exactly one hour, Captain. If your efforts of activation extend to even the most minute of temporal designations beyond that deadline I'll personally see to it that your demise is as drawn out as it is painful."

Captain Blair stopped walking and lowered the clipboard down to his side. He looked on in confusing amazement as his superior officer continued on his way down the corridor. "Sir, that kind of mobilization could take days!"

"For your sake, Captain, I can't tell you just how much I hope that's not true."

Katelyn lowered the book that she held up in front of her face, the sound of the newspaper being slammed down on the table top right in front of the soles of her steel toed boot covered feet that were crossed one ankle over the other distracting her. She untangled her legs and placed both of her feet back on the carpeted floor. "World peace?" she said to him.

"Local hero," Zackery said in response to her cynical attempt at a fake smile.

Katelyn leaned back in her chair and brought the book back up to her face. "Big deal."

"You said it. Someone else just so happened to have wrote it," Zackery said before moving around the small wooden table and dragging a seat up next to hers. He flopped his body down into it. "So what do you say? You up for a little celebrating?"

A sigh escaped her lips. "What are the chances of you leaving if I said no?"

"Hear me out. I didn't have anything too fancy in mind or anything that might run the risk of brining you out of your shell too fast, too soon. It'll just be the two of us. My place for dinner. Eight o'clock." He waited for a response. Katelyn ignored him completely. "Is it okay if I take that as a yes?" Placing a hand on top of her thigh slowly gave him her eyes. They were as steely and threatening as ever. Taking the hint, Zackery gave the top of her black jean covered leg a quick squeeze before promptly removing his hand. "I'll let you get back to your book," he said, rising from the seat and granting her the privacy that she so desired.

Katelyn's eyes dropped back down to the pages of the book in front of her. Did this man's pestering know no end? She was positive that she'd done nothing to provoke or attract this much attention from him. Zackery lavished her with it anyhow. He fawned over her even more than the kind and generous Mr. Jordan Carthright, and the intensity with which he did dwarfed any she'd ever witnessed in even the most seediest of dives that she'd ventured into over the past few years. Had she desperately needed to, Katelyn could have certainly taken steps that would have left no doubt in Zackery's mind that she wanted him to stop bothering her. What kept her from initiating such a contingency? Arguably, she would have had to have attributed her tolerance of him to her own feelings of isolation.

She was different. She didn't exactly know why but she could feel it. Worse yet, she feared it and went about a course of action to shield herself from what she truly believed would be a hostile world had it taken clearer notice of her. Katelyn did what she could to hide, lay low, mask her differential qualities from every prying eye she ever found present. Jordan Carthright had noticed her, on occasion during some of her most revealing moments, as did a number of the Wicker Basket employees. But unlike the others, Jordan welcomed her with a dangerous degree of warmth. Abrasiveness she could handle better. It would have made it easier to stay away. Welcoming her in the way he did summoned that much more suspicion in her as to his motives. It was unfortunate that she enjoyed it the way she did. To say nothing of Zackery's hounding.

If Carthright's warmth were to be equated into the measuring gauge of Katelyn's own presumption of her acceptance by others then Zackery Collins would rank somewhere in the realm of molten to supernova. Needless to say, that factor raised her apprehensions about him as well as her delights in his persistent agenda. Katelyn despised his consistency and at the same time harbored a quiet comfort in the inclusion that his pestering brought along with it. She had no interest in him and little knowledge of his person. He had next to no knowledge of her on a personal level, but his interest remained unmatched.

And what of her interest toward him?

Katelyn remained understandably annoyed by Zack's come-ons but his presence continued to consist of a non-lethal reliability that was shining a very passive light on his latest bout of exasperation. She resented her allowance of his beckoning; hated her very tolerance where he was concerned.

Dinner.

She'd think about it.

Zackery pulled the small pan of lasagna out of the oven truthfully expecting to be enjoying his meal alone that night. Despite his lingering expectations he seriously doubted that Katelyn would even consider taking him up on his offer. It didn't stop him from extending the invitation though. He'd been so taken with this young recluse of a woman that he didn't know what could.

There was a knock at the door.

Zackery sat the pan down on top of the stove. A glimmer of hope resurfaced in him as he checked the clock on the wall and saw that it was just east of eight o'clock. He opened the front door and there she was. Draped in a black waist length leather jacket that hung over the same dark green T-shirt that she had on earlier, Katelyn didn't say a word to him as she moved forward into his apartment. "Come in," Zack said after the fact. He closed the door. "Make yourself at home. Dinner will be ready in a few."

A ringing phone sounded in the distance and Zackery left her to her exploration of his living room to go and answer it.

Looking around the room, Katelyn found Zackery's living arrangement to be one of simplicity. The walls were hardly decorated. The electronics and stereo equipment were moderately out of date. This place and the meager conveniences it held must have been all his job stocking shelves at Jake's Hardware Store must have afforded him at present. Especially with what he shelled out for his part-time classes at the community college. Simplicity. *Not a bad way to go*, Katelyn thought. She hadn't exactly gone off the deep end when it came to furnishing her place. Austerity. Perhaps the first of many ties to bind them.

"Tell me this is some kind of sick joke and you're not actually trapped alone in your apartment with that freak," Tripp's voice said into the phone pressed against the side of Zackery's head.

"No joke. She's in my living room right now." He reached into the refrigerator and removed two long neck bottles of beer.

"This has got to be a new low for you. Anybody else would be looking for something heavy enough to drop on her head and give them a head start for the door. You're making her dinner."

"You know what else I'm doing? Hanging up. Don't bother calling back because I'm turning the ringer off."

Zackery sat the cordless phone down on the kitchen counter. When he went out to set the table he noticed that Katelyn was no longer in the living room where he'd last seen her. His first instinct was that she'd left the apartment, opting instead to spend the rest of her night in the smoke filled confines of one of the bars she frequented.

It wasn't until he saw a few of the large white vertical blades covering the sliding glass door across the room move on their own that he found reason to believe otherwise. The motion of the blades had obviously been created by the breeze coming in from outside which meant the door was still open. He finished setting the table and stepped out onto the balcony to investigate.

He was right. She was out there. A wave of thankfulness swept over him at the sight of her leather covered back. Zackery walked up beside her. Katelyn had her hands placed on top of the metal rail in front of her. She stared out into the night from three stories up. "Food's ready," he said to her, getting no reaction. After a lingering moment of silence he said, "If you want I can have your plate brought out here to you."

Katelyn turned her head to the left and looked at him coldly, an expression he was growing all too familiar with. "I really believe I could do without your attempt at being witty for the duration of the night."

"You sure? Because I've got the sneaking suspicion that if I stopped it would get real boring around here."

Katelyn turned and headed back into the house. "I thought I told you already that I'm not here for your amusement."

Zack watched her disappear through the blinds. "Yeah. This is going to be fun," he said to himself.

"So those guys in the subway," Zackery said as they continued through their meal. "Are you ever going to tell me how you did that?"

"You seriously need to broaden your array of topics to discuss," she said to him from the opposite end of the small table they were seated at, scraping her fork against the plate.

"I could change the topic of discussion but I'm afraid you'd still be at the heart of the subject matter. For instance, how's this amnesia thing of yours work anyway? You can't remember anything about your life before hooking up with Carthright? Birthday? Parents' names? Friends? Family?"

"I woke up that morning," Katelyn said to him, a hint of frustration in her tone. "Beyond that I'm drawing a real big blank."

Zackery chewed and swallowed his next bite. "So for all you know you could be married. Right now there could be some distraught guy out there going crazy trying to find you."

"What makes you think he'd be so distraught?" she said, leaning back in her chair and turning up her bottle.

Zack cracked a half smile. "Losing a gem of a girl like you, who wouldn't be?"

Katelyn sat the bottle back down on the table and took up her fork again. "Could you please just drop it?"

"Alright," he said. "If you're so tired of being the center of attention then what would you like to talk about?"

"I was under the impression that I was invited here to share a meal with you not engage you in conversation." Katelyn tore off a piece of her roll and threw it into her mouth, knowing that she hadn't silenced him in the least.

Zackery stood up and walked around to her side of the table. He picked up her empty beer bottle and headed into the kitchen. He soon returned with a fresh bottle and sat it down next to her half empty plate. "Do you think I asked you over here just to sit and watch you eat?"

"It wouldn't exactly be out of character for you, now would it?"

Zackery sat back down in his chair. "Can you blame me?"

"I could stop you."

"I'm sure you could. But you haven't."

"Doesn't mean I won't," Katelyn said, biting down on a forkful of food before snatching it out of her mouth.

"So how's that work?"

"What, me stopping you from bothering me?" she asked.

"That and pretty much everything else," he said, slowly pushing his right hand into his pants pocket. He removed the switchblade, making sure to keep it concealed beneath the table.

"I'm afraid I don't know what you're talking about," she said, taking another bite out of her plate. She heard the click. The rate at which she chewed her food slowed and she locked her eyes on him without moving her head. *He wouldn't.*

In one lightening fast burst of fluent motion Zackery drew back and flung the blade in her direction. No surprise showed on his face as he watched her ever so gracefully bring her left hand up and take hold of the weapon by the handle before it had a chance to do any damage. Katelyn hadn't so much as flinched. Slowly the two of them rose from their seats, Katelyn's face beginning to twist with fury. The depths to which this man would stoop to sate his curiosity was starting to seriously tick her off. She ran her thumb down the side of the blade, applied pressure, and snapped it off.

"Who are you?" Zackery asked her softly.

"I don't know," Katelyn answered him sternly.

47

5

Tobias McPhearson walked through the door and approached the desk with a placard on top of it that read Gen. Michael Selinski. Sitting behind the desk was a gracefully aged gentleman crowned with salt and pepper hair and dressed in a black, white, and gray camouflage uniform. He failed to look up as the officer neared the front of his desk. "I assume you're here to update me on your progress, Colonel."

"We've secured the medical records and cleared the hospital of all evidence that she ever arrived there. Unfortunately she falsified most of her personal information so we have yet to pinpoint her exact location."

"What are we doing about that?" the General said, shuffling around some papers on top of his desk.

"Her status has been entered into the state and local law enforcement's databases. She, as of current, is a fugitive from justice considered to be armed and dangerous. They've been urged to use the utmost discretion in conducting their search and under no circumstances are they to attempt an apprehension. It's suspected that she'll be doing what she can to maintain a low profile, but with this degree of a search operating under the off chance that she isn't expecting us, zeroing the target shouldn't require too strenuous an effort."

"You assume she's not suspecting anything. What sort of resistance are we looking at if she is?"

"Extreme, sir," McPhearson explained. "But right now all of our focus is concentrated on locating her. Afterwards there'll be an assessment made as to what level of resistance we'll be up against, allowing us to react more accordingly."

"One more thing, Colonel," Gen. Selinski said, still not lifting his eyes to look upon his subordinate. "I want you on site for this op. Keep me posted."

"Yes, sir." The Colonel turned and left the office.

Katelyn pushed open the door to her domicile in the Cumberland Apt. building and slammed it closed after stepping inside. After switching on the living room lights she hung her jacket up in the hallway closet and went straight for the kitchen area. She snatched a beer bottle out of the refrigerator and slammed the door closed with enough force to rattle the items lining the shelves just on the other side.

Katelyn twisted the top off and tossed it back over her shoulder as she started out of the kitchen. Before the lights went out the cap landed smack dab in the center of the pile in the refuse bin. She couldn't believe that Zackery actually had the gall to offer to see her home. As if she'd be any safer moving through the night with his dangerously inquisitive nature right along side of her. Katelyn turned the bottle up and drained nearly half of it. What the hell was he thinking? It would have served him right if she'd taken up that blade and returned the favor, performing her own unnecessary experiment at his peril.

Peril.

From what she gathered about Zackery's past behavior the last thing he'd be capable of is consciously and purposefully instigating a course of action that would lead to the damaging of the current object of his superfluous obsession. He must have known that there was little to no chance that he'd harm her with that weapon. Katelyn certainly knew it the second she'd heard him reach into his pocket to retrieve it. The question was how did he? Or as he would have put it, how did she? Truth was Katelyn didn't know how she knew that the blade she had known was in his right front pocket ever since the moment he'd opened up his home to her wouldn't pose the slightest threat to her person. She had no idea how or why she was able to sense the things she could sense; know what she knew; do the things she was capable of.

What she was sure of was that he could have definitely went about testing the abilities that he suspected she possessed in quite a variety of better ways; had he found the need to do so at all. Katelyn finished her beer and changed for bed. A black tank top and panties fell against black sheets. Pitch dark hair hit against a coal black pillow case. Katelyn jerked a thick padded comforter that matched the hue of everything on the bed besides her skin tone up over her body. She reveled in the warmth of it all, hoping the soothing sensation would drive away the negative thoughts that she currently had in the way of her concept of Zackery Collins. She was so furious at him. Forcing her to reveal herself like that. She hated him so much for it. But at the same time she felt at ease; safe in being so open in his presence. So much about herself continued to remain hidden from her, but what little she was aware of, strangely enough, Katelyn felt next to no danger in revealing to Zackery. Perhaps she should have. Maybe she just didn't have the mind to. It was late and she had to be at work early the next morning. Surely her anger and confusion would save until the next day. It would have no choice. Katelyn needed her sleep. And with that she let her eyelids fall shut to the darkened room.

She glanced over at the clock on the wall once more as she walked past it. Eight twenty three. Her shift at the Wicker Basket was set to start at nine o'clock that morning. If she left right now there was a very good chance that she'd make it to work on time. Katelyn left her apartment building and headed up the block toward the nearest subway station. She wandered the bustling city streets with thoughts of Zackery running through her mind. She wondered if he'd come in today and if so what in the world he would say to her. He'd already apologized many times over for the nonattempted attempted knifing, and for the life of her Katelyn...

She stopped cold in her tracks. A couple of upset pedestrians bumped into her shoulders as they continued forward wondering what her problem was. Katelyn turned around and looked back over her shoulder, turning her eyes up to get a look at the high windows on the tall buildings on the other side of the street from where she stood. One particular building in the cluster caught her eye...and one window. *What now?*

Looking down at the street through a pair of high powered binoculars from a window on the twentieth floor of the building that he and his team were currently hold up in, Captain Blair could have sworn that this woman was looking him square in the eyes. "We've been made," he said into the microphone and earpiece attached to the side of his head. "I repeat, we've been made. All ground units close in. Dark hair. Black shirt. Black pants. North by northwest on my position. Proceed with extreme caution. I repeat, proceed with extreme caution." Captain Blair continued to stare into the face of the young woman who continued to eye his position ever so studiously until a small pack of bodies passed between the target and his line of sight. Once they were gone from the binoculars' view so was she. "Damn it," Blair said to himself, scanning the streets for any sign of his misplaced target and finding nothing.

Minutes ticked by. Captain Blair radioed in to his people requesting a report of any visual on the target. Nothing. She was gone. Countless hours of intelligence gathering, surveillance, positioning, monitoring, all gone to waste in the matter of a few morning hours' worth of activity. So what now? Blair thought as he tried to assess the damage of this fruitless waste of time and manpower. His superiors would be awaiting a report and most assuredly be gravely disappointed by such a setback so early on in this incursion. Perhaps the fact that they had identified a place of address and positive visual on the target would be enough to smooth things over with the upper brass. All well and good, but the Captain knew that even that insurmountable amount of Intel would weigh very lightly against a missed opportunity at capture.

Who were they? Katelyn thought as she moved off at a sprint down the small, tight corridor that was the alleyway she currently found herself in. What did they want from her? The only thing that Katelyn did know for sure was that she definitely did not have time for this. She only wished that the armed gentlemen dressed in all black fatigues that she collided with upon running out into the gaping alleyway intersection had given her the chance to explain that.

Katelyn forcefully took hold of him by the two utility straps draped down the front of his chest, twisted her body violently, and threw the body she had a hold of down the eastbound passageway adjacent from the southbound path that she had originally emerged from. Unfortunately for Katelyn this aggressor hadn't ventured into this gauntlet alone. Six more men dressed in similar uniforms and armed with equally lethal devises had accompanied him and were headed toward her back with an equal amount of eagerness and purpose.

Katelyn leapt up into the air, pushing herself back as she did. Her body was able to tuck and make two full revolutions, allowing the first hurried soldier a more than ample timeframe to pass right beneath her. The soles of his government issue boots skidded to a sliding halt.

Katelyn extended her body to full length and slammed the soles of both of her tennis shoes hard into the back of the man who was now in front of her. His body flew forward. Her back hit the ground beneath her. Five more sets of feet quickly approached the top of her grounded head, all of which were attached to men anxiously waiting to make her acquaintance.

Katelyn rolled backwards and came up on her feet. Raising her left foot, she swung it around behind her, lifting it high enough to connect the heel with the side of one man's face and then lowered it, smashing her foot into the back of the left knee of the soldier next to him. Both men dropped to the ground.

She moved on.

Her next attacker swung the small rifle that he clutched at the left side of her face. Katelyn jerked her upper body back, dodging the blow. When the butt of the rifle came back for a second pass she swung a hard left hook and shattered the weapon. Following through with the spin of her body, Katelyn twirled around three hundred and sixty degrees, finally bringing the back of her right fist into contact with his right cheek.

Time was ticking away.

She had to get out of there.

Katelyn ran off down one of the passageways. She shouldered her way past her next assailant, knocking his body armored covered frame into a brick wall fifteen feet away off to her left. She dealt with the last living obstacle in her path by simply leaping into the air, flipping over him, and continuing on her way. The black clad trooper tried to run after her but found the effort to be one of futility.

Having had the target sighted and her proximity reaffirmed, Captain Blair swelled with a newly replenished faith in the possible success of this mission. He relayed this updated information to the rest of his men on the ground and instructed them to recalibrate their actions.

Although her mind was plagued by the many curious eyes that had turned to absorb the image of her moving at such a fast pace down the sidewalk she continued to do so. It was imperative that she make it to the subway station and these meddlers were making that much more harder than it needed to be. It wasn't far now. All she had to do was hurry.

Katelyn made it down the steps, through the turnstile, and out onto the platform. She melded into the thin gathering awaiting the next transport and joined them all in their anticipation. Katelyn didn't have long to revel. Shortly, several members of the tact team that for some reason continued to pursue her came pouring out onto the platform, their uniforms and weapons startling almost everyone present.

They shuffled through the crowd of high and low murmurs in search of their quarry. Katelyn checked both exits. Armored troops corked both vents, shielding the true multitude of their numbers behind the human blockade.

Her train was only moments away. Engaging them now was sure to impede her departure if not cancel it altogether. Both exits meant trouble. There was an available alternative...but it meant a race against time. Time she didn't have.

Katelyn hopped down off the platform and onto the tracks below before the soldiers spotted her. After that it was off on foot down the darkened tunnel, the light of the oncoming train already visible at her back.

Zackery walked into the Wicker Basket and conducted a search, first for Katelyn and then for Tripp whom he found restocking a display case. "Yo. You're in here early," Tripp said to him. Kneeling down, he used a box cutter to split apart the packing tape holding closed the lid of a cardboard box. "This wouldn't by any chance have something to do with your date last night, now would it?"

"I'll tell you about it later. Where is she? Have you seen her?"

"Calm down, Casanova," Tripp said, raising his left wrist and pulling his sleeve back. "Her shift doesn't start for another fifteen minutes. Which means she should be in anytime between now and the next fourteen minutes and fifty nine seconds."

Katelyn's rate of speed continued to increase exponentially as did that of the train which was now barreling down on her back. The hulking conveyance wasn't close enough to allow the conductor to have a clear view of her fleeing body but it was gaining fast, not that it mattered. Katelyn knew that she was past the point of no return. It didn't matter now *when* the driver caught sight of her and decided to slam on the breaks. Given the current rate of acceleration of the massive heap behind her and the amount of resistance that this mechanism's breaking system was prepared to apply, Katelyn knew that her only chance of survival lie in pressing on harder for the tunnel opening that was quite some distance ahead of her. With a train heading at her on the adjacent track in the opposite direction of the one closing in behind her, Katelyn's salvation solely resided in her making it out of this tunnel and fast; less she take the chance of running into more of her eager pursuers upon her exit.

She felt the heavy gust of wind that the train on her left picked up as it shot by her. Katelyn pushed harder to maintain her present velocity against the opposing force. She heard the high pitched squeal of the applied brakes behind her and despite the small measure of comfort she was able to draw from the knowledge that the train's speed was decreasing, Katelyn knew that the vehicle wouldn't make it to a complete stop before it made it out of the tunnel. The opening was just ahead. With the grinding noise on the tracks behind her growing dangerously close, Katelyn pushed forward for daylight.

The conductor squinted his eyes more with every inch closer that the front of the train neared this young girl's back. As impressed as he was with this immaculate display of endurance and conditioning, the grotesqueness that he knew lie inevitably ahead was a scene he couldn't bare to witness. Eventually his eyes were completely shut tight.

The train exploded out of the tunnel and when the conductor opened his eyes once more he saw no one obstructing the path of the great metal beast that he operated. He feared the young lady's body had been overwhelmed by the weight of the train and dreaded the findings that the medical personnel would have to exhume from the underbelly of this murderous machine.

Katelyn's body was, as of present, in the process of dropping down to the street three stories below the platform supported set of train tracks above her. She'd leapt up and over the perimeter railing to her right the very instant that her body saw the light of day. The rubber soles of the shoes she wore crashed down hard on the pavement and she spun her body around just in time to catch sight of the grill of the van swiftly bearing down on her position.

The driver hit the brakes but it was much too late for the vehicle he steered to avoid slamming into the nubile figure that had just appeared out of nowhere on the street in front of it. Katelyn's body forced a dent in the front end before bouncing off of it and rolling across the street just beyond the dinged bumper. Once the driver of the van, along with his passenger, stepped out of the halted vehicle all they could do was watch as this woman, whom the impact should have certainly crippled if not outright killed given the speed at which they were traveling, picked herself up and continued on her way at a full out run.

Zackery lifted his eyes up from the book he explored and took a sip of cappuccino. He cut his eyes over to the clock attached to the wall near the reading area he currently resided in. *Where was she?*

Katelyn moved her body up onto the sidewalk and continued to pump her arms and legs that much more vigorously as she sped on her way through the scattering of individuals that cluttered the walkway she was using to make her escape. They were still after her. She knew it. Perhaps if she got off of the streets for a while there would be a better chance of losing them.

Katelyn moved through the revolving glass doors of the next office building she came upon and ran through the lobby to catch a pair of elevator doors just before they shut closed. She was greeted by several sets of panicked, confused, and angry eyes after so abruptly and rudely delaying the occupants already onboard.

No time for apologies, not that she'd any intentions on offering any had she had the time. No. Instead she treated them all to yet another shock when she took it upon herself to exit the car no sooner than it had been set into motion.

Straight through the roof.

Katelyn scaled the wall to her left and pushed open a maintenance panel that she found before pulling herself further up into the elevator shaft.

Once she made it to her feet she vaulted straight up and took hold of the elevator cable, leaving the car itself some distance beneath her. With her feet dangling Katelyn used her hands to pull herself up the shaft until she reached the thirty third floor where she pried open the elevator doors and stepped out into the hall.

Not only was her attire completely out of place in this sea of strange looks and business suits that she moved through, the condition of Katelyn's clothes also left much to be desired. Though she maintained her stoic composure, the strain that this whole ordeal had placed on her showed brilliantly throughout her ragged outfit. She imagined that everyone not wanting security to quickly usher her to the nearest exit, preferably one in the rear of the building, wanted to sit her down and allow her time enough to rest so that an ambulance may be summoned. She had no time for either.

Katelyn pushed open a door and stepped inside of a packed conference room, gaining a number of curious eyes as she did. She continued on her way, ignoring every comment directed at her along the way. She moved around the large boardroom table packed with suits, both male and female, and moved through another door that lead into a much smaller office. She went for the window behind the desk to her left.

Just getting the pane of glass open, Katelyn heard the office door that she had previously shut coming open behind her. Ignoring the ranting once more, she climbed out onto the ledge and continued on her way.

Katelyn walked along the concrete shelf looking down at the street far below in search of any signs of her previous pursuers. Unfortunately for her she found plenty. Scattered throughout the wandering masses below were clusters and swarms of individuals all scurrying about with nothing else on their minds but locating her. Individuals that she could see and make out from the rest of the pedestrians and commuters along with the others that she couldn't see but could inexplicably sense and pinpoint.

All Katelyn wanted to know was *why?*

Why were they after her?

What did they want?

She approached the corner of the building and turned her eyes back to the skyline in front of her. Just then a large black helicopter rose up and hovered in near silence directly in front of her line of sight mere meters away from where she stood.

From what she could see of this particular craft with its sleek design and quietly running motors Katelyn rapidly assessed the nature of this vehicle to be one of combat rather than transport. The image she saw through the cockpit window. The dark haired figure draped in black cloth, black body armor, and an even darker intensity stared back at her from the other side of the glass covering the helicopter's cockpit with a glance that promised reprieve; reproach; retribution; relentlessness. Katelyn knew that she wanted nothing to do with him. She turned to the left and dashed off down the side of the building.

"No you don't," Col. McPhearson said through a clenched jaw. He pulled the control stick to the right and veered the helicopter off along the side of the building attempting to keep the nose of the flying vehicle in line with his fleeing prey.

Katelyn's legs pumped furiously and when she reached the edge of the ledge her legs pushed off hard and sent her body gliding up into the air. The apex of the arc that she traveled along brought Katelyn up high enough to clear the roof of the building across the street, but as she watched the helicopter and the spinning blades that kept it airborne move through the atmosphere beneath her Katelyn knew that her downward descent would bring her nowhere near to touching down on top of the building.

Dropping down out of the sky, Katelyn's body smashed through a sixteenth floor window. She tucked and rolled across the floor that was being showered with glass shards. She quickly saw a way out of the large office room as panicked employees either hurried over to investigate or darted off towards the nearest exit.

Once again finding herself with little patience for the elevator, Katelyn made off for the nearest stairwell. Surprisingly enough she didn't find locating one very difficult at all despite having never been inside of this building before. Plenty of time to ponder over that later. Katelyn looked down over the green painted railing at the spiraling staircase that went all the way down to the ground floor. There was an exit at the bottom of this well and she had very little time to make her way to it.

"Have you found anything?" McPhearson said into the radio attached to the side of his head. "Report! Over!" His infuriated eyes continued to scan the streets below as the helicopter he piloted circled the last building his target was known to have entered and swept the surrounding areas.

"Sir, no visual as of yet, sir," a voice coming over the Colonel's earpiece replied. *"We're conducting a floor by floor search of the subject's last known position as well as broadening our search pattern outside of the structure, sir. Over."*

"Just make it quick and keep it quiet," McPhearson ordered menacingly. "If there's no contact, visual or otherwise, within the next half hour regroup and get back to the rally point. Over." He did his best to try and calm himself, but could barely contain his frustration at coming so close to completing the mission that he'd been placed in charge of only to have his acquired target slip so nimble through his grasp. He tried desperately to take comfort in the knowledge that this wasn't by any means over.

6

Katelyn let go of the grit covered fixtures welded to the undercarriage of the large mail truck she had hitched a ride on, unbeknownst to the driver. She slammed down back first against the pavement below, adding to the tally yet another collision with solid matter that she could have done without that morning. The truck itself continued to move on through the traffic in front of the Wicker Basket bookstore, but the car trailing it screeched to a rubber peeling stop at the sight of the tattered young woman coming to her feet directly in its path. Thankfully the stunned woman behind the wheel managed to pause the front bumper a few feet away from Katelyn's body. Applying a sizable dent in her hood would have been the last thing Katelyn needed at this juncture as she turned and went for the front entrance of the bookstore.

She ignored the shocked gasps of the patrons and gawking glances that the Wicker Basket employees sent her way in response to the condition of her and the clothing she wore and headed directly for the back of the store where she would find the staircase leading up to Jordan Carthright's domicile. Having aided her so greatly upon her initial settling in, it was no surprise that a few articles of clothing belonging to her remained in his home to this day. Confident that she'd shaken the all seeing eyes of the horde of troops that had latched onto her, Katelyn felt that she had more than an adequate enough amount of time to wash up a little and hop into some fresh clothes. She just hoped that Jordan wouldn't be too put off by her sudden and uncharacteristic problem with punctuality.

"Hey," Zack called out as he hurried over to the Coffee House. Tripp turned to greet him. "Was that Katelyn that just came in?"

"No. That wasn't Katelyn who just came in. That, my friend, was Katelyn coming in late for work." Zackery crinkled his brow at Tripp's pun and struck out after her, leaving the Coffee House attendee to the open book he had in front of him. "Truly a red letter date in the chronicles of the Wicker Basket."

Zackery calmly knocked on the proprietor of this establishment's apartment door unsure of what his reaction would be having such an action performed by a customer instead of one of his more familiar employees. The door opened and a spectacle adorned, confused looking man poked his head out. "Is there something I can help you with?"

"Yes, sir, there is. I'm sorry to bother you here, but I really need to speak with Katelyn."

"Fine. She'll be down in a minute."

"With all due respect," Zack said. "There's kind of a personal nature involved in all of this and if it were at all possible I'd prefer we discussed it somewhere a bit more private." Actually he would have been willing to seize any opportunity he could to talk to her anywhere right now, but if there was a chance to secure a private meeting with her why not jump at it? "I understand that she's supposed to be at work right now so I'll try to keep it as brief as possible."

"And you are?" Jordan asked him, adjusting the glasses on the bridge of his nose.

"Zackery. Zackery Collins."

Jordan gave him another quick once over. "Wait right here, Zackery."

The door shut closed in his face and Zackery knew that the owner of this place was on his way to consult with his employee about the individual outside of his front door that so desperately sought counsel with her. Zackery figured that once his name was dropped there was a more than decent chance that he might not only be politely asked to go away but to leave the store altogether. Imagine his surprise when the owner returned and invited him inside. "You've got five minutes," he said, raising his right hand and pointing off in the direction of a hallway. "And...try not to touch anything."

Zackery gave him a raised palm, nonverbal acknowledgement of his demands before watching his wiry form slink off into the further recesses of the gadget cluttered place he called home. Zackery turned and headed down the corridor past a small row of doors towards the one directly in front of him at the end of the hall. The one that he just knew was his intended destination.

He grabbed the knob, twisted it, and gave the door a slight push. It swung open wide with a surprising amount of ease and he stepped inside the room. Though there was some illumination present, originating from a standing floor model lamp in the corner across the room from him and the incandescent glow pouring out of the open doorway in the corner of the room to his right, the atmosphere of the quarters that Zack had walked into was one draped in dark shadows.

The array of furniture present clearly let him know that this was indeed the master bedroom of the dwelling. Zackery didn't know if any such junior replicas were present throughout the expanse of this apartment but that was his best guess as far as a first glance went.

The clothes covered leather recliner to his immediate right; the oak dresser in front of him at the foot of the king size bed cluttered two times over with an assortment of what looked to be hand made mechanical devises; the nightstand at the bedside ornamented with an identical arrangement of disorder. This room had definitely been lived in.

Zackery turned his head and his eyes away from the cluttered décor and placed his sight on Katelyn as she stepped into the room from the doorway to his right. She moved at a placid, steady pace toward the bed in front of her. "Jordan said you had something important you wanted to say to me," Katelyn said as she snatched up the black pair of jeans resting on top of the comforter. She stepped into them, pulling the pants up over the black panties that she was wearing.

"First and foremost, I wanted to apologize for what happened at my place last night." He turned his attention to the chair next to him and grabbed up the half shredded remains of her discarded wardrobe. "And to just let you know that it's not everyday that I go hurling particularly dangerous objects at any dinner guests that I happen to have over; female or otherwise."

"I'm grateful to be the exception," Katelyn said as she did up her pants.

"Secondly..." Zack examined the numerous tears, holes, and cuts that he found in her clothes with curiously suspicious eyes and pliant fingers. "What the hell happened to you this morning? You get hit by a train?"

Katelyn snapped her fingers at him and extended her left arm. "Actually, it just missed me." Zackery dropped her soiled clothing to the floor and reached down to the chair seat, gathering up the top and tossing it to her. She stuck both of her arms through the long black cotton sleeves of the shirt before pushing her head through the neck hole. She pulled the remainder of the material down over her black bra covered chest and the rest of her torso. "Is that the only reason you came up here and decided to disturb Mr. Carthright?" she asked him as she walked over and collected her discarded clothing. "To offer up one more of your heartfelt apologies?"

"To tell you the truth, I came up here to ask you to dinner again."

"Is that so," she said, folding her clothes and walking them into the bathroom. "You plan on pulling a gun and taking a shot at me this time?" She dropped her clothes in the hamper and walked out of the bathroom, shutting out the light as she did.

"How about someplace public this time. Just to be on the safe side. Come on. Let me take you out. Someplace nice. We'll make it my final apologetic gesture."

Katelyn was seated on the edge of the bed slipping on her socks and shoes. "Sorry, but I'm reasonably sure that I'll be spending my evenings dining alone from here on out."

"Guess I like what that's saying about my chances."

Katelyn stood up from the bed and moved past him, offering up a sinister glare as she went for the bedroom door.

"What makes you think I would even consider taking you up on that offer?" Katelyn spoke as she descended the staircase down to the ground floor with Zackery at her back.

"Because whether or not you want to admit it, I really believe that you enjoyed yourself last night." Katelyn stopped and the ferocity with which she spun her body around sideways and looked at him caused her raven toned hair to slosh around in front of her face. Zackery grinned at the way he had her seething. A day earlier and he would have felt a tinge of fear at the possibility of incurring the wrath that that sultry set of eyes were now promising. But not today. Today invoking such a reaction somehow amused him. "Tell me I'm wrong."

There was overstepping his boundaries and then there was overstepping his boundaries. And if he thought that song and dance at his place the other night had enough of an effect for him to believe that he had some kind of hold on her then he'd better think again. "Buy something or leave me alone. I'm on the clock."

Zackery watched her turn and continue on her way down the stairs. "Anything in particular you'd like to recommend?"

Colonel Tobias McPhearson pushed open a set of double doors on the forth floor of the abandoned building that he had personally commandeered to serve as the central command center for the small network of command posts that were up and discreetly running in nearby areas of the city. An armed cadre of soldiers followed him inside of the once spacious room that was now filled with state of the art military grade computer equipment being manned by personnel of the highest level of training.

Though the men that followed McPhearson into the room wore seriously stern looks on their faces indicative of years of profoundly intense training and deeply instilled professionalism, neither of them carried with them the ferocious zealousness that filled the dust thick air around their commanding officer.

It was an intensity that was now being directed specifically at the ranking Captain in the room, or building for that matter. Captain Robert Blair. Being audibly aware of the Colonel's presence the second he'd entered the room with his personal army of sycophants, it wasn't until he felt the indistinguishably cold aura of the Colonel and his rabble grow uncomfortably close to him that he turned and visually acknowledged McPhearson's presence.

"I trust you have good news for me, Captain."

"Sir, with all do respect..." Blair started but was instantly cut off by McPhearson.

"Spare me your inept attempt at formalities, Captain. Just tell me you haven't completely wasted the past six hours of my time."

Blair, continuing to maintain the strict self discipline instilled in him, retained his composure even in the face of his senior officer's blatant degradation of the soldiers he obnoxiously regarded to be his lessers. Letting it get to him now would only succeed in making a bad situation worse. "I promise you, sir. You'll be notified the instant we have something, but for now there simply isn't anything to report." Captain Blair suffered the infuriated eyes of the Colonel for a few moments more before turning back around and continuing with his task which consisted of overseeing the work being done by the other men in the room. He could still feel the Colonel's malice filled eyes holding him steady at the center of a pair of crosshairs that melded into one. Eventually he turned, grumbling inaudibly, and took his leave of the room.

Katelyn dropped her time card into the slot atop the clock fixture attached to the wall. Once she was punched out for the day Katelyn replaced the card back onto the rack next to the clock and removed the name tag that was pinned to her shirt. After attaching it to the bulletin board she left the break room. She'd almost made it to the front entrance and out of the store when she once again found herself in the presence of Zackery Collins. It was just past six that evening. Katelyn had seen him leave the store no more than a half hour into her shift. He'd obviously taken the time to find out when her shift ended and made sure that he'd be there to see her off.

"What are you doing here?" she asked him.

"Stopped by to see Morgan," Zack answered her.

"She clocked out over two hours ago."

"There was this book I was hoping to purchase while it was still on sale."

"You're lying."

He stood there in silence for a moment with a strained look on his face as if her were racking his brain to come up with just one more remotely plausible excuse to offer her. "Your eyes," he finally let slip out in his exhaustion.

Katelyn moved past him, pushed the door open, and stepped out onto the sidewalk. It didn't take Zackery long to start out after her. "Aren't there laws against this sort of behavior?" Katelyn said as she continued walking.

"Yes. But it's only when the attention is unwanted."

"And somehow you've managed to convince yourself that this doesn't fall into that category?"

"Alright then. As far as you're concerned I'm just another familiar face in the crowd that just so happens to be heading in the same direction as you." Katelyn turned and looked at him completely overwhelmed by a quiet sense of astonishment.

She tolerated him. Him and his banter all the way from the Wicker Basket to the subway platform where she would meet the transport that would shuttle her back to her neighborhood. When the train finally did arrive Katelyn didn't even put up much of a fuss when he boarded with her. Although she had her doubts about whether or not Zackery would be allowed beyond the threshold of her apartment door she couldn't help but notice the acute difference of making this short trek with Zack at her side after four years of doing it alone.

They *would* have to ruin it.

"Zack, get away from me," Katelyn said to him, interrupting the flow of their words.

"What? What are you talking about?" Right off the bat Zackery took her command to be nothing other than her typical standoffishness; a force field that he was starting to excel at maneuvering around.

"Get away from me. Now!" she said more sternly, offering up a slight shove with her words that moved him across the aisle from her. "Sit down over there," she ordered to the very confused face now staring at her.

"Katelyn, what's going..."

"Just do it! Right now!"

He wasn't sure about what it was she was up to but whatever it was Zackery could see that she was serious about it. He complied, taking a seat while she remained standing. Katelyn stepped out into the center of the aisle and faced the rear of the car. Zack started to say something to her once more but the look she shot him silenced him immediately.

Katelyn turned her focus back to the rear of the car and the large cadre of men clothed in gray suits and ties making their way inside of it. One individual in particular stood out in the crowd. The gentleman leading the pack dressed in all black and cloaked in a floor length trench coat. She recognized the face from the cockpit of the helicopter that was in pursuit of her earlier that day.

Their entrance had also succeeded in capturing Zackery's attention, as did the assortment of well dressed men entering the car at Katelyn's back. Whatever it was that was about to go down he was starting to gain an understanding about Katelyn's unexpected apprehension. The image of the tattered clothing she'd walked into the Wicker Basket wearing that morning suddenly flashed into his mind.

"Well now," the black haired, darkly adorned individual said as he neared her. "Here we are at last...Katelyn."

"Who are you?" she asked, curious as to the fact that he seemed to be somewhat familiar with her.

His approach remained constant as did all of the men who accompanied him. "Someone who's been searching for you...for a very long time." He stopped nearly ten feet in front of her and the crowd with him did the same. His movement and actions appeared to be the conduit by which all the men present in his party based their own actions. Zackery along with every other passenger in the immediate vicinity remained frozen in place, weary that the slightest motion could potentially set off God knows what kind of reaction.

"What do you want from me?" Katelyn asked.

"I want to take you home. To take you back where you belong."

It was then that Zack had found the strength to break through the sheet of ice that his body had previously been cocooned inside of and rise to his feet. The utterance of Katelyn's name by this strange man brought with it a familiarity that Zackery unmistakably knew linked this person to Katelyn's past. But it was the bleakly frightful way in which his vocal tone came across that had been the main driving force that caused him to take such action. "You're not taking her anywhere," Zack said, stepping in front of Katelyn and standing between her and the dark sheathed gentleman before her.

"What the hell are you doing?" Katelyn said to him.

"What are you talking about?" he said over his shoulder. "I'm not letting this guy take you out of here."

"Katelyn, be a dear and apprise this Samaritan, if that is indeed what he truly is, of the dire situation he is attempting to interject himself into."

"Tell me who you are," Katelyn said to the man in black.

"Why? Do I seem familiar to you?" His words were as spiteful as they were meticulously enunciated. The soft chuckle he produced as he stuffed both of his hands into the pockets of the trench coat he wore was both eerie and unnerving. Especially for the many spectating passengers littered all about. "It's McPhearson. Tobias McPhearson. And I, for one, see no reason why anything occurring here should result in an episode of violence." He took a single step toward her. "Wouldn't you agree, Katelyn?" There was a lingering silence between them. "If in fact that is your real name."

Katelyn placed her hand down firmly on top of Zackery's right shoulder and physically moved him from in front of her as she stepped forward. "My name is Katelyn."

His soft chuckling was sinisterly devious. "Tell me, exactly how far back does that memory of yours stretch, huh?" The train they were all on slowed to a halt as it approached the next stop. "Come with me and I'll tell you everything that you want to know."

The doors to Katelyn's left parted and the timid passengers onboard eased their way past the conferencing parties and slipped out unmolested. "My name is Katelyn," she said softly before turning and heading for the door. "Leave me alone." Once she was off the train Zackery hurried off after her. McPhearson and his men remained onboard as the doors closed shut again and the train pulled away.

"Do you know that guy?" Zackery asked her as he sped up the pace at which he walked to keep up with her movement.

"Did it look like I knew him?" she said, starting to scale a small flight of stairs. "And what the hell were you doing? I thought I told you to stay back." They reached the top of the staircase and continued through the station.

Now Zackery was beginning to feel a little put off by her abrasiveness towards him. "What I thought I was doing was trying to help you," he said with a hint of negativity in his voice. "And given what I just saw back there on that train I'd say that whether or not you can confess to knowing that man or any of the people with him, he certainly came off as being no stranger to you. Not to mention your past which, as of late, you have absolutely no memory of."

"I sincerely hope that you don't live to regret that decision."

Once Katelyn and Zackery reached the sidewalk just beyond the stairway entrance to the subway station they were greeted by the sounds of screeching tires leaving black streaks of ground in rubber across the pavement of the street as each black painted unmarked car and van swerved to a strategically positioned and well timed stop.

The stationing of the multitude of vehicles that effectively blocked off the streets from the thru traffic in all directions was one thing, but it was the droves of both tactical uniform adorned and business suit clad men that emptied from the vehicles, took cover behind the large masses of rubber and metal, and trained the sights of lethal weapons on the two of them that had absorbed the majority of Katelyn's attention.

She turned her eyes up and scanned the array of windows on the buildings high above them, singling out the many snipers present on the scene. Still eyeing the well armed personnel facing her, Katelyn began stepping backwards. Zackery instinctively followed suit; still mesmerized by the threat being mounted against them.

Katelyn turned her head to the right and glanced down the subway entrance stairway. After witnessing the gathering of black body armor covered, weapon toting individuals huddle themselves at the foot and turn their violent handheld machinery up toward the couple occupying the sidewalk above them, Katelyn began to shimmy away from the opening taking Zackery with her, shielding his body behind hers.

She stopped moving and turned around to face him. "I'm almost positive that their interests lie completely with me."

"Is that little piece of information supposed to put me at ease?" Zackery took another glance over Katelyn's shoulder at the firepower pointed in their direction. It was all accompanied by a loud booming voice--over barking out orders for Katelyn to surrender herself.

"Once I draw them away I want you to get out of here," she said to him.

"Oh yeah? And just how do you plan on doing that?"

One second later found Zackery's eyes turning up and his head leaning back as he tracked Katelyn's path as she moved through the air. Her sleek body twisted and she came down from a height of nearly twenty five feet on top of the roof of one of the cars in the middle of the street. The tiny glass projectiles that the shattering windows turned into distracted the members of the strike team who were closest in proximity.

Katelyn bounded off of the damaged automobile and came down on the flat tarred rooftop of the small three story building across the street from where Zackery was still standing, his mind lost in amazement. He'd always known that there was something profoundly odd about this woman. He'd even gone about testing his theory in a not so roundabout way and as amazed as he was with his previous findings, what he was witnessing right now was nothing short of impossible.

Katelyn didn't remain on the roof for very long. Placing the adjacent building in her sights, she vaulted up and catapulted herself through a fifth story window, a barrage of gunfire trailing her.

"Sir, permission to use deadly force, sir?" is what Colonel Tobias McPhearson heard coming through the radio he held onto as he moved through the subway station.

He lifted the radio up to his lips and squeezed a button on the side of it. "Negative. I repeat, negative. Your orders for now are to subdue only. Deviate at your own peril. Is that understood?"

"Yes, sir. What about the civilian, sir?"

McPhearson moved in silence for a short period of time before lifting the radio again. "Take him. Find out what he knows."

She'd already disarmed him. Now she was taking hold of the sniper that she'd located by the front of his uniform with one hand and pulling his body into hers. With one firm shove Katelyn launched the man she held through the window at his back. A tact van parked on the street below broke his fall with as much resistance as a drop from that height could be sustained without being lethal. At the moment his safety wasn't on the top of Katelyn's list of priorities. It was the sight of Zackery being drug against his will and placed into the backseat of a car that consumed her.

Katelyn knocked loose some of the glass shards that still remained in place as she placed her left hand against the inside of the window pane that she stood in front of. She watched the car that carried her once upon a time traveling companion pull off down the street. "Zack," she whispered to herself.

Katelyn jerked her body back and the small projectile that whizzed through the window just missing her lodged itself into the wall to her right. She studied the small three pronged object whose spikes held it to the plaster and watched as it momentarily sparkled with a glow of electricity. No more time to waste on curiosity. Katelyn pushed away from the window and sprinted off through the apartment.

When she reached the front door she didn't bother with the knob. All the barrier received from her was a lowered shoulder. The force of her body as she barreled out into the hallway nearly blew the door off its hinges, and though the collision kept up quite a clamor it hadn't slowed her down one bit.

Katelyn's stride quickened as she broke out into a full on run down the corridor. All of her thoughts were on Zack at that moment and she wasn't about to let any barricade stand between her and the target she sought.

Closing in on the next hardwood obstruction in her path, Katelyn threw her right forearm into it and dislodged the door from its frame, tossing it aside as she entered the apartment. The window across the room was in her sights now and in no time she was through it.

Katelyn's body moved through the air high above the street below. Performing a single flip, she was now headed feet first toward the window across the street.

She'd passed directly over the car that Zackery was confined inside of and Katelyn was positive that the solitary vehicle she trailed was anything but. Cutting a swath through the building that she now found herself in, she vowed not to let the numerous vehicles and armed personnel that had since lit out after them both sway her from her task in any way.

Every fiber in her being beckoned her to abandon this senseless pursuit and seek out shelter somewhere far away from this ensnarement. But she couldn't leave Zack. Not like this. She couldn't abandon him to the malevolent clutches of that Tobias McPhearson. Logistics and dialectics were being betrayed by sensations that Katelyn neither knew the source of or reasoning for.

His continuing struggle with his two captors in the backseat of the car he currently occupied finally afforded him a squarely placed elbow to his solar plexus that belted the wind from his lungs as it doubled him over. His head still hovering just above his knees, Zackery struggled to find his breath once more. Turning his head to the side as he gasped allotted him just enough time to catch a glimpse of the image of a night black cloaked body outside of the window on his left. It exploded through a glass panel, vaulting over the small building below before touching down on the outside portion of the fire escape railing attached to the outer skin of the building next to it. What the hell was she doing? Zackery thought. And better yet, how the hell was she doing it?

"All sources are in accordance, sir," the gentleman sitting in the passenger seat in front of Zackery announced into the radio he held. Zackery's chest continued to heave expansively in and out as he finally managed to bring his upper torso back upright and take in vast sums of much needed oxygen. "She's using the surrounding buildings to acquire a measure of cover from both our air and ground units, but it's become clear that evading capture is definitely not her primary objective."

"What exactly are you trying to tell me, Sergeant?" Tobias said from the front passenger side seat of the humvee that he was traveling through the city in.

"She's tracking us, sir!" the Sergeant said, speaking into his handheld radio once more. "Our girl's nose open for the carryon we recently took into custody. Please advice. Over."

"If she's locked on to your position then draw her out into the open," Tobias said, the tone in which he spoke clearly conveying his annoyance. He let go of the button on the side of the radio. "Moron," Tobias muttered under his breath.

"Make a left at the next corner," the man sitting in the passenger seat in front of Zackery said. "Head for the freeway."

Zackery had no idea where these people were in such a hurry to usher him, and clearly Katelyn, off to or what they had in mind for them once they arrived but he was positive that he'd regret finding out. No sooner than the car had made the corner Zack felt his body lurching forward as the driver smashed on the brakes. Whatever mass he'd been hoping to avoid saw him fail miserably at the task.

Zackery had winced at the onset of the collision and when he finally pried his eyelids apart he looked out of the front windshield and got an eyeful of Katelyn's splayed out form resting comfortably on top of the dented in hood of the car that was currently still in motion. Zack noticed that she hadn't really paid much attention to him as she alternated cold, steely glances between the driver and the passenger to his right. Two quick jerks on the steering wheel and the car swerved hard enough to throw her.

"Katelyn!" Zackery called out to her as he once again took up his struggle with the two men holding him hostage in the backseat. Finding his efforts as futile as ever, all he was eventually left with was the esteemed pleasure of watching her body tumble across the street behind the car until his captors forced him to turn back around in his seat. "Bastards!" Zack growled at them, his spite rousing little effect if any.

Katelyn slowly came to her feet, her eyes locked on the automobile that was speeding away from her with Zackery inside. She was quickly becoming most displeased with their elusiveness. She wanted Zackery back and she wanted him now. The reckless motion of the car she'd just been thrown from had been successful in sending the traffic all around it into disarray. Katelyn's discarded body even managed to bring a few vehicles to a complete stop altogether; one of which she was now in the process of approaching.

"Are you alright?" the driver of the black Miada said as she approached his window. Katelyn's only response was opening his door, snatching apart the seatbelt mechanism holding him in place, and pulling him out of the vehicle. "Heeey!"

Katelyn took his place behind the steering wheel and shut the door, ignoring his frantic protests of her actions. The engine was still running and Zack was waiting. She pressed her foot down hard on the gas pedal.

Katelyn weaved through the traffic that cluttered the streets in front of her as she desperately sought to close the distance between her and the transport she was after which was no longer anywhere in sight. It was all happening just as it had been before. She traveled along the busy streets in the same manner as she'd previously moved through the various hallways and quarters of the many buildings as she bounded from one to the next.

She turned all the right corners; moved in all the right directions; constantly gaining on and keeping in close proximity with the quarry that she could neither physically hear nor see. And yet somehow she continued to successfully track her prey.

She could feel them; inexplicably feel the swelling numbers of her enemies beginning to close in around her on all sides. The freeway onramp was near now and so was Zack. She felt it. Katelyn gunned the engine of the car she was in, pushing it for all it was worth. She fought every impulse present within her in order to remain stubborn in her pursuit of him.

"There she is!" Tobias said, leaning forward in his seat, barely able to contain his excitement at the sight of the sporty two-seater that was forcefully merging its way into the freeway traffic not too far ahead of the armored vehicle's front bumper.

Katelyn zigzagged through the lanes of traffic until the vehicle that she had so longed for came into view in the center lane just ahead of her. She maneuvered the car around until there was nothing between her front bumper and the rear bumper of the car containing Zackery aside from twenty feet of rapidly moving pavement.

Glancing up at the rearview mirror, Katelyn suddenly became more concerned about her own rear bumper. Struggling with the steering wheel with both hands, Katelyn was barely able to keep the car in the lane after the humvee slammed into her. She momentarily turned her full attention back to the numerous vehicles still in pursuit of her. Emphasis on the numerous. No matter. Zack was in her sights. It was time to make her move.

Katelyn swung a punch at the windshield. The glass in front of her was instantly covered in fractures. Next she slammed her palm into the glass, knocking the entire fixture away. The damaged windshield slid across the hood and slipped down to the rushing freeway concrete below to be crushed completely by the rugged tires of the humvee that followed.

Maintaining a firm hold on the steering wheel with one hand, Katelyn slid over to the passenger seat. The instant that she let go of the wheel Katelyn bolted up and moved through the now open portal just beyond the dashboard. After crawling across the front hood of the car she quickly forced herself upright on her feet. The uproarious sound of the traffic all around her wasn't enough to drown out the noise of the multitude of whirring engines belonging to the black helicopters that swarmed through the airways above this stretch of the freeway that she now found herself traveling along. On top of the hood of an unmanned moving car, no less.

Slowly, the car began to shift off course. The humvee was closing in fast for another hit. She had no more time to waste. Katelyn rushed forward and leapt from the hood, coming down on top of the roof of the car in front of her. Kneeling down, Katelyn quickly found both her balance and her grip as the driver of the car instantly reacted to her presence, swerving in the lane.

"She's on the roof!" the driver yelled out.

"Well do something!" was all the sympathy he received in light of his plight.

Still kneeling down on one knee, Katelyn drew back her right fist as she prepared to deliver a blow to the top of car when a sudden flash of electricity rushed through her body. She was barely able to maintain her grip on the car as her body collapsed down on the roof. Katelyn reached up her right hand and pried loose the projectile that had lodged itself into her right shoulder.

Letting it drop from her fingers, Katelyn turned her eyes up towards the sky and the many helicopters that filled the horizon, specifically the one nearest her with the soldier posted on its flank, once again trying to retrain the sights of the sniper rifle he held on her.

That last jolt that he'd given her packed enough of a punch to momentarily take her feet out from under her. She was in no mood to wait around and find out just how many shots this man could get off until he ultimately put her out of commission for good.

It was close enough. She could make it. Katelyn found her footing again and pushed off of the car roof in the

direction of the rifle wielding trooper. Zack was simply
going to have to bide his time. Her body moved through
the air. Across the next lane of traffic. Past the freeway
railing. Over the water that filled the riverbed below.

She hit against the side of the helicopter right next
to him. Grabbing the stunned soldier by the back of
his uniform, Katelyn gave a sharp pull and ejected him
from the flying vehicle before moving further on inside.
By the time the first man she had accosted onboard the
helicopter splashed down into the river below Katelyn
had sent two more flailing bodies down to join him. She
now found herself alone inside of the helicopter with the
pilot. She simply took him up from his seat and shoved
him toward the rear of the helicopter, taking his place
behind the controls.

"Sir, she's commandeered Delta-23, sir. Please advice.
Over."

Col. McPhearson was growing ever more infuriated
with the squawking device that he held clutched in his
palm. Furiously he brought it up to his lips. "If at all
possible I want that gunship back in pristine working
order. Aside from that, anyone of you that gets a clear
shot at the girl take it." Tobias fought every urge that he
possessed that beckoned him to smash his radio against
the dashboard in front of him. In the end it was the
years of discipline instilled in him that won out, allowing
him to refrain from destroying such a source of outright
aggravation.

Discipline.

He clutched his fingers increasingly tighter around
the radio as he lowered it.

This time.

The former pilot of the helicopter that Katelyn now
steered above the cars that moved along the freeway
lanes below looked on cautiously as this dark haired
young woman went about working the controls within
her reach. She went about her tasks seemingly oblivious

to his presence. Despite all he knew of her, for a moment he thought to use her apparent distraction to mount an offensive maneuver. One step in her direction and the slight tilt of her head in his halted his movement and simultaneously quelled any and all thoughts of a repeat performance on his part.

Not only had Katelyn caught up with the automobile carrying Zackery, she'd moved ahead of it. The helicopter did a one eighty and lowered itself down into the feverishly protesting freeway traffic. The drivers hurled curses; the vehicles swerved to get out of the way, but eventually traffic in the westbound lanes did come to a standstill once the helicopter touched down.

Katelyn got up out of her seat and turned around, making eye contact with her passenger. "Get out. And get lost," she said to him. His compliance came in the form of his back being turned to her followed up by his eagerly mobile body shuffling off through the open portal to her left. Once he'd exited the assault vehicle and hurried along his way across the freeway pavement Katelyn turned her eyes toward the opening to her right and started for it.

She bolted out of the helicopter and lit out over the hoods, roofs, and trunks that stood between her and Zack. The car he was in remained trapped in the stalled traffic and Katelyn was closing in fast. Zackery watched her approach along with the four gentlemen holding him hostage until Katelyn's body leapt up into the air and they all lost sight of her. Without warning, the window behind Zackery's head exploded into thousands of tiny shards that showered the occupants of the backseat, throwing the entire interior of the car into disarray.

Next, Zackery felt a hand grip hold of the back of his shirt and he found himself being pulled out of his seat. The next time he opened his eyes he was standing on top of the trunk staring Katelyn in the face. "Come on," she said to him, hopping down to the ground. Zack followed suit. "We have to hurry."

All too pleased to have been liberated, Zackery stayed on her heels as she weaved through the standstill traffic toward the very large object that was obstructing it. Millions of questions flooded his mind and as the spinning propellers that he approached forced him to duck his head down as he moved, he couldn't deny number one million and one. He climbed inside of the helicopter and looked on in astonishment as Katelyn climbed into one of the seats and began working the controls under the guise that she might have actually known what she was doing. Had she truly possessed the capabilities to get them out of this horrendous mess that the both of them were now mixed up in then he might consider making the question of how she was able to accomplish such a feat number one million and two.

Zackery sat down in the seat next to her and clutched at the cushion in a brief moment of panic as Katelyn brought the helicopter up from the ground. She forced the machine through the air at an alarming rate of speed, hoping to put some considerable distance between the two of them and their opponents who were currently in the process of changing course. Katelyn cut her eyes over to the fuel gauge.

This bird clearly held enough gas for her to give Tobias and his men a fairly decent run until she ultimately found a way to lose them, but dragging Zackery along for the ride would not only drag out the ultimate conclusion but hinder it considerably. Might as well do what she could to try and put an end to this agitating pursuance right now if she could.

Katelyn, much to Zack's surprise and outright shock, got up from her seat and abandoned the controls for the rear of the helicopter without uttering so much as a single word.

"What the hell are you doing!?!" he exclaimed, jerking his head around to get a look at her. "Does this thing have some kind of automatic pilot or something?"

"You're free to have a look," Katelyn said to him as she stared out of the right side of the helicopter at the water rushing by below. "Or you could come with me."

"And do what?" Zackery said in a state of complete distress. Katelyn turned her eyes to him and conveyed her every intention. "Are you insane? I'm not jumping out of this thing!"

"Then I take it you know how to operate it?"

At that Zackery quickly went about undoing the fastening mechanisms that held him in place and hurried over to Katelyn's side. "I would just like to officially go on record as saying..."

Katelyn stepped behind him and took his body up in her arms. "Save your breath," she said, stepping over the edge and holding him firmly as they dropped.

Their bodies hit and went under. After the initial sinking Zackery's arms and legs began thrashing as he tried to make a go for the surface. He was on his way and would have most assuredly accomplished his task had he not snagged his left ankle on something. Turned out it was the viselike grip of Katelyn's hand that was preventing his ascension. He struggled against her hold but it was no use, and instead of joining him in a stride for the waiting oxygen above, Katelyn set her body in motion and drug him down deeper into the murky depths beneath them.

7

Tobias just stood there, his hands in the side pockets of the black trench coat he was wearing, staring out at the small rolling crests that covered the surface of the waterway laid out before him. The treading on the soles of his polished to a night black shine military issue combat boots were sank into the soft moist earth of the bank he stood on. It was rapidly closing in on thirty minutes since his team last had a visual on the target they sought so feverishly. At this point the Colonel was secretly operating under the assumption that the timeframe between that previous moment and the next time that they laid eyes on her would most likely occur sometime in the distant future, if at all.

Regardless. He ordered his men about their respective tasks in the off chance that there was even a minute opportunity that their efforts would yield something even closely resembling that of anything fruitful. Given the outright erratic behavior that this soldier had been granted the recent privilege of witnessing from a subject that he had been trained to hold to a significantly higher standard, Col. Tobias McPhearson could honestly admit to himself that he had his doubts about his predictions as to what his target's next move would be.

Fleeing when there seemed no point in her doing so. Making herself a visible target when remaining unseen undoubtedly allotted her a definite advantage. Her actions defied logic at every turn, but as long as his didn't

Tobias' confidence in this campaign remained unshaken. Besides. He still held one more trump card to play.

"Colonel," Capt. Blair called out to him as he approached him along the riverbank on his left. Tobias turned his eyes away from the water and placed them on him. "We've gone over every inch of this place for a mile in both directions along both shores. There's no sign of where she came out anywhere. You want me to bring the divers in? Drag the place?"

"That won't be necessary. In the off chance that she is still in the area I'd much rather prefer a confrontation on land. Gather the men. Tell them to fall back." Tobias turned his eyes back to the water.

"Yes, sir," Capt. Blair replied before turning and heading on his way.

Katelyn's body emerged from the depths of the riverbed along with Zackery's not too far from where they initially entered the water and they swam for the shore. Zackery's necessity for oxygen had been sustained courtesy of one of the tires of a rusted out old heap that Katelyn had led him to. Seeing as how she remained at his side during the duration of their stay, never partaking of any herself, he wondered just what it was that was sustaining her. Some set of lungs perhaps. Number one million and three.

Katelyn made it up to the riverbank thrashing her soaked, black sleeve covered arms down towards the ground on either side of her. She stormed off without so much as turning to look back at Zackery who struggled to the shore behind her. Mumbling inaudibly, she appeared to him to be examining the damp and torn clothing that she wore. She brought her right forearm up to her nose and inhaled. Her reaction was one of odious revulsion. "This is the absolute worst day of my entire life!" she yelled out. "Probably," she said after a moment's thought.

"Hey!" Zack shouted to her back as he struggled out of the water and onto the shore. Katelyn stopped walking and turned to look back at him. "Do you mind waiting up? I just so happened to have had the misfortune of joining you in this not so stellar event in your life and I, for one, can vouch that seeing you home is definitely a spectator sport. So if it's no problem for you, I'd rather not sprint the rest of the way."

Katelyn removed some of the wet strands of hair that were dangling in her face out of the way so that she could get a clearer view of him. Was he serious? She couldn't believe that after all she'd been put through this man had actually expected her to suffer his presence as she sloshed her way back to her apartment.

The light in the evening sky was fading, turning it a light shade of purple. The comfort of her home was where she so desperately wanted to be right now and though she continued to possess more than the required strength necessary to wage a monumental protest, something deep down inside of her lacked the desire to do so.

Katelyn conceded to its draw, turning a deaf ear to every voice of defiance that echoed through her mind. After all, she'd once found a small measure of solace in his company before having to deal with the onslaught that had claimed to go by the name of Tobias McPhearson. Perhaps even a small fraction of that level of repose would do her a whole world of good. At least until she made it back to her bathroom shower.

Zackery pulled open the door of the apartment that he stood inside of and stepped aside allowing Tripp Manning and Morgan Paleto to come inside. "Hola," Tripp said, looking all about the living room as he stepped inside of the very personal space of his fellow Wicker Basket employee. "Bienvenidos a la casa de freak show."

"Take a pill," Morgan said, slapping a backhand against his left shoulder as she moved into the apartment behind him. "And try and act like you're a guest in someone's home. Which you are." Morgan turned her eyes to Zackery just as he was shutting the door behind them. One glance at the ensemble that he was draped in and she could tell that something was profoundly off about the whole picture in front of her. "What are you wearing?" she asked him, referring to the navy blue cotton sweater he wore that hung loosely over his upper torso and the dark blue jeans he had on that his waistline was barely able to hold up without the use of a belt. It most definitely wasn't the outfit that she had seen him adorned in earlier that day; the brightly colored T-shirt that hung snuggly over the Dockers he'd had on.

"Katelyn lent these to me," Zack told her. "I had to swap mine out."

"What?" Morgan said, her face twisted in confusion.

"Come on. I'll tell you all about it."

Zackery recounted the events of the evening he'd just experienced to both a captivated and skeptical audience. Between the two of them, Tripp was more inclined to take it all with a grain of salt while Morgan was more willing to place some validity in the notion that Zackery might actually be speaking the truth. Soon Katelyn emerged from the depths of her bedroom and moved into the living room wearing a pair of black silk pajamas. She stopped moving at the sight of the trio making themselves comfortable in her home.

Tripp turned his head and locked eyes with her. "Katelyn. How are you? That's good to hear. Hey, do you think I could bother you for a beer?"

She didn't speak a word as she took up walking again and made her way towards the kitchen. Tripp turned back to Zack and Morgan and after giving them a look that drew out a slight grin from both of their faces he got up and headed after her.

When Tripp reached the kitchen he hopped up on one of the counters and gave the room a good eyeballing. "You keep a pretty clean place of residence here, Katelyn. What's your secret?"

Katelyn was standing on the other side of the room off to his left with her back to him. Shutting the refrigerator door, she turned around and walked towards him. Katelyn handed him one of the two clear beer bottles that she held. "My secret is not polishing the countertops with my ass." With a smile on his face Tripp twisted off the cap on his bottle and swallowed a swig from it. Katelyn did the same with the bottle she held. "That was a hint. I could be more direct if you'd like."

"Don't bother," Tripp said, sliding down to his feet. "Word on the street is that you're some kind of fugitive from justice. Would I be safe in assuming that your crimes against humanity don't fall anywhere under the violent offender category?"

Katelyn glared at him as Tripp dangerously tested the boundaries of her patience and tolerance for his presence in her apartment. "The only concern you should have for your safety should involve you getting out of my kitchen, going back into the living room, and trying not to break anything. Otherwise you'll find yourself wishing that the words floating around the street regarding your demise were greatly exaggerated."

Tripp never let his eyes fall from the ice sheet that was her face as he slowly inched his way out of the kitchen. All speculations of her lethality aside, Tripp felt that he was definitely in too close of a proximity to this potential threat to chance provoking an unwanted reaction from her. He flashed her a quick smile before turning and making off for the living room. Yes, the living room. Where he could once again keep company with the sanely predictable. It certainly sounded better than continuing this one on one with the exact opposite.

The hours passed and the constant trickling away of time eventually found four slumbering bodies occupying the interior of Katelyn's darkened apartment. Katelyn, of course, was resting snugly in her bed. Morgan had drifted off on the living room couch. Tripp snored softly on the loveseat. Zackery slept comfortably in the recliner. At least he did until a tickling sensation in his nose roused him to a somewhat awakened state of consciousness.

Rubbing his right hand down his face, Zack retracted the footrest that his legs rested on as he leaned forward and opened his eyes. His vision retained a small portion of blurriness but he was easily able to make out the time on the digital clock embedded in the cable box atop the television that consumed the area of the corner across the room from him. It was just after 2 A. M.

Cutting his eyes to the right, Zackery soon caught sight of Morgan's stretched out body on the couch. His neck continued to twist further and his eyes suddenly located Tripp's still form over his right shoulder.

They both slept soundly. Zackery stood up from the recliner, rubbing his face awake with both of his hands. He moved off toward the hallway located in the area to his left. Katelyn's bedroom lie at the end of that passage.

He grabbed hold of the knob and gave it a turn. The door to her bedroom, much to his surprise, was unlocked. Zackery pushed it open and stepped inside. He walked on, stepping slowly and softly until he reached the foot of her bed where he came to a stop. Turning his head to the right, Zackery took a moment to soak in the shadow covered image of Katelyn sleeping soundly, silently... safely beneath the comforter that covered the mattress supporting her body.

Mentally freeing himself of the rapture that had consumed him brought on by such a vision, Zackery continued forward toward the window across the room from him. He spread open the dark shaded curtains that Katelyn had in place and parted the blinds just beyond with the fingers of his right hand at eye level. This allowed him the privilege of somewhat secretly peering out into the night coated city. His eyes scanned back and forth, up and down, everywhere in search of anything that could possibly be perceived as an unforeseen threat to himself, Tripp, Morgan, and, most importantly, the woman that slumbered at his back.

"What are you doing in here?" Zackery heard a soft voice call out to him that could have only belonged to Katelyn.

Slumbered?

Zackery turned and when he placed his eyes on the bed he watched the shadows covering it move. "Sorry. Just checking to make sure that you were okay. All of us actually."

When Zackery had raised the argument of him being allowed to remain at her place even after he'd showered and been awarded a fresh change of clothes it didn't take much prodding for him to coax Katelyn into agreement. His company that evening hadn't been altogether that unpleasant and neither would it be had she been forced to stomach it a bit more, she'd imagined.

Katelyn even found it possible to scrounge up a lingering scrap of tolerance when he suggested inviting Tripp and Morgan over. Recommending that they all be allowed to stay the night for safety's sake had pushed Katelyn further past her threshold of comfort than she cared to venture.

She protested adamantly and was seriously close to placing her foot down firmly on the issue, if not down on top of one of the two that he stood firmly on. In the end, after Tripp and Morgan had been reluctantly brought onboard, it was his gently soothing and non-threatening manner of speech that had once again tipped her over into the ravine of acceptance.

But this?

This was too much. Zackery was inside of her home. It was well into the late hours; the darkened hours that had been notorious for cloaking both the underlying intentions and the individuals they belonged to in a blackened shroud of mystery. And although the two of them weren't exactly alone in the apartment they were, in fact, alone in her bedroom at this particularly presumptuous moment in time. It was a level of familiarity that Katelyn currently remained averse to even consider lending him. All rhyme and reason be damned.

"I'm fine," she said, rolling her body over in his direction. Katelyn opened her eyelids and stared right at him. The golden glow of the street lamps just outside of the building produced a bright aura of illumination behind the dark figure standing near the foot of her bed. "So either go back to sleep or go home. Come first light I seriously doubt you'll find your options so pleasing."

"First light?" he said, folding his arms in front of him, his eyes still fixated on her form splayed across the mattress she rested on. Zackery turned and started moving away from the window. "Is that my cutoff time? First light?" he said to her as he slowly moved across the carpet just beyond the foot of the bed.

"All luck pressing aside," Katelyn replied, her eyes following his movement as her back continued to rest firmly on the mattress beneath her.

Zackery's eyes continued to remain locked on the sublime figure lying on the bed as he took one soft step after the other, watching the body's features slowly assume an ever more clearer definition as he continued to move and she sat up and braced herself against the pillow covered headboard. "I'm not leaving you alone in here."

"You will if I tell you to," Katelyn said in a voice that matched the soft tone in which he spoke.

"What is it?" he said as he rounded the corner of the bed and started her way. "Why are you like this?"

Katelyn felt her body tense as the dark figure neared her. When Zackery sat on the bed and slid his body next to hers she pushed herself back as close to the headboard as she could get. "Like what?" she said.

Zack stretched his hand out in an attempt to place his fingers against the side of her face, a maneuver that was instantly thwarted by Katelyn as she lightly took hold of him by the wrist. "So defensive. So afraid to let anything touch you."

Katelyn slowly let go of his arm, gently stroking her fingers across his skin as she lowered her hand. "I'm not sure anything should," she said to him. "You don't know me."

"The way I hear it neither do you." Zack inched his body across the mattress, bringing his face that much closer to hers. "So how can you really be sure?"

Katelyn remained silent as she was at a complete loss for words. What could she say to him? How could she explain to him the multitude of instincts that were, at the moment and for reasons unknown to her, beckoning for her to back away from him both physically and emotionally in a way that would make sense to him? How could he understand when she herself remained in the dark about it all? "I can't," Katelyn said to him. "I just feel it."

"What?" Zackery continued to inquire. "What do you feel?"

He leaned in closer to her, his darkened face moving down nearer to hers. Katelyn had no where else to go. Her back was pushed as far back as the headboard would allow. Zackery was getting closer. Closer to her now than anyone had ever been or dared venture, in both the physical and emotional sense of everything present in this moment. Katelyn stopped resisting. Not the urge to retreat from his presence, but the desire to embrace it. Slowly. Gradually. She lifted her chin and...

Suddenly and without warning Katelyn perked up on the bed, her back stiffening as straight as a board. Zackery was forced back a few inches. She turned her head to the left and then quickly back to the right, her eyes fixating on her bedroom window. "They're here!" she said, turning back to Zack.

"What are you talking about? Who's here?" When the once gently illuminated window over his left shoulder suddenly blinked out to a dull gray Zackery found his attention momentarily distracted. It didn't take him long to come to the realization of who the *they* that Katelyn was referring to actually were. The same *they* that had just cut the power on the streets below and most assuredly that which was being utilized by the occupants of this building. "They're here?" Zackery said, rising to his feet as he felt the mattress shift beneath him as Katelyn made for the area of the floor just beyond the foot of the bed.

"Hurry!" she said to him, throwing open the doors to her closet. "We have to get out of here."

Zackery moved as swiftly as he could through this unfamiliar dwelling and did so without the use of his eyes until he reached the living room. He searched the floor for his shoes, quietly calling out to both Tripp and Morgan for them to get up. In the end it would take him physically jostling them for Zackery to rouse them from their slumber. After that, even more time was wasted trying to convince Tripp that this wasn't all part of some practical joke.

The quartet spilled out of the apartment and into the darkened hallway that awaited them, thus confirming what Zackery had already suspected to be true. The building's power had effectively been shut off. The only illumination that the four of them enjoyed was being produced by a single window at the far end of the hall at Katelyn's back. Outside of that faint smidgen of incandescent it was the sound of their footsteps and voices that helped the small rabble approximate each other's proximity to one another as well as their position in the hallway. "What is this?" Tripp asked, clearly peeved at the extent of this annoyance. "What's going on with the lights?"

"They cut the power," Zackery explained. "How many times do we have to go over this?"

Tripp was sleepy, annoyed, and at his wit's end. If they wanted to keep up this pointless charade then they could have at it. "Oh, will you just drop it already. If you guys want to roam around here in the dark hiding out from G-men then be my guest. I'm going home." And with that, Tripp's feet began to beat a path down the hallway away from them.

"How are you going to get out of here?" Morgan called after him. "Aren't the elevators down?"

"I'll take the stairs," Tripp slung back over his shoulder.

"You can't get out that way," Katelyn spoke up in warning.

"Oh yeah, princess?" Tripp stopped walking and turned around. "Why's that?"

"Because they're on their way up."

"And you know this how?" Tripp posed to her. He was answered with silence. "Right. Of course. See you around." Tripp turned and continued on his way.

"How *do* you know that?" Morgan asked her.

Again with the silence.

Katelyn could feel Zackery's eyes examining her right then and there in the darkened hallway as he also awaited an answer to that question. Katelyn herself would make for number four.

Tripp leaned against the bar and pushed open the door that led out to the staircase. Remembering the area of placement of the once lit up light fixture that had been emblazoned with the letters *E X I T* above a door down the hall to the right of the elevator that he had stepped off of previously that night aided Tripp in successfully locating that particular port of thru traffic. But something wasn't right. Moving toward the railing that barred the opening between the first step leading down the staircase to his right and the step that started up the staircase to his left, Tripp leaned forward and peered down into the swirling funnel of steps.

Lights.

He saw lights.

Not the ones that should have been coming from the electronic fixtures that had been professionally installed by the individuals initially commissioned to perform such electrical engineering on the building, had such features currently remained in operation, but from another source altogether. These lights existed in the form of several small beams. Beams that slithered and crawled over everything they came into contact with as they wound their way up the staircase in Tripp's direction, their numbers too numerous to count.

They weren't tenants. Tripp had figured that out for himself. Their movements contained too much precision; their actions, too concise and objectively driven. Slowly. Quietly. He hoisted his upper body up and stepped back from the rail. The sudden shock that the elevators were currently inoperational finally settled in on him as he moved backwards through the stairwell door and began to once again attempt to fathom a plausible exit strategy. He slowly began to accept the fact that Zack's wild-eyed conspiracies just might hold some measure of weight.

"Hey!" he called out to the shadowy figures he saw still occupying the corridor off to his right. "Somebody's coming. There are..." He extended his right arm and pointed his index finger out as he forced his back against the concrete wall behind him. "...these guys! They're coming up!"

"This way," Katelyn said, turning and walking in the opposite direction of the door leading out to the staircase. From what she could tell there was only one way that she was going to secure an exit from this building that would see all four of them out safely. But they would have to hurry. Her adversaries were closing in and closing in fast.

When Katelyn reached a bend in the hallway she stopped and ushered the others around the corner. Remaining in place, Katelyn stood there and watched as several beams of light spilled out into the hall and started moving in her direction. When the spotlights began to dance along the wall right next to her Katelyn continued on her way.

"Where to now?" Tripp said to anybody willing to offer him up some kind of explanation. Katelyn walked over to the wall and pulled open a panel that was next to him. The smell hit him instantly as Katelyn took hold of the handle at the top of the metal plate and pulled down. "Aw," Tripp cringed, bringing his fingers up to block his nostrils. "The garbage shoot?"

"Unless you'd prefer the alternative," Katelyn commented.

Having prior knowledge of the intensity of the foe that was currently on their heels, Zackery, realizing the consequences of the dwindling timeframe within which they operated, moved to the front of the open portal. "Screw it." Gripping hold of the ledge he found inside of the shoot that lined the upper rim, he hoisted his body up and shoved himself inside feet first.

Morgan took her turn next.

Tripp approached the opening and turned to Katelyn about to voice another grievance to her. "We're wasting time," she said, cutting him off.

Tripp was expelled from the shoot and his body deposited into a large waste bin filled with refuse, some bundled and some scattered loosely all about. Neither of which made any difference to Tripp. He continued to find the entire ordeal revolting. "Yeah," he said, wading through the trash toward the edge of the bin. "This is exactly how I had planned on spending my night." Reaching the edge, Tripp climbed over the side to the sound of Katelyn's body crashing down behind him. "Do me a favor, Zack. Lose my number."

Katelyn soon landed on the ground next to Tripp.

"I assume our next move is to make a break for Tripp's car," Zack said. He spoke softly but the acoustics of the large bay room they were in managed to carry his voice exceptionally well. The area across the room from them that was home to two large open garage doors allowed what little light the night provided to slip into the room.

"Provided you especially," Katelyn said to Zackery, "keep a reasonably low profile, I'm sure the three of you could just walk on out of here. I shouldn't have much problem slipping past them afterwards."

"Are you sure you're going to be okay?" Morgan asked her.

Zackery began to boil over with an emotionally charged mixture consisting of worry, anger, and utter confusion. He couldn't believe the absolute ridiculousness of the plan of action he saw taking shape right before his eyes. Surely Katelyn wasn't delusional enough to believe that they were just going to cut out of there and leave her to fend for herself while they saved their own necks, Katelyn's freakish chances at success be damned.

Zackery approached her and his chest expanded drastically with all of the oxygen that he sucked into his lungs. "If you think for one second that we're leaving here without you then I strongly suggest that you..."

His voice had rose significantly along with the finger that he now held up in front of his chest. As he neared her Katelyn reached up and took hold of his hand, silencing him. "Your place. In one hour," she said, hoping to calm him with the promise of a speedy reunion.

Witnessing the soothing effect that her words were starting to have on him, Katelyn took the time to relish in both the accomplishment of the strategy she was in the process of implementing in order to get rid of him along with the knowledge that she was actually planning on making good on her promise.

Her mind screamed at her to send Zack home with his false hope, elude her pursuers, and head out on her own in search of much more safer venues to occupy. Preferably venues much much further away. "Wait for me," Katelyn said to him. "I'll be there." Watching the trio begin to move away from her, Zack backpedaling, she secretly cursed herself for even considering upholding the vow she'd extended to him. Really. What was the point?

He stepped out onto the balcony and forced the sliding glass door closed behind him somewhat aggressively. The metal and glass barrier had been effective in cutting Zack off from the unrelenting back and forth banter between Tripp and Morgan as they went about their heated argument in his living room regarding various government conspiracy theories and the validity there of. Though he was free of that nuisance, the slightly chilled night air and the view of the virtually pedestrian free streets below brought him little comfort.

Where was she? She'd said one hour. By his count, courtesy of every comparable time keeping mechanism in his apartment, she was approximately fifty three minutes into the debt of time lapse that she had waged against her arrival. What if she hadn't made it out? Zackery's mind flashed back to the last image of her that his mind had on record as he backed out of that apartment building. The shadow drenched picture of the slender femme flooded his every thought.

Asshole, his mind called out to him.

What was he thinking leaving her there? What if she'd been captured? What if she'd been able to escape? What reason did he have to believe that her most sanest strategy would lie anywhere in the realm of finding a way back to his apartment? Back to him? Given what he'd witnessed of her uncanny abilities it was quite plausible that Katelyn was miles away by now and still in the process of placing considerably more distance between the people that so eagerly sought her out as well as himself.

That certainly would have been the wisest course of action to take. What purpose would possibly be gained in showing up here? he thought as he stared out at the cityscape just beyond the railing in front of him. Whatever Katelyn's decisions consisted of Zack chose to maintain a sense of hopefulness that they would see her through to the safety that he knew she both sought out and desperately needed. At the same time he suffered under the quiet resentment that he selfishly harbored towards her for having the audacity to seek out such solace in his absence. Who'd she think she was anyway?

Katelyn.

Katelyn Bree.

Zackery turned his head to the left and saw Katelyn standing there on the balcony with him. She was as poised and calmly looking as if she'd been standing there this whole time. "Where'd you come from?"

"Does it matter?" she said to him.

That was it. The bull's back had officially had it. That was without a doubt the very last straw. No longer would he stand idly by and let unimaginable feats of human strength and endurance coupled with swarming hordes of tact gear strapped militia men continue to go about their existence unquestioned.

"Who are you?"

She let out a long sigh and turned her eyes away from him to get a look at the city lights out past the balcony. "You already know the answer to that."

"No. No I don't. But I think it's long past time that I did."

8

Tripp Manning was sitting behind the steering wheel of his car guiding it along the freeway. The light of the oncoming sunrise had already began to fade out the starlit sky and paint the once pitch dark canvas with hazy shades of light blue and purple. The very early morning hour explained the thin layer of traffic that was obstructing their path, but Tripp himself was still somewhat in the dark regarding both the purpose of this spontaneous trek as well as the destination. "Where the hell is Wilderbrook, Kansas anyway?" he asked.

Morgan Paleto had been accompanying him on this strange spur of the moment voyage that had originally been initiated in order to delve deeper into the enigma that was Katelyn's past. Morgan was seated in the passenger seat next to him. Katelyn was occupying the seat at her back and Zack's body was trying to find rest on the cushion behind Tripp.

"Just keep going on this stretch," Katelyn said to him over the music pumping out of the car's speaker system. "You're going to need to veer south after the next hundred and fifty seven miles."

Tripp cut his eyes up to the rearview mirror in search of a view of her. His search yielded bupkiss as she as of current was sitting much too far to the right of his automobile for him to acquire a clear view of her. "The only place I'm veering off to is the next exit and after that I'm pulling into the nearest motel parking lot." A weary eyed Zackery shoved a knee into the back of his seat. "Oh screw you, man. I've been driving for hours. Anyone willing to take their shift at the wheel, be my guest. But as for me, personally I'd much rather spend my recoup time in a warm bed than in a car seat. Any objections?"

"Whatever," Morgan said to him, sensing the overwhelming air of exhaustion floating around the interior of the car. "Pull it over. I'm sure we could all do with some much needed rest right now. A few hours at least. Let's just bed down for the time being and see where we're all at come daylight. Agreed?"

Tripp came walking back to the car after a short visit to the Travel Inn's manager's office. After pooling all of the cash that they had on hand he was able to secure two singles for them to rest and get washed up in while still leaving a reasonable amount of spending cash for the duration of the trip, however long or short it might be.

He tossed a set of keys over the roof of the car and Katelyn raised a single hand up in the air, catching them. They officially had lodging for the night.

Zackery stayed on Katelyn's heels all the way up until she put the key in the designated lock and opened the door to her motel room. She stepped inside and Zackery would have followed had it not been for the firm hand that Morgan placed against his chest as she stepped in front of him. "Is there a problem I need to know about?" Zackery said to her.

She turned around and watched as Katelyn went straight for the bathroom, shutting the door behind her. "We're looking at an early start tomorrow and we're all going to need as much rest as we can scrounge up in the next few hours. And don't get me wrong but somehow I doubt that you attempting to bunk with Kate is going to mean solace for anyone tonight. You catch my drift?"

Zackery stared vaguely at the halfcocked smirk she wore, desperately trying to find some logic in her

SoulSeeker: Rise to Chaos

reasoning. Watching Katelyn emerge from the washroom over her shoulder, it could truly be said that he'd done nothing short of fail miserably. Either way, trying to get past Morgan right now would no doubt prove to be more trouble than he needed. "Tripp?" he said, raising a thumb up and pointing it to his left.

"Tripp," Morgan replied with a nod as she stepped back into the room and closed the door.

"Why is he like that?" Katelyn said to her once they were alone.

Morgan turned around to find her sitting on the opposite side of the bed from her with her back to her as she alleviated herself of her footwear. She'd asked the question, but Morgan would be hard pressed to come up with a quick answer.

Really, what was the attraction?

Morgan had been acquainted with Zack for quite some time and there was nothing about this bleak malcontent that held any similarity to any past consort that she had been aware of. "Not sure," Morgan said to her back as she moved over to the nightstand that was on her side of the bed. "Guess something about you just rubs him the right way."

"And you?" Katelyn continued as she turned her head toward her right shoulder. "I don't rub you the right way?"

Her fingers had been working at the controls on the alarm clock in preparation for the day that lie in wait for them until that last remark froze her fingers mid function and pushed all thoughts of the journey that lie ahead of them out of her mind. Morgan thought back to the countless times that she had joined in in ridiculing and mocking her. True, she had done so out of little more than her own momentary amusement but in hindsight, attributing any valid feelings on Katelyn's side of the line, Morgan could see how she might have come to that conclusion.

Morgan stood up straight and turned to face her profile. "It's not like that, Katelyn. And I don't mean anything bad about this but...you're just different, that's all. Not everybody understands that. Including me."

Katelyn faced forward again and let her eyes drop down to the carpet just in front of her bare feet. "Guess that makes two of us," she said to herself. Katelyn stood up from the bed, pulled her shirt up over her head, and dropped it to the floor before heading for the bathroom once more.

Courtesy of the quick scavenger session in Zackery's closet before embarking on this trek, along with a quick stop in at the nearby supermarket, they were all allotted the esteemed convenience of stashing their sullied articles of clothing in the trunk while they adorned fresh outfits. It also allowed them to stock up on an assortment of snacks for the road but they still found it necessary to stop over at a diner for breakfast that morning before heading out of town.

Zackery held open the door and Katelyn moved out past him. "Did you sleep okay last night?" he asked her, letting go of the door and following her out onto the parking lot.

"Of course. Why wouldn't I have?"

"I don't know. I just assumed what with you being on the run and having to spend the night in a strange bed with a woman you hardly know might have had some effect on your log sawing."

Katelyn opened the backseat door on the passenger side of Tripp's car. "Sorry to disappoint you," she said, climbing into her seat.

Zackery got in on the other side. He just sat there for a moment waiting for a response from her. All Katelyn did was rest her outstretched arm against the window sill and lean her head over her right shoulder. She stared forward out of the front windshield in total silence. "So this place we're headed to," Zackery said, refusing to let the peace endure, "what's it like? Is there going to be anybody there to welcome you back? Somebody not dressed in government issue fatigues perhaps? Preferably unarmed?"

Katelyn sucked in a large swell of air and hissed it all out slowly. "It's just a few acres of land out in the middle of nowhere," she answered him, still staring ahead. "And no. Nobody's home. Shouldn't be, anyway."

"So it's like some kind of farm we're talking about?" he asked her.

"Something like that," Katelyn sighed.

"And you have no idea how you wound up there? Whether or not you were brought there? Born and raised there?" That did the trick. Katelyn lifted her head up and swiveled her neck, placing a set of ice cap covered eyes in line with his. "Right," Zack said, his face turning to look forward. "Been there. Done that."

Morgan pulled open the door in front of Zackery and climbed in behind the wheel. "Where's Tripp?" Zackery asked her. "It's going on eleven o'clock. We've gotta get going."

"Hold on," Morgan replied calmly. "He'll be right out."

Zackery was finding that the closer they approached this one particular puzzle piece that belonged to the woman sitting beside him the more eager he was becoming. Morgan had called Jordan Carthright first thing that morning and explained to him about the nature of their expedition, being careful to tiptoe around the specifics of the circumstances that had set them off. Jordan, of course, wasted no time in forgiving their absence from work and asking her to extend Katelyn his wishes for the best of luck to her.

With the all clear given for them to pursue any leads that they had on the origins of the young amnesiac in their company, Zack couldn't have been more on edge.

He'd wanted to know everything he could possibly find out about Katelyn even before the bombshell of the strange talents that she possessed had been dropped. Since then his desire to unravel the mystery of the raven haired femme sitting next to him had extended well beyond the realm of uncontrollable. They were getting close to something. He could feel it.

Tobias McPhearson took a seat behind the desk in the room that he had cordoned off for the purpose of being his own private office deep within the confines of this abandoned office building. Flipping up his laptop and switching it on, Tobias didn't have to wait long for the high tech, state of the art piece of equipment to produce a small window in the top left hand corner of the liquid plasma screen covered with data. The window contained the very crystal clear image of Tobias' commanding officer Gen. Michael Selinski.

"I understand that we've incurred more complications than initially perceived in the apprehension of our misplaced parcel. Now the thing I was wondering about was whether or not this was a result of a mere lack of manpower...or just piss poor planning on your part. Feel free to inject your own astute input at any time now."

"Negative on all accounts, sir," Tobias said, remaining uncharacteristically calm. "And begging the General's pardon, sir, I believe the chain of command was very well informed of the difficulties that this specific campaign could present."

"Then allow me to inform you that your faith in the tolerance of your ranking officers in light of the ongoing lack of progress on your behalf is sorely misplaced. This entire operation is becoming entirely too public. If there's either a problem with personnel or personnel equipment then voice your grievance now. Otherwise get this mess cleaned up, Colonel. Is that understood?" Tobias' teeth couldn't have been clenched together any harder, his already insurmountable anger being forced over the edge by the condescension being put on display by his senior officer. Prying his jaw apart, he said, "Consider it taken care of, sir."

"See to it that it is."

The window disappeared from the corner of the screen and the General was gone, leaving Tobias alone in his office with nothing but his fiery ire and, after a low grunt accompanied by a swift backhand blow with his left hand, one shattered laptop computer. "Katelyn," he breathed out softly as he leaned back in the seat and collected himself. "Where are you, girl?"

The road that they traveled along was composed of nothing but dirt and rock and kicked up a dusty cloud behind the car as it kept up its slow and steady pace. Aside from the sky having taken on a bright shade of blue in contrast to the dull grays that she'd last seen here, the place was exactly as Katelyn had remembered it. The overgrown lawn to her left. The weed strangled, untended fields to her right. The two story white painted home in the distance that was the only place of residence for miles in every direction. She had no idea what they were hoping to find on this barren stretch of land. Ever since she'd woken up here some four years ago, finding nothing and no one here of any discernible interest to her, Katelyn had wanted nothing else but to leave.

Morgan pulled the car into the driveway of the home that was composed of roughly the same material as the road aside from a few more patches of weed sprouts. She brought the car to a stop behind a blue and white Ford pickup complete with camper cover and everyone immediately got out of the vehicle.

"So this is it?" Tripp said, leading the pack off to the right of the driveway toward the front porch. "This is where it all started for you, huh?" He climbed the steps on the side of the porch and walked until he came to a screen door. With the door on the other side of it open wide he was able to lift a hand over his brow, lean against the screen, and peer straight into the house. "Looks like nobody's home." Tripp pulled open the screen door and Katelyn pushed past him as she moved into the home. "After you," Tripp said before following her in along with Morgan and Zack.

Four sets of padded feet clunked across the creaky wood planked floor and soon each pair began heading off in their own separate directions. Morgan moved forward, away from the front door, toward a staircase running up to the second floor along the wall to her left. "Anybody home?" she called out suddenly and without warning to the balcony running perpendicular to the two walls, startling both Tripp and Zackery.

"Who are you expecting to get an answer from," Tripp said from the area off to her right near the kitchen entrance, "the termites?"

"How do you know this place is empty?" she replied.

"Hey," Zackery said, interrupting them. "We'll check it out." Zackery started up the staircase and made it to the fifth rung before he noticed that he had been climbing the steps all by his lonesome. He stopped and looked back over his shoulder. "Katelyn?"

"There's no one up there," she said to him, clearly frustrated by the invitation.

"Fine. Then just humor me if you don't mind."

Katelyn rolled her eyes and abandoned the area of the den behind Morgan's left shoulder. Moving past her, she started up the stairway after Zack.

The clicking noise caused by Tripp flipping a light switch attached to the wall next to him averted Morgan's attention back to him. "Nothing. Not a drop of juice in the place."

"Well what did you expect?" she said to him snidely.

Zackery made a right at the corner when he reached the end of the hallway and continued forward with Katelyn by his side on his right. All of the walls up here were as barren as the ones downstairs. Not only were there no decorative ornaments hanging anywhere there wasn't a single portrait depicting any resident, past or present, adorning any wall or article of furniture anywhere in the house. When they came to yet another white painted wooden door Zackery pushed it open and stuck his head inside of the bedroom. "Hello?" he called out, once again being answered by silence.

"What are you doing?" Katelyn said to him, reiterating her previous indication to him with slightly less irritation in her tone.

"Alright. I'll take your word for it," he conceded. Zackery was mostly reveling in the fact that it hadn't taken much arm twisting to get her to come along with him. She'd even offered up something in the way of a verbal exchange without much prying. "How bout a change of subject. Which one of these was yours?" he asked her as they rounded the next corner.

Katelyn moved through the hallway in silence, suddenly coming to a halt in front of a window on her left. Zackery had moved a step ahead of her before turning to see what the hold up was. Katelyn reached up and wrapped her fingers around the cords attached to the blinds and pulled them down, allowing a flash of daylight to pour into the dank and musty hallway. Zackery approached. He closed in on the window and stood behind her, peering out at the greenery overrun yard in the back of the old home. In the distance, ramshackled and barely being held together by the pile of wood and nails that it was composed of, stood a rickety old barn. Katelyn had yet to speak again and she didn't have to for Zack to know that whatever it was that they had come out here to locate lie somewhere within the confines of that crumbling structure.

Morgan was in the kitchen going through the cupboards. After searching the refrigerator and finding nothing inside of it aside from a few pitchers of water, she decided to give the rest of the room a once or twice over for any signs that this place had been lived in at one time or another.

Canned foods.

Nothing but canned foods in every cupboard that didn't contain dust covered dishes. Beans. Fruits. Meats. Was this place someone's home or a fallout shelter?

Morgan had been squatting down next to the refrigerator going through a cupboard packed with dehydrated packages of milk when out of nowhere she heard the machine's compressor switch on. She rose to her feet in utter disbelief as several of the electrical devises came humming to life all about her.

The clock on the microwave in front of her was blinking either midnight or noon at her in bright green numbers. The central heating and air unit began to blow a warm gust of wind on the back of her neck from the vent above her head. Her next surprise came in the guise of Tripp Manning who was in the process of bursting through both the hard wood and screen door to her right and rushing headlong into the kitchen from outside of the house.

"Can you believe that?" he said to her. "This place still actually has power. Someone or...something had tripped the breaker."

"In other words the owner of this place could still be lurking around here somewhere and could just show up at any time without us knowing about it," Morgan said, letting her eyes roam around the interior of the room once more.

But Tripp had been too intrigued to let her caution sway him too much. They'd come all this way and now he was eager to explore. After years of speculation as to the true origins of Katelyn Bree, it would be a shame to pass up a chance at finding out how close to the mark he'd actually gotten. "I'm sure Katelyn wouldn't mind vouching for us, assuming she's on familiar terms with the current residents. Hey," Tripp said, looking around the room. "Where is she anyway?"

Katelyn reached out her hand and took hold of the barn door. Her feet went into motion and she began moving backwards, pulling the already slightly ajar door open that much further. Zackery took to the other obstruction barring their entrance to her left.

It was a muggy and soot filled atmosphere that had come out to greet them. The clattering sound of several applauding sets of wings echoed throughout the dimly lit expanse inside as the gathering of feathered creatures present fled through the gaping holes in the roof and open shutters lining the walls along the second level of the barn, frightened off after finding their long standing sanctuary being disturbed.

Katelyn moved on inside, the dull yellow and brown straw covered floor beneath her feet muffling the sound of her steps. Zackery stayed close, allowing only two steps in length, three at the most, to exist between the two of them as they conducted what he knew had to have been the first incursion made into this squalor in years.

He let his eyes roam all about them in every direction. The grit covered leather saddles. Pitchforks. Grappling hooks. Handheld reaper blades. The multitude of hay bales stacked up on top of one another on the tier above their heads. From what Zackery knew of such things this place looked well equip for whatever livestock it was designed to hold. Livestock that had left no sign that they had ever been there at all.

"Well now," Zack heard a too cheery voice call out from behind him. He turned to see Tripp and Morgan making their way through the barn entrance that he and Katelyn had pried open, Tripp taking down a coil of rope that was hanging on the back of one of the barn doors. "Just what did you two wander off back here and find?"

"Not sure yet," Zackery said, turning and starting after Katelyn once more. "It's probably nothing."

"Oh yeah?" Tripp said. He examined the coil of rope he held, toyed with it for a moment, and then tossed it into one of the horse stalls. "Well whatever it is hurry up and get it bagged and tagged. We've got power up at the big house and wanted to run into town later and pick up a few supplies."

Katelyn continued to lead the way, retracing the steps that she had made here once so many years ago. The memory of this place remained crystal clear in her head. The sound of the shuffling hay beneath her feet was almost identical to the noise she had kept up when she last took her leave of this place and as vivid as her memory was of the damp, chilly air that had filled this noiseless place that morning, clearer still was the notion that a need for her to ever return here again may never arise.

And now...here she was. And with a small band of curious marauders at her back no less, following her into one of the horse stalls waiting both patiently and impatiently for her to reveal the significance of this place.

They gave her room as Katelyn used her right foot followed by her left to shove away the straw bedding covering the floor of the stall, undoing the work that she had so diligently took care to put forth the last time she was here. Upon completion Katelyn had revealed the two large panels embedded in the wooden floor.

"Sooo. Any guesses as to what's behind door number two?" Tripp said as he stared down at the floor.

"Only one way to find out." Zackery stepped around Katelyn and took hold of one of the protruding metal handles attached to one of the wooden doors embedded in the floor. Tripp went after the other and together they pried open a gaping portal in the barn floor. A portal that came readily equipped with a concrete staircase that led down into a darkened sinkhole beneath the earth.

All eyes turned to Katelyn who stood emotionless before the apex of the steps. She didn't move. She was stone. Whatever was down there she didn't seem to have any immediate interest in reconnecting with it. Zackery didn't let his eyes linger on her long before turning them back to the void they had just uncovered. Standing off to Katelyn's right on the opposite side of the opening from Tripp, he took a step down inside the manmade cavity and found his footing with no problem. The other one followed suit and soon he was moving down into the darkness one slow and careful step after the next. "Like I said...there's only one way to find out."

9

"Colonel!" Capt. Blair shouted as he moved off down the hall at a quick pace after Col. McPhearson's back. "Colonel!" Capt. Robert Blair called out once more, sure that his commanding officer could hear him just as sure as if they'd been standing side by side. Still, Tobias hadn't so much as slowed down a single step, let alone voiced an acknowledgement of the Captain's presence even as he made a left and stepped onto an open elevator.

The quick pace at which Robert Blair moved nearly turned into a slow jog as he hurried to catch up with the Colonel before having to bear the burden of waiting on the next car. He wound up having to shove his forearm into the six inch space that was left between the closing elevator door and the frame just before it shut completely, gaining him the privilege of being left to stand there and wait as the sliding door slowly began to move in the opposite direction.

Colonel McPhearson's expressionless face was soon visible to him. "Something I can help you with, Captain?"

He stepped onto the elevator car and turned to face the closing door. "Yes, sir, I believe there is." He lifted his eyes and watched the digital numbers above the elevator door increase in value one floor at a time.

"By all means, Captain, don't keep us in suspense."

"Sir, I was just curious as to our next course of action. I noticed that you've pulled more than two thirds of our resources including personnel off of active duty and cut their orders to be shipped out of here, all by day's end."

"Impressive, Captain. You've proved to me that you can actually read an itinerary. Now would you mind getting to the point at your earliest convenience."

Capt. Blair had about as much patience for his senior officer's glibness as Tobias had for him in general. Over half the units in his command had orders to pack up and ship out, most of which he didn't even have a final destination for, while his mission orders continued to remain unchanged. "Am I to understand, sir, that you've located the target?"

"That would be a negative, Captain."

"Then can I ask why the majority of the resources that I need to successfully complete this mission are being diverted to...where exactly are you headed to, sir?"

The elevator stopped and the doors opened. Colonel McPhearson stepped off and Capt. Blair hurried to keep in step behind him. "Our girl's in the wind, Captain," Tobias said, making a right at the corner at the end of the hall and heading up a flight of stairs. "And despite the very uncharacteristic behavior that she's been displaying, if she hasn't already abandoned this city for a safer haven then there's no doubt that she's well on her way to doing so."

"That still doesn't explain..."

Tobias reached the top of the staircase and pushed open a door that lead him out onto the roof of the building. "And if there's even the slightest thread of common sense present in that empty vacuum that she calls a brain..." The whipping wind and whirring engines that accompanied the rapidly spinning blades of the twin helicopters present on the roof forced the Colonel to raise his voice in order to be heard. "...then she has to realize that her impending safety is going to rely on her figuring out who I am." Tobias stopped moving and turned to face the Captain. "Which is going to inevitably mean unearthing the truth about her past."

"Presuming she opts for this detour down memory lane, am I to understand that while me and my men are left here to quite possibly keep inadvertently chasing our tails around you've found a way to use this to your advantage?"

Tobias took up his walk toward the awaiting transports once more. "Let's just say I'm going to see if I can't cut her off at the pass."

Zackery continued moving down into the shadowy depths beneath the barn one carefully placed step at a time as he did what he could to mind his footing on the concrete staircase. With the sound of his friend's footsteps behind him he continued on down into the unknown clinging to the confidence that had he been unfortunate enough to stumbled into any sort of malice then perhaps at least their numbers would be enough to see them through the calamity.

Zackery continued his descent and upon reaching the bottom step he ran into a solid stone wall. A faint glow of light broke through the darkness and lead him around the corner of the stone barrier to his right where he found the glowing aura of several tiny flickering and steadfast points of lights in the distance across the room from him that varied in a wide spectrum of colors. He ran his left hand across the wall next to him and eventually located a panel that allowed him to activate the overhead florescent lighting and bring the entire underground facility into bright shining view.

"What the hell is this place?" Tripp said, moving around Zack and heading over toward the area of this uncovered addition to the barn upstairs that was literally covered with a strange assortment of electronic and mechanical equipment. There were desks and tabletops cluttered with numerous laptops and desktop computer consoles.

Wires of all shapes and sizes were coming and going in every direction, attached to articles of machinery, the likes of which seemed alien to their wandering eyes.

The three of them let their curiosity run unfettered as they went about exploring everything within this compound that they could get their hands on. They tinkered with the unusual equipment present, rifled through the drawers and cabinets everywhere that were cluttered with all sorts of medical equipment (small vials of chemical solutions, syringes, gauze, blood pressure gauges, stethoscopes), loose-leaf papers, and stuffed manila folders.

Katelyn stood idly by as the associates that she'd arrived there with bounded from one room of this underground labyrinth to the next. She remained content to just pace the tile floor reliving the details of those few moments that she could remember spending within the confines of these walls some four years prior.

Everything around her was silent. Everything indoors that is. Somewhere in the distance high above her Katelyn could hear the faint rumbling of the rolling storm clouds that cluttered the morning sky. When her eyelids parted she saw nothing but darkness and became almost instantaneously aware of the fact that she was completely alone.

"Katelyn!" Tripp called out to her. She was currently standing in a room that was obviously meant to serve as some sort of den by the look of the couches and lounge chairs all around. Tripp was bellowing out her name from another portion of the dwelling. Reluctantly, Katelyn made off in the direction of his voice.

She found him near the entrance they had used to climb down into this mockup of a home that for all she knew could have been her legitimate place of residence. What a strange and dreary life that must have been, she imagined. A life spent living underground, for some reason in hiding, she thought, suddenly remembering the more than adequate living arrangements that the home residing topside looked as if it could provide. What other sort of purpose could a place like this have existed for other than that which could have consisted of trying to avoid someone else's prying eyes. Hiding. An image of Tobias McPhearson forced its way to the forefront of her mind. Perhaps there was something to that theory.

Tripp flagged her over to some sort of metal containment unit attached to several of the various electronic mechanisms on the opposite side of the room by a multitude of thick snaking coils of black insulated cords. Looking inside of the container and seeing the white padded bed lining running the length of it and the foam rubber pillow inside, Katelyn recognized it instantly. She could still remember the distinct feel of the cushion that supported her head and neck as well as the padding that the rest of her body had been resting on top of.

Hanging down along the right side of this capsule was an L-shaped metal and glass panel that Tripp attempted to hoist up and fold back over the top of the container. Katelyn stood at the foot of the contraption watching him work with a concerned look of disdain on her face.

Having been successful, Tripp moved around to the opposite side and repeated the process, effectively sealing the empty coffin. The two glass panels embedded in either side of the two halves of the lid now came together to form a window that would have allowed for an excellent view of the upper portion of whatever body just so happened to be lying inside.

Remembering that she herself had once woken up inside of this thing, Katelyn wondered just who it was at one time or another that had been using that viewing portal to spy on her slumbering form.

"You mind clueing us in on just what the hell this thing is supposed to be?" Tripp asked her, taking a step back from the contraption that he'd just been tinkering with.

"You know about as much as I do," she said to him.

Tripp cocked his head over his left shoulder and took a step back from the chamber. "Alriiight." He moved back another two steps, his head still leaning. "Then how about this? *K...A...O...S...S*," he said, reading the letters inscribed across the lower portion of the container from left to right. "Any idea what that means?"

Katelyn was getting fed up with this pointless expedition and she had no intention on wasting anymore time shuffling around the cobweb covered, dusty depths of this basement tinkering around with forgotten relics. "No. I don't know what it means. I haven't the slightest clue," she said, raising her arms up beside her and turning her head from side to side, "what any of this junk means." Her arms dropped again. "And suddenly I'm finding myself not all that interested in finding out."

She did an about-face and for the second time in her life she headed for the staircase that would take her up to the surface and ultimately far away from this place of seclusion.

The difference this time was that she didn't have to peel away several large white circular patches with tiny red blinking bulbs at the center of their circumference from her skin as she rose from the bedding that she lie across.

And she wasn't barefoot and dressed in a pair of plain white cotton pajamas. So there would be no need for her to scrounge around the bedroom closets of the main house for suitable articles of clothing before striking out for parts unknown.

"Wait," Zackery called out to her as she reached the straw covered floor of the horse stall at the top of the concrete staircase. Katelyn heard him calling after her but refused to let his words halt her departure. "C'mon, Katelyn. Hold up a minute," Zackery said as he moved out into the open bay of the barn. "Stop!" he yelled at her back when every attempt he had instated to reason with her fleeing form fell on deaf ears. Katelyn stopped once she made it to the open doorway of the barn and she turned around to face him. Zack continued to walk until he caught up with her. "Hey. What's the matter with you?" he asked her.

"Nothing. Just not my idea of a good time, that's all. You can go back down there and finish rummaging with them if you want. I'm going into town."

"Well, wait up for a minute. We'll drive you. Morgan was going on about us holding up here for the night. We were just about to head into town to stock up on some supplies."

"Whatever," Katelyn said, turning away from him and staring out at the stalled farm vehicles being overrun with tall grass and weeds in the field just beyond the open barn doors. She was in no mood to argue with any solution that resulted in her putting some considerable distance between her and this place. And the quicker the mode of transport the better. "Just tell them to hurry up."

Katelyn was once again seated in the backseat of Tripp's car. She stared out of the window at the small buildings and shops that composed the outer edges of the downtown area of Wilderbrook, Kansas. Morgan had been enroute to the nearest supermarket with a big enough variety and surplus of the inventory that she claimed would be absolutely necessary to make their stay at what the mailbox claimed to be the Beckman household as comfortable as possible.

Among other things, she was most insistently in the market for a much more appeasing and readily available source of food and drink than the kitchen cupboards or the refrigerator of the long abandoned home had to offer.

Seeing as how the home came equipped with its own washer and dryer set, securing a small box of laundry detergent in order to clean the muck out of their discarded wardrobe and freshen up the clothes that they were wearing right then might not have been such a bad idea either.

Katelyn, on the other hand, had been scouting out the scenery for a suitable after hours spot, preferably a watering hole that didn't cater to Wilderbrook's everyday ordinary citizenry. She could really go for a nice variety of spirits right now and a dark corner to enjoy them in.

Morgan located her supermarket and after she pulled into the parking lot and brought the car to a stop they all exited the vehicle and headed for the front entrance. All of them except for Katelyn who'd struck out across the lot in an entirely different direction. "Okay," Tripp said after noticing her veer off course. "What's this about?"

"Nothing," Zack said to him. "You guys go ahead. We'll catch up to you later." Zackery broke away from them and started out after Katelyn.

"Uh, will that be before or after we're back at the hacienda?" Tripp beckoned to his friend who had began moving away from him across the parking lot at a slow jogger's pace.

"You've got your cell phone on you, right?"

After waving a slap at the air in Zackery's direction Tripp turned his focus back to the electronically sliding glass doors of the supermarket in front of him and the surplus of valuables that awaited him and Morgan inside.

"Where are you off to in such a hurry?" Zackery said to Katelyn once he caught up to her.

"I caught sight of this place just up the road. Looked like it would be a nice place to go and clear my head for a while."

"Don't suppose you'd mind if I tagged along."

"Long as you don't bother me I don't care where you go."

Zackery handed over the cover charge for both of them to a shaved head individual in a leather vest on the other side of a panel of bullet proof glass. The bare skin of both his arms were covered in tattoos. After handing Zackery back the change from his twenty spot he cracked a sneering smile at him before hitting the buzzer that released the lock on the door barring them entrance into the nightspot that Katelyn had sought refuge in.

Zackery collected the singles and followed her through the door. "You know, I'm not really sure we can afford to be throwing away money like this," he said to her after stuffing the bills into his pocket.

His ears as well as his thoughts were suddenly overtaken by the smoke filled atmosphere that pumped and pulsated with the thunderous sound of metal music and clamoring billiard tables that covered the floor of the room that they had just stepped into. Zackery inhaled the stinging aroma of cheap cigars and motor oil as his eyes looked all around at the denim and leather clad bodies that filled the interior of this establishment.

Even in the most brightly lit of areas the florescent white light bulbs glowed at a dim twenty five watts. Most of the other heavily trafficked areas flickered with alternating flashes of dark blue and red. Zackery couldn't have felt more out of place here if he'd tried. Snapping out of the trance he'd momentarily slipped into due to his initial shock, Zack had failed to notice that Katelyn was already in the process of moving deeper into the belly of this beast while he stood alone next to the entrance.

The next patron through jostled his body with an abrasive shoulder bump as he made his way inside, cutting an angry looking glare at Zackery as he moved past him in all his shaggy haired glory. His feet went into motion and he hurried after Katelyn's back.

"What is it with you and these places?" Zackery said after catching up with her at the bar. She'd already ordered a shot and a beer.

"Their uncanny knack for warding off individuals such as yourself. Although their potency does seem to be lacking a bit these days."

"Perhaps you've just been overlooking a newly acquired fixture they seem to all be acquiring."

Katelyn quickly downed her shot of whiskey and took a drink from her bottle of beer. "Oh yeah? What's that?"

"You."

Zackery ignored the menacing look that she gave him and ordered himself a beer. Katelyn secured herself another shot and moved away from both the bar and Zackery. She wasn't sure if whether or not his continued presence at her side for the duration of this evening would wind up being distractingly comforting or simply an annoyance all too common whenever his company was in question. Either way it was nothing she wouldn't be able to handle.

She was away from that house and nursing at the tap of a more than adequately stocked house of libations. The rest of the evening she'd take as it came at her.

The bright blue sky above the Luna Vista had started to fade into hues of brilliant burnt orange shaded over with graying clouds as the sun began to set over the western horizon of the town of Wilderbrook. Zackery raised his watch up to his face to check the time once more. It had been quickly closing in on three hours that he and Katelyn had been hold up at a small table in a dark corner in one of the more lightly frequented areas of the establishment.

Tripp and Morgan had ended their shopping expedition some time ago and were back at the Beckman residence preparing the place and themselves for the stay that they would all have to endure for the duration of the night. Exactly what time they would be pulling out of there the next day, assuming that they actually would be, was anybody's guess. The threat that Tobias McPhearson and his men still posed and the fact that they couldn't by any means plan on holding up there indefinitely remained a factor in all of their minds. After that it was simply a question of where they would be off to next.

Zackery brought the chilled tip of the bottle away from his lips. "So what do you think of all that stuff that was stashed underneath that barn?" he asked her, sitting his bottle down on the table. "Any idea at all what to make of it?" Remembering how uncomfortable she'd become while in the presence of all the strange equipment that they'd unearthed earlier that evening, Zackery had made it a point to try and avoid the subject as best he could. But continuing to imbibe the numerous alcoholic beverages that their waitress ferried back and forth between them and the bar had loosened his tongue and left his curiosity unchecked.

"Just someone's idea of a practical use of storage space if you ask me," Katelyn answered him. "Outside of that I'm afraid I don't have much of an opinion on the subject."

"How can you be this cavalier about the whole thing? I mean, your life pre-Wicker Basket is a complete blank; this McPhearson guy shows up out of nowhere with his own private battle unit looking to drag you back off to who knows where; and your old bedroom looks like a place that Dr. Frankenstein would love to call home. And in light of all of this you're just like..." He hunched his shoulders at her and she finished off the contents of her bottle. "Didn't the sight of any of that tap into anything you might have repressed at least?"

"It was about as mentally stimulating as this conversation," Katelyn said to him. "But if you find it so terribly interesting you're free to pick up and head back to your little treasure trove anytime you feel like it."

"Yeah, we probably should be getting back. It would probably make more sense than wasting anymore time in this dive blowing money that we don't have," he said, looking around at the seedy scene that had engulfed them around every turn.

"What do you mean we?" Katelyn spoke up. "I never said I was going anywhere."

Zackery turned back to her and let a sneaking smirk take over his lips as he reached into his right front pocket. "Oh yeah? Not only are you leaving with me but you're going to be civil if not outright and overtly nice to me for the rest of the night." It must have been the alcohol coursing its way through his bloodstream right then that had emboldened him with enough courage to allow him to direct such a statement towards her. He pulled his hand out of his pocket and brought it up beside his head, twirling a shiny quarter between his fingers.

"Pardon me?" Katelyn replied.

"Come on. Heads, we cut our losses, get out of here, and try and catch a ride back to your old abode, during which time you have to think of at least three, count 'em three things to say to me that can't in any way be construed as an insult. And nothing in the realm of casual conversation counts."

"And tails?"

"Tails?" Zackery looked at the coin he held and then back at the dark brown eyes hiding behind the sable strands of her hair that dangled in front of her face. "If it's tails we stay here. For as long as you want...but you have to dance with me."

"How very inventive," Katelyn said, standing from the table and grabbing up the bottle of beer that sat on the table in front of Zack. "Heads, you win. Tails, I lose. Too bad I won't be indulging you in this desperate plea for attention."

He watched her walk away from the table for a few moments before turning back to the quarter he held. In one fluent motion he dropped his arm and let the coin slam down against the wooden table. Upon doing so the quarter instantly bounded up into the air again and came down dead center into a shot glass resting on the table in front of him.

His concentration was stolen away from the small glass that he had just sank the coin in by the sound of Katelyn's voice in the distance being overlapped by the very masculine demeanor of the individual attempting to converse with her. Zackery cut his eyes over in her direction and took in the image of the lean figure obstructing her path back to the bar with a growing sense of uneasiness.

He'd offered to buy her a drink and after Katelyn promptly refused his generosity he extended his invitation to include a seat with him at the booth that he shared with a few loyal compatriots of his where she would be assured that her money would be of no further use to her for the duration of the night. Again Katelyn said no and once more found her potential suitor unfazed by her rejection as he neglected to remove himself from her path when she tried to continue onward to the bar.

"Hey!" Zack called out to them both. He'd gotten their attention as well as a few other patrons passing through that section of the bar. "What's it take the get the message across?"

"Excuse me?" Katelyn's gentleman caller said as he titled his body to the side in order to get a look over her shoulder at the area at her back.

"Come on, pal. You heard her. She's not interested, and the longer you keep this up, the longer I have to wait on her to get back here with my beer. So if you don't mind."

Zackery's comments were enough to draw a few chuckles out of the guy as he brought his eyes back to the nubile beauty standing in front of him. "Who is that guy?" he smiled and said to Katelyn. She was suddenly wondering the same thing as she turned her head to look over her shoulder.

Zackery stood up from his seat and walked over to where the couple was standing. "Seriously, man. She said *no*. Now why don't you kindly back up out of the lady's way and we can all get back to what it is that we were doing."

"Speaking of which," Katelyn spoke, "do you mind me asking just what it is that you think you're doing?"

"For one, saving you a hell of a lot of wasted time. And I really would like for you to hurry and go get me another beer."

Katelyn stood there sandwiched in between a pair of utter and complete nuisances unable to decide which one was responsible for the greatest level of aggravation in her life right at that moment. Needless to say, she wouldn't have long to suffer the inconvenience of either of them. From what she could see their attention was slowly but surely drifting away from her and towards one another.

"How about I kindly drag your sorry ass outside and back the tread of my bike tire across your face. Maybe that'll help teach you the value of minding your own damn business."

"Listen, man..." Zack started. He was set to continue but found his words instantly cut off by the sound of a pair of snapping fingers. The next thing Zackery knew both of his arms were being hooked up into those of two grizzly men who had appeared out of nowhere on either side of him. "Hey! Wait a minute! What's going..." They practically lifted him up off of his feet as they dragged his struggling body off past Katelyn and her suitor. "Katelyn!" he yelled back to her before being shuffled off into the crowd of patrons. The man who once stood in front of her attempting to shower her with his hospitality headed off after them and Katelyn continued on her way to the bar.

The exit door on the front of the building flew open and Zackery came tumbling out. The force with which he was thrown sent him crashing down to the parking lot pavement. He recovered and made it back up to his feet just in time to witness the two very same burly individuals that had just tossed him barreling down on him once more. "Come on, guys. Is this absolutely necessary?" Zackery said just before swinging a right hand haymaker that connected with the jaw of the man approaching him on his left. He had no time to gauge just how much of an effect the blow had had on the man he'd just hit due to the fact that he was already being wrapped up around the waist by his partner and carried off across the parking lot.

Zackery felt the intense pangs of the blunt force trauma he'd received after being slammed down back first on the hood of a car pulsate throughout his entire body. Rolling over to his right, he dropped down off of the car to the cold uncaring pavement below.

He didn't have long to revel in his misery as he soon felt the collar of his shirt being taken up into someone's fist and his body being jerked violently off of the ground. After his arms were subsequently bound in the clasps of the two men holding him hostage his body was swiftly spun around to greet the menacing visage of Katelyn's once insistent gentleman caller.

"What's the matter, tough guy?" he said to Zackery. "You leave that smart mouth of yours inside?"

He buried two swift punches into Zackery's gut; a hard right followed by an even harder left. After a moment of hacking and wheezing Zack summoned up enough strength to lift his right leg up and plant his foot squarely between the guy's legs, doubling him over.

Once his upper body dropped Zackery had a clear view of the crowd who were standing outside of the Luna Vista waiting to gain entrance. It was the sight of the young brunette making her way through the crowd that reveled in levity at the scene unfolding before them that he had really taken an interest in. "Katelyn!" he called out to her mere seconds before the guy in front of him rose again and smashed another closed fist into his belly that knocked a great deal of the wind out of him; following that blow up with a right hand to the side of Zack's face.

Katelyn turned up the bottle she held and finished off the contents as she closed in on the squabbling rabble. "Something you want to say to me?"

Zackery struggled against the hold that the two men had on him and this time he was forced to suffer a hard left to his right cheek. "Katelyn, for God's sakes! Will you help me here!?!"

"How about this?" she said to the tune of him taking two more blows to the gut. "Heads, I get you out of this and you don't so much as look at me funny ever again." Another fist smashed against the right side of his head. "Or tails, I leave you here and these guys will pretty much see to that themselves."

"Anything you say! Just help me!"

The guy standing in front of Zack drew his fist all the way back past his head and upon releasing all of its pent up energy he delivered an overhand blow to the front of his face that sent his body careening back (after the two kindly gentlemen standing on either side of him turned him loose first, of course) and crashing into the small gathering of motor cycles behind them, causing the vehicles to spill over into one another. "Aw! You see that? Now you've gone and dinged my ride. That's really gonna cost ya."

Katelyn tossed the empty beer bottle back over her shoulder. "Alright, boys," she said, moving closer to them. "I think that's about enough roughhousing."

"You just hang tight, little lady," Zack's primary abuser said to her, his eyes still on Zack's body as he was being hoisted up off of the heap of cycles he'd just toppled. "We'll pick up where it was that we left off in just a few moments. I don't think junior here's done with his lesson." Once Zack was lifted up into position again he drew his fist back to deliver another blow to him but found the maneuver interrupted mid-flight by Katelyn's hand gripping tightly around his wrist.

"I said, that's enough."

Katelyn twisted her body to the side, using the force of her motion to pull him across the pavement and slam his body into the left fender of the car at her back. A swift side kick that placed the sole of her shoe against the back of his head sent his face smashing down to the hood of the car that was still bearing the dent forged by Zackery's back.

She used the same foot to smash in the back of his right knee, knocking loose his balance and allowing gravity to take his body the rest of the way down to the parking lot.

The man standing next to Zackery on his right released his hold on him and stepped toward Katelyn. Three right jabs to his face in a lightning fast succession brought him to his knees right in front of her. Katelyn shifted around him and moved over to Zackery. "What is it with you and picking fights?"

The last guy gripping hold of him let go and threw a punch at Katelyn's head. Without hardly exhibiting any effort or so much as turning her head in his direction, she raised her right hand and closed her fingers around his knuckles the second they slammed into her open palm. "I don't know," Zack said over the moans and cries of the man standing next to him. Katelyn had begun to apply an increasing amount of pressure to his hand the more he struggled to loosen himself from her hold.

His free hand had clasped around her wrist as he tried to pull away from her. Finding all of his efforts fruitless and the pain becoming ever more unbearable, he slowly started to sink in his stance. "Guess it's a new habit I recently picked up," Zackery finished.

"You should think about quitting," Katelyn said to him.

His irritation with the screams of the man standing next to him as well as his earlier actions prompted Zackery to draw back and swing a punch at his head that knocked him to the ground as Katelyn let go of his hand. "I'll think about it. Now let's get out of here."

"Hold up a minute," Katelyn said, walking back over to the downed gentleman that had once been so kind as to offer to buy her quite an assortment of beverages before abandoning her side for the parking lot that he now lay against.

She delivered a kick to the back of his kneeling cohort on the way over to him that sent him all the way down on his chest. Katelyn rolled her former suitor over and ripped open the left front pocket of the pants he wore; spilling its contents. She scooped up the wad of bills she found that was bound together in a brass money clip and tossed it in the air over her shoulder. Zackery clumsily caught the small bundle. "Cash," she said, reaching back down for a pack of smokes and a Zippo lighter she saw lying at her feet.

"What's this?" Zack said as he examined the wad of money he held. "You're robbing him now?"

"You said we were running short of money." Katelyn removed a single cigarette from the pack and placed it between her lips before tossing the rest aside. Going though the pocket on the other side landed her a set of keys.

"Hey..." the guy groaned as he began to come to a little. Katelyn smacked her palm against his forehead and knocked his skull hard enough against the cold pavement below to put him back into his daze.

Standing, she proceeded over to the pile of downed motorcycles that Zackery had once had a run in with. Climbing astride one, she lifted it off of the pile and smashed her right foot against the toppled bike nearest her. It, along with a few others, slid away from her across the pavement to the tune of a nerve racking grinding sound created by the abrasiveness of rock against metal.

She put the key in the ignition and turned over the roaring engine of the small beast before flicking over the lighter in her possession and bringing a flame to the cigarette dangling from her lips. Katelyn gripped hold of the handlebars and gunned the engine a couple of times. "Get on."

Reluctant to obey at first, Zackery cautiously made his way over to her and climbed onto the seat behind her. "And now we're stealing a motorcycle."

Katelyn pulled the cigarette out of her mouth and tossed the lighter. "I also distinctly remember you saying something about us needing a ride out of here." She replaced the smoke between her lips and took a long drag. Removing it once more, she flicked the flaming stick back over her shoulder and picked her feet up as the back tire of the bike she and Zack were seated upon spun furiously enough to cause the rubber to smoke.

The cigarette landed hot end first into the pool of spilled fluids that had been leaking out of the slightly trashed motorbikes as Katelyn pulled out of the parking space. The blaze ignited and the three trounced men did what they could to help each other scramble away from the burning trail that the fire moved along toward the toppled bikes resting in a heap across the parking lot.

The explosion rocked the area outside of the front of the night spot as Katelyn pulled the bike out onto the street, leaving a billowing cloud of flaming black smoke in her wake that rose up to find its way toward the purple sky above.

A blackened sky saw Katelyn and Zackery pulling into the driveway of the Beckman residence onboard their requisitioned conveyance. Katelyn guided the bike around Tripp's car and the pickup truck, pulling around to the back of the house before shutting off the engine. After dismounting, the two of them gained access to the home through the kitchen entrance.

"What happened to you?" Morgan asked after taking notice of the wounds on his face and his blood splotched shirt.

"Don't ask," Zack replied, continuing to keep pace at Katelyn's back as she moved through the kitchen.

Katelyn pushed open the door to one of the upstairs bedrooms and switched on the light after stepping inside. "Sit down," she said to Zackery as she continued off to the left of the room toward an open door in the wall. After watching her switch on the light in the small washroom Zackery moved over to the side of the bed and heeded her advice.

He rubbed his hands across the eggshell white linen beneath him and glanced around the room. The sound of water running began to emanate from the washroom that Katelyn had stepped into and had ceased to exist just as quickly as it had come into being. She came back into the room carrying a small white washcloth with her.

Pulling the chair out from under the desk next to the bed, she slid it across the wooden panels that made up the floor and took a seat in front of Zackery. "Come here," she ordered him.

Zackery scooted forward on the bed and offered her his slightly battered face. "Is this going to sting?"

"Shut up," Katelyn said, pressing the damp cloth against the cut above his left eye and drawing a wince from him. "It would have served you right if I had let them finish the job on you. You care to explain the meaning behind that outburst?" Katelyn pulled the cloth away from his face and refolded it until she had a much cleaner surface to dab against his wound once more.

"Like you said, just trying to get your attention."

"Well, for future reference a gin and tonic tends to work a whole hell of lot better that getting your face pushed in. Is that what they teach you up at that college of yours?"

Zackery cracked a grin. "What do you know about it?"

"Just what I saw in your apartment." Katelyn pulled the towel away from his face and stood up. "Biology; Economics; Composition," she said, heading back into the washroom. "You're skipping out on quite a few hours for this mundane excursion, aren't you?" She dropped the towel in the sink and began to run some more water over it.

He hadn't so much as given it a second thought. Zackery had simply picked up and headed out after her past while at the same time shoving his present and any possible effects such an act might have on his future to the inevitable wayside.

For the moment it would seem that Katelyn had taken more of an interest in his higher education in one sitting than he had displayed ever since that night in the subway station when she had first allotted him something besides her striking physical attributes, unsettling quirks, and mysterious ambiance to intrigue his senses. "I'm sort of betting it all on some sympathetic professors and a set of midterm scores that'll boggle the mind with the realm of impossibility that they fall into."

Katelyn reemerged from the washroom and took her seat in front of him again. Zackery reached for the damp cloth she held and Katelyn slapped his hand away before going after his cuts and scrapes again. "What about the people at Jake's Hardware?" she said to him. "Are you that valuable an employee or are you counting on them to be as sympathetic as you're hoping your instructors will be?"

Zackery was so floored that he jerked his head back at the next touch of the towel to his face. For someone he believed to have regarded him with all the attention one might give to a passing face on a crowded street, Katelyn had been surprisingly well versed in the monotonous comings and goings in his day to day life.

Had he not been so aware of how fleeting her personal interest in him could be he might have actually taken the time to be flattered. "I'm hoping so," he said to her with a mild amount of cheer in his voice. "But on the off chance that they aren't, perhaps you could put in a good word for me over at the Wicker Basket. From what I saw, you've got yourself some kind of pull with the boss."

Turning his head to the side, Katelyn lifted her free hand up and stroked her thumb down across the red smear in front of his right ear in search of the well from which this flow sprang. Locating the fount, she cleared away some of the drying runoff with the cloth and then compressed the slit. "You don't seriously think I'd jeopardize my standing with Mr. Carthright by staking my reputation on someone as blatantly irresponsible as you?"

He straightened his head on his neck again and Katelyn was forced to pull back away from him. His eyes aligned with hers. "Come on now. You couldn't possibly think that little of me."

Katelyn pressed the towel to his face again. "You'd be surprised."

"Besides. It's not like I'm planning on spending the rest of my days slaving away in Jake's storeroom."

"Well, just what else did you have in mind? Assuming you're not planning on letting all of that collective knowledge you've been gathering go to waste on a career in barroom brawling."

He let a soft chuckle slip from his lips. Katelyn's attitude remained as serious as ever despite her ridiculous speculation. Zackery reached a hand up and wrapped his fingers around the back of her hand. She shooed him away and went on with her nursing. "What about you?"

he said. "Is the Wicker Basket a one stop shop or are you planning on moving on anytime soon?"

A wave of uneasiness washed over her and Katelyn allowed for a brief pause in her motions as she went about wiping his face clean. "Just...Don't worry about me," she answered him. "Mind your own business." Having been drawn into such a candid discussion with him of her own volition, Katelyn felt strangely awkward about backing out of it so abruptly. But as oddly as that may have registered with her, continuing on with such a line of discussion could only prove that much more worse for the wear.

Zack stared at her in silence for a moment, intrigued by the level of concentration she showed in tending to the cuts and scrapes on his face. Eventually her trained eyes began to alternate their glances between his somewhat minor wounds and the green glowing orbs that stared at her so intensely. "What?" she said to him, curious as to what was going on behind his piercing emerald irises.

"It's not fair, you know?"

"What isn't?"

He reached his hand up and took hold of her wrist, ceasing her nursing altogether. Her eyes locked on his. "The fact that you get to touch me." She tried to pull her hand away from him but he held on. "It's not fair you getting to put your hands on me like that. How would you like it if it was the other way around?"

She tried to pull away again but Zackery continued to hold on to her. "How would you like it if I made your face a little more symmetrical?" Katelyn tried to make her tone as abrasive as she could in the hopes that it would mask any of the warmth that she was secretly indulging in while administering this rudimentary first aid. Putting her hands on Zackery in this manner; the gentle caution; the care involved, awakened dormant senses within her that she would have otherwise never known existed.

As far back as she could remember no physical contact that she had ever endured between her and any other sentient being could rival it. Not the handshake from a satisfied Wicker Basket customer. Not pounding her combative fists against an aggressor. Handling him in this way felt nice but she couldn't let him know that for fear of what he might do armed with such knowledge.

"What's it feel like?" he asked, still holding on to her wrist. She jerked her arm again but he refused to relinquish his grip.

"What's what feel like?" she asked him, her voice reflecting more anger now. He was teetering on the very edge of the amount of levity that she would be willing to put up with from him tonight. The thrashing that he'd taken in the Luna Vista parking lot had afforded him some leniency but there was only so much of him that she was willing to tolerate.

"Being this close...and not being able to pull away."

Katelyn dropped the washcloth and jerked her arm back with an extreme amount of force as she stood from the chair. Continuing to maintain his grip on her arm, Zackery found himself being pulled up from his seat on the mattress. The chair Katelyn had been sitting in toppled over as she spun her body around and drug Zackery with her.

With a single shove she threw his body up against the wall that had once been at her back and penned him there. Zackery still had a hold of her wrist. "You having fun yet?" he asked her. He leaned forward and attempted to reach up and touch her face with his free hand but Katelyn slapped it out of the air hard and, at the same time, snatched her other hand free of his hold.

Shoving his body back against the plaster, she placed both of her palms against the wall on either side of him, keeping him boxed in. Brow lowered; eyes squinted; her elbows slowly bending, she inched her glowering face ever closer to his. "It doesn't have to be this way, Katelyn,"

Zackery said to her softly, quietly. The expression she wore on her face relayed her every violent intention had he not ceased his present course of action immediately, but he refused to adhere to any of it.

"Then what?" she snarled at him. "What should it be like?"

Slowly.

Gently.

Zackery stretched out his hands and let his fingers come into contact with the black denim covering her hips. Katelyn quickly dropped her eyes down and brought them back up again. "It should be easier," Zackery said to her. His fingers continued to move around her waist.

"Stop it," Katelyn said, refusing to remove her hands from the wall.

Zackery applied pressure and his hands began to pull at her hips and move her body into his. "Easier," he said. "Better."

"Stop it," she whispered. Katelyn wanted him to stop. She needed him to. Every voice inside of her head screamed for her to pull away from him; leave the room in its entirety had she so desired, but at the very least pull away from him. The front of her pelvis pressed against his and she realized that there was no way that she would be able to comply with such a demand. Her only hope now was that Zackery would come to his senses and put a stop to his actions before it was too late. "Please," she said to him softly.

Zackery leaned his head forward and pressed his lips against the corner of her mouth. Katelyn's body shuddered at the sensation but she didn't move away from him. Moving his lips to the side and squaring them up firmly with hers, he pressed harder. His skin. The moisture. The pressure.

Indulging him in this foolish recreation, it wasn't long before Katelyn started to push back...and push back hard. Slamming him back into the wall again, Katelyn peeled her hands loose and pressed them against both sides of Zack's face as she feasted feverishly in his lips and his touch.

His touch.

She knew that she shouldn't but with her every inhibition forsaken there was nothing and no one there now to prevent her from denying her own forbidden impulses. Zackery definitely wasn't up for the task and maybe...just maybe for one night she didn't have to be either.

Katelyn drug her fingers down across the skin of his cheeks that had began to prickle over with the sprouts of his budding facial hair and moved them down along the smooth contour of his neck. With their lips continuing to remain intertwined, Katelyn lowered her hands until she felt the fabric of the T-shirt he wore beneath the open black and gray flannel shirt that he had on against her palms. Her fingers curled into fists and she forcefully removed his body from the wall.

Turning around, she shoved his back down against the mattress and climbed on top of him. Ripping his T-shirt down the middle, she found his lips again with hers and allowed her fingers to caress the warm flesh of his chest and lower abdomen while Zackery's hands were busy beneath her shirt just above her lower back. His hands moved upward as her lips trailed down the side of his neck.

He'd been questioning his motives even before he'd entered the bedroom and found the opening to put his devious thoughts into action. Katelyn had left him with no reason at all to believe that his advances would incite little more than an annoying rise out of her that might have capped his night off with a small amount of amusement.

After the beating that he had taken in the parking lot of the Luna Vista he could have certainly used it. But now, even as he actively participated in the unexpected fruition of a very long awaited and generously sought after episode with none other than Ms. Katelyn Bree herself, he had no idea what sort of reaction to expect as each sensual second lead into the next.

As if coaxing Katelyn into dropping her long standing guard wasn't enough, Zackery now had to relinquish his own inlaid defenses against his preconceived notions of her and find a way to move with her as they both ventured into the unknown together.

10

Zackery brushed the pitch black strands of hair out of Katelyn's slumbering face. With the moonlight pouring in through the window behind the bed and cascading a pale radiance across the white linen sheets they were both lying beneath while facing each other, he now had a much better view of the defining outlines of her stunning facial features.

Listening to her take one soothing breath after the next, he stroked his fingers through her dark mane once more. Lying there in bed beside her he realized that this was without a doubt the most serene image of this woman that he'd ever seen in all of the years that he'd known her. Just like that all the bitterness, rage, anger, and indifference had all melted away leaving her to rest. Leaning over and placing his lips softly against the corner of her mouth he thought to do the same as he slid out from under the sheets and stood from the bed.

The wooden planks of the floor of the home felt cold and moist against his bare feet as Zack moved through the kitchen. Closing the refrigerator door and shutting off the kitchen light Zackery abandoned the room carrying his ham and cheese sandwich and tall glass of iced tea for the dimly lit living room.

Morgan Paleto was inside stretched out across one of the couches with an open book lying across her stomach. Whether or not she had opted to spend the night down here instead of seeking out one of the bedrooms upstairs or had simply succumbed to her own exhaustion where she lay was anybody's guess. Regardless, Zack did what he could to see to it that he didn't disturb her sleep as he slowly crept across the room.

It was the low hum in the distance and the churning of something hulking and electrical somewhere deep within the confines of this dwelling. Something that was definitely the cause of the vibrating floor and walls all around him. Zackery took another bite out of his ham and cheese on white as he rounded the next corner and continued on down the hall.

He stopped after he passed an open doorway that lead into a small room with a single hanging light bulb lighting the nook. Taking two steps back, Zackery looked inside and saw Tripp seated on top of a small white clothes dryer. He seemed engrossed in the stack of papers that he held up in front of his face in his left hand. His eyes remained glued to them even as he poured a cap full of fabric softener into the open lid of the washer to his right.

Zackery made his way into the small room and headed over to the small window embedded in the wall opposite the doorway. Sitting his glass down on the top shelf of a dusty rack nailed to the wall on his right that was covered with tins and small brightly colored glass jars overflowing with safety pins, buttons, clothes pins, and other knickknacks, he undid the latch on the window and lifted up the pane of glass.

The blaring sound of the chirping crickets that consumed the night outside of the house spilled over into the confined space of the laundry room through the screen covering the outside portion of the window. He peered out into the darkness and looked over the dark silhouette of the barn that was set against the shady tree line in the background just beyond it before turning his eyes toward the very studious Tripp Manning. "Anything of any particular interest there?"

Tripp lowered the lid of the washing machine. "Like you wouldn't believe," he said, taking up flipping through the papers with both of his hands now. "I clipped these papers from Dr. Mangalo's playpen across the way over there. Vital statistics. Heart rate. Palpitations. Pupil response." Tripp flipped through a few more pages and even unfurled a few fold out portions. "Electroencephalographic readings of alpha rhythms. Brain scans. Blood pressure. Breathing rates." Tripp squinted his eyes and pulled the stack of papers in closer to his face. "Comparable tolerances to E-grade biochemical and pathological agents," he said, reading aloud. Tripp jerked the papers away from his face and looked over at Zack. "On and on with this stu...What happened to your face?" he asked just noticing the small assortment of battery marks that decorated Zack's mug.

"Don't ask." He snagged another bite of his ham and cheese on white. "Any of that nonsense you just spouted off supposed to mean anything?"

"I'm not sure," Tripp said. He began fishing through the paperwork again. "You say our girl Katelyn used to reside down in that hole. If it's true then it most definitely would explain why she has a tendency to come off as so...her. Because whoever all of that equipment and medication was brought here for underwent an insane amount of treatment and observation. I mean some of these readings account for as much as ninety six hour blocks of time that are broken up into half hour increments."

Zackery took another chunk out of his sandwich and grabbed up his glass of tea again to wash it all down. The woman who slept so soundly upstairs had once again engulfed every thought in his mind as he tried to imagine what she must have suffered through and at the hands of whom during her time here. Time that was now completely lost to her. "Did you come across anything that might let us get a handle on who exactly

147

this Beckman person was?" Zackery asked him, the name on the mailbox outside suddenly coming to mind.

The urge to locate this individual or individuals and grill them however aggressively about the incidents that had taken place at this residence so many years ago grew more overwhelming with each second that ticked by. Had he been armed with this Beckman's current whereabouts right now Zackery would have been tempted to rouse the entire household in the hopes of leading the expedition out of there right this second.

"Nada," Tripp replied. "There isn't even so much as a single barcode or logo on any of that equipment out there to trace it back to wherever it came from. And this place? The water? The power? All paid for by direct deposit through an account that was started with cash and still has enough bulk to keep this place running well into the next decade." Tripp had really been busy rummaging through this place, Zackery thought, going over the chunk of time that he had pilfered away earlier that evening getting wasted and shooting the breeze with Katelyn when he wasn't getting into scrapes with the local hooligans. "No television. No phone. Newspaper subscription. Internet connection. There's no sign that anybody's been out here in ages and there isn't so much as a single scrap of junk mail out there in the box. As far as I can tell this Beckman guy is a ghost."

"Great," Zackery breathed out harshly. "So we've got nothing." He drained the tea in his glass until there was nothing left but the stack of clattering cubes. *Perfect*, he thought. He couldn't help it but something inside of him burdened him with a sense of guilt that was brought upon by the feeling that he had somehow let Katelyn down. They'd come all this way and it didn't seem right for them to have done so only to walk away with substantially more questions than the ones they had arrived there with.

"Well, there's nothing solid here. I'll give you that. But I did manage to come out of that refuse with a name. Thomas Donavan. I found it on an old airline receipt from a flight out of Carson City, Nevada to Dover city."

It wasn't much to go on but Zackery was still ecstatic that they were able to get that far. "You wouldn't by any chance happen to have an address on Mr. Donovan would you?"

Tripp nodded his head and Zackery cocked a single eyebrow. "Santa Fe."

The four of them loaded up the car the next afternoon in preparation of their departure from the Beckman estate. They had quite a drive ahead of them and no one was in any desperate need to stay at that farmhouse residence any longer than need be. After making sure to pack up as much of the edible provisions that they had secured the night before as they could carry to cut down on their stops they all piled into Tripp's car and were soon pulling out of the gravel driveway of the Beckman home.

Zackery was seated in the backseat along with Katelyn. Her body was once again pushed up against the car door on the passenger side behind Morgan, her head leaning to the side against the window, and her eyes staring out through the glass, taking in the scenery outside of the car.

She had a look about her that was as distant as it was disheartening. Zackery, still floating on the intoxication of the high she'd put him on the night before, was compelled to react to her emotional state in the hopes that he could somehow bring her back to the level of bliss that she had appeared to exude in his presence so many hours before.

He edged himself over and moved closer to the center of the backseat. Stretching his arms out across the top of the seatback cushion, he still failed to gain her attention. Zackery lowered his right hand and stroked two of his fingers through her ink black hair. When Katelyn turned to look at him he flashed her a smile. She offered him up one in return that was significantly less bright and was one of a much shorter duration than his.

Taking this as the welcome mat that he knew it to be, Zackery couldn't resist attempting to further close both the emotional and physical gap that he could still see lying between them. He removed his right arm from the seatback behind Katelyn's head and lowered his palm down over the back of her hand that was resting on top of her thigh. He gave her hand a gentle comforting squeeze. One that she didn't seem to mind. She even went so far as to slowly move her hand out from beneath his grip and place it on top of his, clasping her fingers around the back of his knuckles.

Zackery was beside himself with the sensation of it all. The two of them were really making progress and in more ways than one. He could feel it.

And then...

He felt it.

The pressure that Katelyn began to apply to his hand soon became unmistakably aggressive. The needle sharp sparks of pain shooting up through Zackery's arm drew a closed lipped wince of agony out of him. It would have been a high pitched yelp but he didn't want to clue the occupants of the front seat as to what was going on right over their shoulders.

He tried to pull his hand away but she wouldn't let go. Continuing to stare out of the window ahead of her as if nothing was going on, Katelyn put the squeeze on his hand just as nonchalantly as if she were sitting there lovingly holding it. Ultimately, Zackery had to place his free hand down on her wrist for leverage and slowly pry himself loose from her grip. "Damn it!" he blurted out as one final tug freed his hand. He slid back over to the other side of the car.

"Everything alright back there?" Tripp called back to them.

"Yes!" Zack said with a little too much anger in his voice. "Yeah. Everything's cool."

Despite the intimacies that they had shared the night before Katelyn had yet to display any easily visible signs that any of it had had any effect on her disposition where she and Zack were concerned. Massaging his aching hand with the other one, Zackery secretly chastised himself for jumping the gun the way he did and having to be reminded the hard way that the barriers in place around whatever it was that Katelyn had to be overprotective of weren't going down without a fight. Whether or not he would retain the same tenacity on his end still remained to be seen.

Before departing the town of Wilderbrook, Kansas Tripp stopped off at a gas station to fill up. Zackery and Morgan stepped out of the car for a moment and headed inside the gas station convenience store. When he returned he climbed into the backseat and nudged a bottle of water into Katelyn's shoulder. She turned around and placed her eyes on it then turned them up to him. "Here," he said to her. "And try not to take my fingers off."

Katelyn snatched the bottle away from him. "That won't be a problem as long as you continue to keep them to yourself."

"Funny. Last night I don't recall you minding where I kept them. Even came through with a few suggestions if I'm remembering right."

Katelyn twisted the cap off of the bottle of water and took a drink. "Momentary lapse of judgment."

"Bullshit," Zack said to her. "Last night you let me in and you and I both know that the only reason was because it was exactly what you wanted. Blame it on the alcohol; fate; the alignment of the stars. You wanted me; you've got me."

Katelyn started to respond to Zackery's comment but Morgan's return to the front passenger seat silenced her before she could speak. Tripp was done pumping the car's fuel not too long after that and in no time at all they were back on the freeway and the town of Wilderbrook became an ever shrinking spec in the car's rearview mirrors as the sun began to set over the western horizon.

By the time they crossed the border into New Mexico Katelyn was at the wheel of the car. Zackery was sitting next to her in the passenger seat holding a fold out map in front of his face as Katelyn usher them ahead into the daylight hours along the long stretch of highway that lay out before them. Morgan and Tripp continued to sleep away in the backseat as the rolling hills and barren desert plains moved past the windows all around them. Zackery folded the map closed and stuffed it into the glove compartment in front of his knees.

He glanced up, took a look out of the windshield, and saw the tops of the many buildings embedded within the city in the distance begin to rise over the desert horizon in front of them. A city that was supposed to be home to a Mr. Thomas Donavan.

With any luck they'd find him there and he'd be of sound enough mind and body to provide them with some much needed answers about the identity of the illusive Mr. or Ms. Beckman and perhaps even shed some light over the dark cloud that was Katelyn Bree's past.

She parked the car on the curb up the street from the front entrance of the apartment building and stepped out onto the sidewalk. "This is a complete waste of time," Katelyn said as she turned and stared up at the apartment building in the middle of the block.

Zackery climbed out and walked around the hood of the car in her direction. Stepping up onto the sidewalk he closed in on her right shoulder. "Nobody's keeping you here against your will," he said to her. "I'm sure Mr.

Carthright is missing you back at the Wicker Basket right about now."

Katelyn glared at the side of his face and then at the back of his head as Zackery moved past her and continued on down the sidewalk. True, she wasn't as overzealous to see this thing through to its conclusion as a few other members of her party might have been but she did possess a tad bit of curiosity that was enough to keep her from forsaking the lot of them for her responsibilities to Jordan back at the bookstore.

Staying the course might even see to it that once she did return to Chicago she would be able to go about her once daily routine unmolested by certain outside forces that had recently reared their very pestering head in her life. There was only one way to find out for sure.

Zackery stepped out of the elevator onto the fourteenth floor of the eighteen story building with the rest of the pack at his back. The hallway floor was carpeted with a gray fabric that was lined with a wine red coloring on either of its edges. It still bore the streaks that were left by the vacuum cleaner after the morning's tidying up.

The walls were all covered in expensively framed paintings and portraits that were offset by various other gold trimmed fixtures and decorations. There couldn't have been more than a handful of apartments residing on the floor. Just one more feature hinting at the severely elevated price range that someone would have to be comfortable forking over several times a year in order to enjoy the privilege of calling this place home. This Mr. Donovan had to have been one such well-to-do individual.

After locating the apartment door that coincided with the address Tripp had given him Zackery rang the doorbell a few times and was answered with a deafening silence with each corresponding toll. He shook the door handle, attempting to test the locks keeping the door sealed. They appeared to all be in place. "Looks like our boy's not home," Zackery said. "So unless you guys feel like sitting outside and staking the place..."

Katelyn moved up to the door and nudged him out of the way. Taking hold of the door knob, she gave it one sharp shove and the sound of snapping the wood and metal could be heard reverberating in the small area of the hallway that the four of them inhabited as Katelyn broke through the initial security measures of the apartment and pushed the front door ajar. Both Zackery and Tripp began twisting their heads from side to side in search of any potential witnesses in the immediate area.

"Or we could go somewhere and look up the laws on breaking and entering in this state," Morgan said.

Katelyn pushed the door open wider and stepped into the apartment. The others quickly followed her inside with Morgan trailing the pack, leaving her with the responsibility of shutting the door closed behind them.

There weren't any lights on inside but enough sunlight poured through the windows to allow for a more than adequate level of visibility.

Katelyn was able to take full advantage of that fact the moment she stepped into the corridor leading away from the front door and deeper inside of this domicile. It was the array of studio portraits that aligned the walls on both her left and right sides that initially stole her attention away from her pursuit.

She would have thought it nothing more than a hanging mirror had she been allowed to continue on her way but slowing down in order to further inspect the piece, she found that it spoke to her of a very different story indeed.

Katelyn had entered the apartment at almost a full on fast paced walk but the sight of the portraits, particularly the stills in which her likeness was present, robbed her sails of the very wind with which they needed to maintain her momentum. She was stunned beyond words.

Tripp Manning moved up beside her on her left. "Now she certainly looks familiar. Not too sure about that weird thing she's doing with her lips and teeth but I've definitely seen that face before. You wouldn't happen to have a sister, would you?" Katelyn didn't even look in his direction as she turned and continued on her way down the hall. "Right. How would you know?"

"Oh my God," Morgan said as she slowly stepped down the corridor gawking at the display along the walls. "It's really her. It's Katelyn." Head shot after head shot passed before her eyes. Photographs of Katelyn from multiple angles in various states of elation and glee. The portrait of a complete stranger wearing an unmistakably familiar face eerily staring her in the eyes as she continued to walk past each one.

"Yes indeed it is," Tripp said. "I suddenly feel inclined to scream out the word *jackpot* before one of you clowns beat me to it. Any takers there, Zack? Zack?" Tripp turned away from the wall he was facing in search of his friend but found no sign of him.

Katelyn's eyes crawled and glossed over everything; over every spec of inventory that crossed in front of their path with meticulous precision. Beige sheets covered every stick of furniture in every room that she stepped into. Mr. Donovan wasn't home.

He hadn't been for a while and from the looks of things he wouldn't be returning anytime soon. The walls in almost every direction that she turned bore a still shot of her reflection, all of them staring back at her like ghosts from a life long dead to her that she had absolutely no memory of.

Nothing.

Nothing at all about this place sparked even the most minute grain of familiarity inside of her. Not one turn of the corner. Not one room. Not one sight, sound, or smell. Nothing. Nothing but the image of her face at various stages of growth looked like anything she had ever seen before.

What was this place? What was this place to her? Had she been here before? Had this been the house she'd grown up in? If it was then...when was the last time that she'd walked these halls? When had she last eaten breakfast here? When had she last slept the night and awoken to the sight of the high spackled ceiling above her head? Four years ago? Five? Seven? Was this her home? And if not then whose and why weren't they here to greet her or to explain any of the multitude of questions perplexing her right now?

Katelyn pushed open a door she had come to and stood there as still and as quiet as she could be while listening to the soft squeak of the hinges as the hardwood barrier moved within the frame. Nothing. She listened to it as if hearing it for the first time before making her way further into the room. There was a large bed inside. The rest of the furniture present had sheets draped over them. Katelyn walked over to the large standing object to the left of the bed.

She took up a portion of the sheet covering it between her fingers and after clenching hold of a firm enough portion she jerked her right arm forcefully across her body. A small layer of dust was poofed out into the air above her head and she let go of the sheet allowing it to float back down to the floor as gravity would have it fall.

The sudden shedding of the tarp revealed an artifact covered dresser top complete with, among other things, a music box whose lid abruptly flipped opened and whose underlying mechanisms let loose with the composition they had been holding back for quite some time.

Katelyn paid little attention to the harmonics spilling out of the contraption and instead reached her hand out to lay fingers on one of the many Polaroid photos pasted on the mirror that resided at its back. She peeled the snap shot away and brought it closer to her face. The image was that of a young dark haired child sitting astride a miniature rocking horse with a fully grown man at her side and a decorated Christmas tree in the background.

"Cute kid," Katelyn heard Zackery's unmistakable voice speak out from behind her. Lifting her eyes she saw him moving past her in the mirror toward the other end of the dresser. "Hey. Look at this." Zackery picked up a small folding partition from the dresser top. "High school diploma. Katelyn Breanne Donavan. Hmmph. Guess that's you."

"My name is Katelyn Bree," she said, dropping the Polaroid she held. She picked up a small picture frame this time and examined the image it held.

Zackery replaced the small partition. "You don't say?"

"Do you think she..." Katelyn took a moment to poise herself. "Do you think I look happy?" she said, vocalizing what she suspected to be the truth but in her head still doubted.

Zackery moved in closer to her and looked down at the photograph she held. It was a picture of her kneeling down on a plush green lawn hugging a Golden Retriever. Kneeling on the other side of the full grown animal was an adult masculine figure with a beard and mustache covering his face that was the same shade as the hair on Katelyn's head. Thomas Donavan, he imagined. Katelyn's father. Both of them wore smiles as bright as the day showing down on the pair. "Yes," Zackery answered her. "Yes. You look happy." Happier than he'd ever seen her before.

"Come on, Daddy! Hurry!"

He'd heard it too but Zackery wasn't quite as thrown by the sound of Katelyn's voice emanating from some other part of this home than the woman standing next to him. The joy it held; the vibrancy was what had initially struck him as odd. Katelyn on the other hand was utterly perplexed by the fact that a vocal tone and resonance so similar to the one that she possessed could somehow be present on the air in this apartment without the aid of her windpipe and vocal cords. Strange thing to feel seeing as how there were so many other things within these walls that bore a more than striking resemblance to her.

Anyhow.

Katelyn placed the picture frame back down on the dresser top and started for the door. Zackery was right on her heels.

"Now make a wish and blow out the candles. Oh, and don't forget you have to keep it a secret. If you say it out loud it won't come true."

Katelyn walked the hallways of this strange place following the sound of her own laughter; her own voice. Where was it coming from? she thought, referring to both the physical presence of the sound she was hearing as well as the ticklish joy that formed the pitch behind all of her words.

"Come now. It's not my birthday." This time it was a man's voice that stirred the dust cluttered atmosphere. *"What should I be bothered with wishes for anyhow?"*

"Daddy?"

Her voice was louder now. Katelyn made another left and stopped moving. Standing there in the open doorway she stared across the room at the television that Tripp and Morgan had pulled the sheet away from.

Right there; in front of her; center stage on the television screen for all to see was an image of her covered from head to toe in pastels from the spaghetti strap top she wore to the kapri pants that covered her legs.

The panning camcorder followed her as she moved behind a large wooden picnic table that was covered with decorative paper place settings, one for each individual that composed the small crowd of young adults gathered and seated outside on what looked to be an extraordinarily beautiful day.

Katelyn examined each face that found its way into the frame with her as the camera lens zoomed in and out on the festivities. Each one mimicked the odd euphoria that she herself appeared to be filled with. Especially the man that moved into the shot and stood next to her behind the table.

Tripp turned around and looked back over his right shoulder and watched as Katelyn slowly made her way inside of the room toward the television. Looking off to his right at Morgan he saw that she too had turned around to get a glance at the silent, slowly approaching brunette who looked about as curious as she was awestruck.

"It was in the machine when I turned it on," Morgan said to her coworker. There was no response. Katelyn didn't even look in her direction, refusing to let her eyes drift away from the television as she moved. Morgan let her gaze drift farther back behind her to Zackery who was standing in the doorway leaning his right shoulder against the inside of the frame as he observed the video playing on the television. When Morgan locked eyes with him all he did was shake his head gently from side to side and that was enough for her. She turned back around to the show.

Katelyn recognized him instantly; the man standing next to her wrapping his right arm around her shoulder and pulling her in for a side by side hug. It was the man from the photograph on top of the dresser in the room she had just left.

"Would it be too much of an inconvenience for you to just humor the poor girl?" This voice was clearly coming from the man holding the camera that zoomed in on the two faces as he spoke. *"After all, she did have the decency to go through all of the trouble of putting this thing together."*

"Exactly. You tell him, Mr. Mercer. For once in your life would you at least try not to be a complete killjoy." There she went again, rippling with uproarious laughter and merriment. *"It's not like it's everyday that we get to celebrate a promotion like this."*

"I told you, it's not a promotion. It's more of a lateral move than anything else. And Frank, you would do well not to encourage her."

"Promotion. Lateral move. It's one hell of a step up in pay grade, that's for sure." Now everyone at the table was in stitches. *"Now blow out the candles, damn you, and make a wish for Heaven's sake."*

"Alright then. But I'm afraid I've nothing to wish for. Especially seeing as how everything I'll ever need is already right here with me." He pulled Katelyn into him once more and placed a kiss into the pitch black mane draped down across her left temple.

Lightly stepping across the carpet floor, Katelyn slowly closed the distance between her and the television. She stopped once she was shoulder to shoulder with Tripp. His neck craned in her direction and he watched her eyes lift up from the television screen and come to a rest on the large bay curtain covered window behind it. "What?" he asked her. "What is it?"
"Get down!"

160

11

The glass across the room in front of them exploded into millions of bits and the curtains that covered it were shredded to ribbons as the cannon outside continued to open fire on the apartment. The television screen shattered into tiny bits of wood chips and electrical sparks as the onslaught of projectiles ripped through the device and continued to cut a swath through the living room across the carpet. Katelyn shoved her body into Tripp's and took him with her as she made strides across the room to avoid the artillery fire attempting to shred the room in half.

Letting out a shrill scream as she threw her arms up to cover her face, Morgan stumbled off to her right with a clumsily reflexive maneuver, tripping over a lounge chair on her way, as she did what she could to get out of the way of whatever this was that was threatening to rip her and anyone else in its path to pieces. Zackery merely rolled around to his right, placing his back against the wall next to the doorway just outside of the room as he saw the mayhem coming his way.

"Morgan!" Zack called out to her, the sound of her panicked scream sending an icy shiver through him. Surely she hadn't been hit. He tried to slow his mind down and remember the last image of her that he'd taken notice of. No. She hadn't been hit. She couldn't have been. "Morgan!" he called to her once more.

There was a pause in the firing and Zackery eased his head around the corner until he was able to get a look

161

inside the room with only his left eye. There she was, huddled behind a chair with her knees pressed against her chest and wrapped up in her arms. She had her head down and her eyes shut tight. "Morgan, come on!" he barked out.

Just as she made it up to her feet the reports started again. She didn't know it but thankfully the firing was veering off from her position as she hurried over to the doorway, to Zackery, and hopefully to a much better source of cover from the menace bearing down on them. When she got close enough Zackery reached out and snatched her into him, pulling her around the corner as he did. His mind suddenly flashed back to the friends of his that still remained in the room that was under attack.

Katelyn.

His heart was in his throat.

The horrifically loud noise of the constantly repeating report filled the room with a thunderous racket, the reverberations of which shook to the core every piece of matter that the rounds being fired from the cannon of the gunship just outside the window failed to touch. Katelyn slammed Tripp's body against the seatback of a couch that she helped to toppled over when she came crashing down on top of him. When the back of the couch hit the floor Katelyn rolled off of him. There was another pause in the firing.

"What the hell is that?" Tripp demanded to know.

"Tobias," Katelyn answered him. Lying on her back she shoved her hands down into her pants pockets and came back out with a set of keys. She grabbed Tripp's wrist and smashed them down into his open palm. "Get out of here!"

"What?" he said, looking at the twinkling articles he held as if he were trying to figure out what they were. "Where are you going?"

Katelyn rolled over onto her stomach and with one quick pushup motion she was up on her feet. Feet that were now sprinting across the carpet toward the glass covered portal embedded in the wall directly in front of her. Katelyn burst forth through the window and out into the daylight to the chorus of shattering glass and the sound of her name being called out by the very distinguishable voice belonging to Zackery Collins.

Katelyn's right arm hooked around the landing gear on the side of the helicopter hovering outside of the fourteenth story apartment window. The abrupt stop jerked her body around and she wrapped her legs around the long bar extending to the rear of the flying machine.

The helicopter spun away from the apartment and Katelyn clamored up to her feet. With one hand clasped around the edge of the frame of the open portal on the right hand side and the other hand pressed against the glass covering the cockpit of the helicopter the rest was all balance. She stared through the transparency at the two faces between her and the ripped open hole in the side of Mr. Thomas Donovan's apartment.

The face directly in front of her held very little interest but the one on the other side of it, the one belonging to Tobias McPhearson, she couldn't take her eyes off of. The gun he drew from his side holster and trained on her managed to momentarily avert her sight. To the extreme surprise of his copilot the Colonel flexed his right index finger and the weapon came blaringly and explosively to life. Two rounds broke through the shield next to Katelyn's head. The third one would have smacked her squarely between the eyes had Katelyn not pushed off of the hovering conveyance and forced her body back through the air.

Her feet flipped up over her head and when they came back down beneath her Katelyn's back was coming into contact with the building across the street from the shattered window she'd leapt out of only moments before.

Tobias brought the nose of the craft he flew around in tune with Katelyn's airborne body. He aligned the revolving cannon attached to the undercarriage of the helicopter up with her body and started the multitude of barrels spinning. Unfortunately for him the effects of gravity had already began to display its effects on Katelyn's body and she had already started on her downward descent just as the high caliber rounds began to shred the concrete above her.

Tripp was finally able to get his breathing slowed down to a somewhat normal rate. Taking his eyes off of the window that Katelyn had recently dove through he once again took notice of the set of keys that he held in his hand. The set of keys that she had handed him before bounding out of the apartment. The set of keys that belonged to a car sitting against the curb on the street fourteen stories below. Fourteen stories. Tripp's eyes found the window again. Katelyn had just went out of a fourteen story window without so much as a second thought. What the hell did she do that for? Where the hell was she? Was she okay? Was she still alive at all? Why the hell would she do something like that?

"Tripp!"

The sound of his name being yelled out ripped his attention away from the window again. It was Zack. He was calling out his name from the doorway across the room. "I'm right here!" Tripp reciprocated, voicing his beacon and assuring both Zack and himself that he was still in one whole piece.

"Well quit screwing around and let's get out of here! Come on!"

Screwing around? Assuming the two of them made it out of this alive Tripp was going to be sure that Zackery received an in-depth lecture on the true meaning of that particular word phrasing. But for right now saving his neck would have to take precedent over any thrashing that he had in mind for his friend.

It had been a few moments since he'd heard any further response from the arsenal outside of the apartment window. Perhaps it was safe to venture out and away from the seclusion of his hiding spot behind the toppled sofa; if only for this fleeting moment. It wasn't as if that delicate piece of furniture would have provided him much security had the vicious beast of a machine that previously took to decimating the living room turned its sights back on the flat; specifically the area of the room where he had been residing.

Clutching the keys he held in his fist, Tripp hurried up to his feet and shuffled around the sofa in the direction of Zackery's voice.

With both of her knees slightly bent and her right leg extended out a little further than her left, the rubber soles of Katelyn's shoes picked up hardly any traction as they remained pressed against the side of the building with the ground below rushing up quickly to meet her. Both of her arms were extended out beside her and the palms of her hands felt the rapidly moving concrete beneath her fingertips grow warmer with ever meter that she closed in on the sidewalk beneath her vertical body.

Katelyn's elbows bent and before the cracked walkway had the opportunity of coming into contact with her person, utilizing her weight and the rate of speed with which she fell from the sky to inflict whatever damage was due to her, she pushed off of the building wall and came down right shoulder first on the roof of a passing car.

She rolled off of the top of the moving vehicle and smashed into the side of one that was parked against the curb in front of Thomas Donovan's apartment building, shattering all of the windows on the passenger side as her tumbling body dented in the metal construction.

Katelyn dropped down to the cold gray glass covered pavement of the street. She did what she could to cushion her fall with her hands and forearms but the concrete that she dropped face side first against held little mercy for her. Rolling over on her back, Katelyn hoisted her upper body up on her forearms. It was just in time for her to see the front bumper of a SWAT van casting its shadow down over her feet and ankles as the front of the vehicle passed over the lower portion of her body on its way to eclipsing the entire sum of her.

The back of Katelyn's head slammed down hard against the unyielding street, the impact of the blow forcing her eyes to squeeze shut and her teeth to clench hard as her ears bore the burden of the booming noise of the engine passing by overhead. Her body had dropped quick enough for her to avoid any contact between her forehead and the shiny chrome of the bumper that kicked up several strands of her hair as it sped through the air mere inches above her front hairline. The driver hit the breaks hard and Katelyn's face had to suffer the tiny pinpricks of debris that the tires threw at her as the halted steel belted radials slid across the asphalt.

The van passed over her and Katelyn used the momentum of force that the vehicle had created in the surrounding flow of air to help aid her as she rolled her body up onto her neck and brought her feet into the air above her face. Finishing out her backwards roll onto her feet, Katelyn quickly spun her body and darted off after the transport with the menacing sound of the propeller blades attached to the flying dreadnaught that Tobias McPhearson operated thumping against the air high above her.

The doors swung open and Katelyn ran headlong into the armed and armor covered individuals that poured out to engage her. She snatched the semiautomatic rifle out of the clutches of the first soldier she met, spun, and used it to whack the next man who filed out of the van behind him against the side of his protective helmet covered head.

Just as he was meeting the awaiting pavement of the street Katelyn completed her three sixty turn and returned the rifle back to its original owner after slamming the butt of the weapon into the side of his helmet with enough force to open up a gash in the hard plastic. Both men lay near unconsciousness on the ground next to each other as their brethren continued to spill out of the van in the hopes of aiding them in their venture.

Needless to say, Katelyn would have none of it. The blows she delivered came swifter and harder as she dispatched of each aggressor in turn until one by one they each lay limp and useless on the street before her.

Katelyn threw her hand up in the air and caught hold of the middle of the rifle as the last standing trooper tried to smash the butt down on the bridge of her nose. Pulling his body into her, she spun him around and placed his back against her chest. With a hard, quick snatch she tore the weapon from his fingers and wedged the front of his neck against her forearm.

She leaned both her body and the struggling physique that she held restrained against the side of the van near the rear on the driver's side as she trained the sights of the weapon out in front of them at the approaching humvee in the distance. Katelyn squeezed the trigger and watched the rounds that expelled from the barrel in rapid succession splatter across the windshield of the off-road hulk leaving very little damage in their wake.

Apparently the rounds that the foot soldiers had been issued were the same electrically charged projectiles that Katelyn had run into during her previous encounter with them. Despite the vicious force that Tobias had opened up on her with their primary objective still appeared to center around her capture rather than her termination.

167

Something she could use to her advantage? Perhaps in the long run. Right now she wasn't taking any chances.

Katelyn threw down the weapon and spun the soldier she held around to face her. Stepping back she pulled him into the spin she made with her body, dragging him around to her left and his right. She twirled around in a complete circle, stepping back behind the van and releasing his body when she had him aligned with the open bay at the rear of the van. His armor clad body flew threw the interior of the vehicle and was expelled through the front windshield. Hitting the pavement, he rolled to a stop and caused the approaching hummer to break and come to a cattycorner stop in the middle of the street. Katelyn had since climbed into the van through the back and moved up to the driver's seat. The engine was still running and she could see several troops ejecting from the hummer through the broken windshield in front of her.

She put the gear in reverse and stomped down hard on the gas. The downed soldiers scrambled to clear a path for her. The van shot back a few feet and then the squealing tires slid to a halt on the blacktop. Katelyn put the van in drive and sped out toward the firing artillery in her path.

The soldiers steadied their aim as best they could as Katelyn guided the van in their direction. She managed to scatter a few of them before jerking the steering wheel to her left and making a U-turn that brought the vehicle halfway up on the sidewalk.

Parking meters were knocked loose one at a time as she continued on in the opposite direction from the stopped hummer, their payload of loose change lying scattered all about the wayside behind her. More assault vehicles approached her, these four wheeled freights coming at her now from the direction that she drove towards in the hopes of thwarting her escape.

Escape.

Zackery and the others would be exiting the building on her left soon in an attempt to secure their own safe passage out of this melee (as well as make an attempt at reacquiring her, she thought, anticipating what would surly be Zackery's primary motive upon making his way down to the street). Perhaps the more distance she put between herself and her compatriots the more discouraged they would be in forsaking their own getaway in lieu of rescuing her from Tobias' brigade.

It was doubtful that such an option would prove successful but at the moment it was the only viable option laid out before her. Katelyn swung a right at the next corner and stepped down harder on the gas pedal. She glanced over in the mirror mounted on the side of the van and watched as the cadre of assault vehicles made their respective turns and hurried after her.

Leading the small horde away from the apartment building, Katelyn barely had sufficient time to enjoy the apparent fruits of her well laid plan before the right fender of the van suffered a collision with the front bumper of an all black hummer. The impact knocked the van Katelyn steered over onto its right side and spun it around, front end facing the rear, as it continued forward along its current path, leaving a trail of metal shards and broken glass behind as it slid across the asphalt. Katelyn held onto the steering wheel and braced her feet against the cushion of the seat and the van's ceiling until it finally came to a metal grinding halt.

She could hear them all. Even over the piercing symphony of the displaced traffic that had been turned into complete bedlam thanks to the ensuing accident. An accident that had disrupted what was once a steady flow of movement being guided by an array of blinking lights and strategically placed color coded signs of various geometrical shapes. Each set of military issue boots stomping across the blackened pavement as the soldiers moved in to surround the overturned vehicle resonated crystal clear in her ears and through means unbeknownst to her allowed her to pinpoint their every position outside of the small enclosure that encased her.

This little turn of events was surly going to make escaping that much more difficult. Fortunately for Katelyn she no longer found herself in the frame of mind of achieving such a goal. At least not at this particular point in time. From this vantage point she gathered that not only would abandoning her passive tactics of fleeing in observance of a much more aggressive stance prove more advantageous it might actually turn out to be something she enjoyed.

These men were, after all, becoming nothing short of an intolerable nuisance and now they were growing dangerously close to inflicting some serious damage to her person. She could hear the chattering cadence, stomping feet, and projectile chambering weapons of the surrounding troops closing in all around her.

She wanted out of this debacle and on her way. They were in clear and present opposition. Katelyn turned her eyes toward the displaced tact gear that had been spilled all around the interior of the van when it had been knocked over onto its side. A cluster of round grenades nestled in a patch of bullet resistant vests down on the side wall to her right caught her eye.

So be it.

Colonel McPhearson guided the helicopter he piloted through the sky along the street toward the obstruction that was causing so much havoc in the midday traffic. His bird along with several of the other helicopters present in the sky slowed their approach as they neared the tact van that was being surrounded by foot soldiers that were emptying from the humvees all around it. Witnessing the scene taking place on the street below him prompted Tobias to get on his radio and send up a com-link to every member of the strike teak in broadcast range.

"Attention. All ground troops, proceed with extreme caution. I repeat. Extreme..."

The ball of flames and dislodged sheets of metal that the van exploded into forced him to instinctively jerk the control stick between his knees to the side and veer his helicopter off away from the rising cloud of smoke, fire, and debris. Every other hovering gunship in the immediate vicinity of the explosion did the same. "Damn it!" he yelled out into the headset.

Maintaining her grip on the steering wheel, Katelyn lowered her body before pulling at the wheel hard enough to eject her body up through the driver's side door. Bringing her knees up to her chest, Katelyn tucked herself into a ball as the exploding grenade that she ignited detonated every flammable in its small surrounding radius and propelled her rotating body further up into the air.

Below her the armor clad bodies of soldiers were being thrown in every direction by the blast. Some of the airborne bodies came down on the street. Others landed down on top of the hoods and roofs of the assault vehicles that had shuttled them there. All that had somehow managed to keep their feet planted firmly beneath them backpedaled to a safe distance as Katelyn descended back down through the smoke and ash and planted the soles of her footwear down on the charred pavement.

Zackery exited the front entrance of the apartment building and headed up the street toward Tripp's car. "Where's Katelyn?" he asked, turning his head in every direction and finding no sign of the young vixen who he'd last seen leaping through the glass of a fourteen story window. "We have to find her and get out of here!"

When he reached the driver's side door Zackery suddenly came to the realization that he wasn't in possession of the keys needed to start the car. Turning back around on the sidewalk he reached his hand up in the air just in time to catch the jingling ring that Tripp had tossed in his direction. "Any bright ideas on where we should start looking?" Tripp asked him.

An explosion sounded off in the distance to Zackery's left and he turned his head in that direction hoping to catch a glimpse of Katelyn. Nothing. "A few! Come on! Get in!"

"Will somebody tell me what the hell is going on down there?" Tobias said into the radio attached to the side of his head. He tried his best to assess the situation taking place on the ground below but was having some considerable trouble maneuvering to a vantage point that would give him a clear visual of what exactly was taking place beneath him. He'd only been able to remain in radio contact with any two or three individuals on the ground before one by one their shaky, panicked, and unsteady voices were replaced by inaudible grunts and eventually deafening silence. "Status report! Over!"

He stumbled backwards as he tried to steady his erratic breathing while the sound of Tobias McPhearson's commanding voice bombarded his eardrums. At the same time he was busy trying to block out the screams and weapon reports coming from his fellow soldiers as he trained the sights of his own weapon on the shadows stirring within the moving fog sliding across the street in front of him.

When his back hit against the driver side door of one of the humvees left abandoned after the explosion he stopped and found himself having to duck and roll out of the way to avoid being hit by the body that came soaring through the air in his direction. The black clad body slammed awkwardly against the side of the vehicle before dropping down to the concrete. He stared down at the moaning heap for one alarmed moment before the piercing sound of Tobias' voice in his ear snapped him out of his trance.

Unfortunately he didn't have long to enjoy his newly acquired focus before he found himself being snatched off of his feet and down onto his back where he was then drug screaming across the asphalt underneath the hummer.

Katelyn came up to her feet in the spot this soldier once occupied and stared up at the swarming mechanical beasts that hovered around in the sky. Ridding herself of the pests that crawled through the cracks and crevasses of these city streets was one thing but if she didn't do anything about those cluttering the space above her head then her problem would remain only half solved.

"Watch out!" Tripp yelled from the backseat as Zackery swerved to miss a car in his path that had slowed due to the sound of the oncoming police sirens blaring through the air in the background.

"You're going to get us killed!" Morgan said to him.

When they reached the area of the street that contained the smoldering remains of the overturned van Zackery brought the car to a stop and climbed out. "Katelyn!" he yelled as he looked all about at the writhing, moaning bodies dressed in black fatigues lying around everywhere and struggling to their feet with the aid of one another or whatever they could get their hands on.

Katelyn was nowhere to be seen and the sound of sirens was getting closer. Whether they belonged to the fire trucks that should have been in route, the paramedics, or the cops Zackery hoped to have Katelyn in his possession and be well on their way out of town before whoever it was arrived. But with Katelyn still in the wind he figured the chances of their escape being anything resembling expedient was farfetched at best. "Katelyn!" he called out to her again.

"She's not here!" Morgan shouted to him. She was standing outside of the car on the passenger side with the door open.

"No but the cops are," Tripp said. He was standing behind Morgan looking down the street behind them. Two cruisers made the corner at breakneck speed and came firing down the street straight at them. "Whatever you guys are planning on doing you'd better do it fast."

Zackery spun around once more and soaked in the Katelyn free scene in frustration before cursing quietly to himself and calling it quits. He staggered back around to the driver's side of Tripp's car and climbed back in behind the wheel. Morgan got back in on the passenger side and Tripp pulled the door open wider as he prepared to climb back into the back.

He managed to touch his left foot down on the floorboard but when he tried to pry his right shoe away from the blacktop and place the rest of his body inside of the vehicle he found his entire right leg to be immobile due to the fact that his right ankle had been taken hold of by one burly, black clad soldier.

Tripp's eyes nearly bulged out of his head at the sight of the battered individual holding on to him with a grip that was most uncomfortable and bordering on quite painful. As surprised as he was looking down at this man it was nothing compared to the shock he received when he felt the automobile that he had been trying to board pull off rapidly, leaving him standing there on the street. He watched the car door he had been holding open close shut with the force brought on by the gust of wind that had been picked up with the car's current rate of speed.

"Wait a minute!" He tried to take a step but the soldier's hold on his ankle was unrelenting and he tripped. No matter. The car was going too fast and there was too much noise being carried around on the wind for his voice to reach the ears of either of his two fleeing companions.

With the distance between his downed body and the car carrying his friends growing wider while the sirens of the police cars continued to close in Tripp found his situation growing more dire with each second that passed.

Rolling over onto his back, he began kicking at the hand wrapped around his ankle as well as the bloody face staring back at him. "Let...let go of me!" he said as he threw his foot furiously back and forth. Once he got himself freed he left the beaten man where he lay and staggered to his feet. Present company consisting of gawking strangers and a severely disoriented tact team excluded, Tripp was all alone amidst this madness and now it was up to him to get himself out of it. He did the only thing that he could given the circumstances. He ran.

"Tripp? Tripp?" Morgan turned completely around in her seat in search of her friend whom to her disbelief was now missing. "Where's Tripp!?!" she said, turning back around to Zackery.

"What do you mean *where's Tripp*?" Zackery said, trying to keep his eyes on the road while taking more than a few looks behind him in the backseat. "Where is Tripp?"

"Attention all units," Tobias spoke into his radio as he looked down at the activity on the streets below from his seat in the cockpit of the helicopter he piloted. "The local authorities have began arriving on the scene. Refrain from interfering in their progress as best you can. I want all of your energies directed toward a broadening sweep of the area. Over." The Colonel lifted his eyes up from the scene unfolding on the streets below and placed them on the skies in front of him; specifically the gunship rounding the corner of the tall buildings two blocks down. He had recently been made aware of the positions and search patterns of every copter they had in the sky, making the sight of the one that was approaching him now quite strange indeed. Tobias began to look over his instruments. "Who is that?" he said mostly to himself. "Delta 4, is that you I have on approach? Over?"

Silence.

Tobias lifted his eyes again and stared studiously at the gunship that continued forward in his direction. "Delta 4?" he said with a gruff and harsh tone of voice. His upper lip began to curve up the right side of his cheek as his mouth took on a snarl of aggravation. His breathing began to quicken and his teeth clenched tight. Tobias pulled hard on the stick but it was too late.

Katelyn flipped up the latch on the front of the joystick in front of her with her fingers and squeezed the trigger that was underneath. The cannons mounted on either side of the gunship that she had control of began firing and she watched as small clumps of fragments began chipping away from the side of the target that she had selected.

Katelyn knew exactly who it was that was piloting the ship she was in the process of bringing under assault and she imagined that right now he was wondering just where the crew that was supposed to be occupying this shuttle had gotten off to. Little did he know that only moments earlier after this aircraft had made too low of a sweep over one of the nearby building rooftops Katelyn had boarded it and quickly dispatched of the members operating it. Now Katelyn had the helicopter and Tobias McPhearson between the crosshairs of her very own brand of retribution.

She pushed forward on the accelerator and pressed on ahead while keeping an eye on the clouds of black smoke that were now coming out of the machine that carried Tobias. Watching him veer off out of her path, it wasn't long before Katelyn was distracted by the instruments in front of her as they picked up on the two helicopters that were now approaching her from the rear.

Katelyn picked up the pace as she dropped down lower amidst the cluster of buildings. Her two pursuers gave chase as she lead them through the air, above the downtown city streets, rounding one set of buildings after the next. When she spotted a building up the block from her that was still in the process of being constructed Katelyn dropped down to an even lower altitude and headed straight for it.

Katelyn stood up from her seat and moved toward the rear of the cockpit as the nose of the helicopter neared the wall of the shell of the building she approached. An alarm somewhere near the controls she had just abandoned began to fill the air all around her. It was designed to signal anyone interested that the twin vehicles that were trailing had acquired missile lock and were preparing to fire.

The space between the front of Katelyn's helicopter and the side of the building was diminishing drastically with each second that passed. Two missiles were released and were now rocketing in her direction. She took the running start and bounded through the front of the cockpit window. Continuing forward through the air, she eventually burst through the newly installed window of the building.

Katelyn tucked and rolled across the floor before bouncing back up to her feet and darting out into a sprint across the wooden boards covering the floor. The helicopter wasn't far behind and after the missiles struck it Katelyn was being pursued by a wall of fire as she made strides toward the wall on the opposite side of the room.

Katelyn didn't let that small barrier stop her either. Pumping her arms and legs, she forced her body to continue on through the barricade of plaster, piping, and two by fours until she came out on the other side. The explosion that had threatened to send the molten inferno through the wall after her had only succeeded in producing a highway of cracks in the punched in structure and shaking loose a few bits and pieces of the wall, causing them to fall to the floor where Katelyn's body had collapsed shortly after breaching the next room.

Katelyn rose to her feet and turned to look back at the hole she had just made in the wall behind her. As the blaze died down she could see through to the other side. The blurry image of the two helicopters caught her eye and when she saw them change their course and head away from the destruction they had just caused Katelyn did an about face and headed on her way through the skeletal structure of the building.

"I don't want to hear about what you think; what you believe; or about any other possible theories that may have wandered into that microscopic organism you call a brain," Tobias spoke loudly into the handheld radio he carried as he struggled to make his voice heard over the fading engine of the helicopter that he walked around. The black smoke spilling out of the perforated hull of the downed aircraft that he breathed in and choked back as he stared out at the adjacent rooftops only helped to fuel his growing rage. "Until you bring me a body the target is still to be considered active. Now find her!" Tobias drew his arm back and let fly the communication devise he held, casting it out over the edge of the building that he had been forced to set down on thanks to the unexpected damage done to the helicopter he had been piloting.

Tripp Manning hadn't made it far before being stopped by the local police and questioned about his involvement in the turmoil that had been responsible for disrupting the serenity and disturbing so much of the peace that had previously enraptured their fair city streets. Needless to say, the answers that he so nervously stuttered and stammered his way through fell on very unconvinced ears. Regrettably those ears happened to be attached to bodies that were in possession of a patrol car with an empty fenced in backseat. He eventually found himself being cuffed and loaded into the car where he would remain until everything got sorted out.

Once that was done then his involvement in the incident would be more thoroughly examined and the length of time he spent within their custody more accurately determined. It was just his luck. He was extremely too far from home in a town that he was a stranger in, separated from his friends, and, as if being mixed up in the unpredictable dangers of the life of someone that he hardly knew wasn't enough, he now found himself in the hands of the law under less than reputable circumstances. Perfect. What else could possibly go wrong?

The sound of forced grunts and groans coming from the uniformed men who were standing around outside of the car distracted Tripp from his own grievances and alerted him to those being vocalized on the other side of the window he was sitting next to. The groans had morphed into threats of retribution and reprisal but none of it seemed to have any effect on Katelyn.

Tripp watched two police officers fall back past the window next to him and then turned his head to the front and stared through the gate as Katelyn opened the car door and climbed into the front seat behind the steering wheel.

"What the hell are you doing?" he asked her, shifting in his seat and taking another look outside of his window at the policemen who were getting back up to their feet.

"Getting us out of here," she answered him. Katelyn put the key in the ignition and turned the engine over. She pulled the gearshift down from *Park* to *Drive* and pushed her foot down on the gas hard enough to make the tires squeal as she pulled off. One of the officers that was still in the path of the speeding cruiser wound up having to roll over the side of the hood to get out of her way.

"Will you watch out!" Tripp yelled from the back seat. With his hands still cuffed behind his back he struggled to remain sitting upright as Katelyn tore through the street, weaving around every obstacle, both man and machine, that got in her way. "Geeze, where did you people learn to drive?"

The earsplitting sound of sirens and a cadre of police cars trailed after the one Katelyn drove as she made her way out of the downtown area via the expressway that she had turned on to. She had managed to keep the car on the road at speeds that reached up to over ninety miles an hour for quite a number of miles before running smack dab into the roadblock that the police were able to get up on the highway in front of her. Katelyn hit the brakes and slid the car to a stop.

"Now what?" Tripp said.

Katelyn got out of the car and walked around to the backseat. She opened up the door and pulled Tripp out of the car and up to his feet. Turning his back around to her, Katelyn took hold of the metal around his wrist and snapped the brace loose from its locking mechanism, first one and then the other.

The handcuffs dropped to the ground and Tripp brought his wrists up in front of his chest, taking turns rubbing each one in his palms. He glanced at the peace officers training their weapons at them from the cover behind their cars that were blocking their exit in both directions. "Now how exactly am I about to regret this?"

Katelyn led him around the car and toward the guardrail that overlooked the highway lanes running perpendicular to the platform bridge they were standing on. The officers were giving them orders to step back away from the rail and surrender themselves and though

Tripp was tempted to obey, Katelyn didn't appear to be the least bit moved by the voices calling out to them.

Katelyn threw her left leg over the rail and Tripp took a step back. "Wait a minute! What's going on here?" Katelyn refused to let him put anymore distance between the two of them than he already had. She reached her hand out and took hold of the front of his shirt. Tripp tried but he was unable to resist the force of her pull. "Katelyn! No!"

Another swift jerk of her arm and Tripp was being pulled over the edge of the bridge along with Katelyn down toward the lanes of streaking traffic below. Neither of them collided with the harsh and unwelcoming pavement or the shattering shards of a speeding windshield as Tripp had initially expected. Instead they both came crashing down through the chicken wire covered bed of a large truck that continued on its way down the expressway as they wrestled around on a padded floorboard composed of loose straw and feathers.

12

Zackery tilted his head to the side and placed his left temple against the palm of his hand as he leaned over against the window. Staring in front of him at the lingering police activity that remained out in front of the apartment building down the block from the car he was sitting in, he couldn't help but let out a sigh of uneasiness. The sunlight overhead had been fading for the past forty five minutes and as the sun began to set on this city Zackery still couldn't force himself to abandon this selfappointed post until he had ascertained the whereabouts and wellbeing of Katelyn. It had been hours since he had heard from either her or Tripp and clinging to the hope that they would somehow find a way to double back to this locale was the only thing keeping him going right now.

"Wherever she is I'm sure she's okay," Morgan said from the passenger's side of Tripp's car. "We should probably get out of here."

"I can't leave. Where would I go? Damn it!" he exclaimed as he smacked his right hand against the steering wheel. "Where the hell is she?"

A smile stretched across Morgan's lips and she turned back to face front. "Man. This girl really does it for you, doesn't she?"

Zackery just shook his head from side to side. "It's the strangest thing. I don't think that anybody has ever fascinated me the way that she does. You know?" he said, turning his head in her direction. His eyes went back to the windshield just beyond the steering wheel. "I don't think anybody's ever hated me as much as she does either, but..."

"Oh come on," Morgan said, letting slip a little chuckle. "She does not hate you."

"Oh yeah? Then where is she? Huh? Can you tell me that? Just where the hell is she?"

"Most likely scenario, somewhere trying to save her own neck. Just like we should be doing."

"What about Tripp?"

"Well we've searched the area as best we could. We've checked the local police stations. Assuming that he wasn't snatched up by those black helicopter types or that he didn't strap himself down to the hood of the first thing smoking heading back to Chicago then your guess is as good as mine. I'm all ears if you have any other suggestions about where to look next, that is unless you're still content to try and hold up here all night."

The chirping sound of a ringing telephone sounded from somewhere inside of the car and both Zackery and Morgan looked at each other with shock in their eyes. The chirping sound again. "Where is it?" Zackery said as he began to scrounge all around in his seat while searching every crevasse that his hands could reach.

"Here." Morgan reached down on the backseat floorboard behind his seat and came up with the noisy cell phone. She punched a button on the keypad and placed the phone to the side of her head. "Hello? Yeah. Hey, where are you?" She pulled the phone away from her ear. "It's Tripp," she told Zackery.

"Give me the phone," he said, reaching his hand out for it. Morgan placed it in his palm and he put it to the side of his head. "Tripp. Where are you? Where's Katelyn?"

Tripp looked around at the scenery outside of the phone booth that he was standing in. He let his eyes follow the next car that passed by him and pulled into the parking lot of the dingy motel at his back. "I don't know," he said, turning back around and speaking into the phone he held. "Some out of the way town about two and a half hours out." He picked up the phonebook that was in the booth and flipped it over to get a look at the cover. "Clarksville, I think."

"What about Katelyn? Is she alright?"

"Let me tell you something about her, okay? The last thing that Katelyn is is alright. Do you know that lunatic threw me off of a freeway overpass? Then she tossed me out of a moving truck and down an embankment. After that..."

"Alright, Tripp! I get it! Just let me talk to her for a second."

"She can't come to the phone right now."

"Why? What's the problem?"

Tripp spun around in the booth again and took a look back at the motel. "I don't know. She's either out getting us a room for the night or boosting a car. Either way I'd say we should be clearing out of here before too long. I just called to tell you to make sure you keep that phone charged up and to get your ass in gear. Whoever these guys are that are trying to get their hands on our little princess here don't appear to be in the mood for giving up anytime soon."

"What exactly did you have in mind?" Zackery asked him.

"Don't know yet. There's a few things I want to try and check out about our good friends Mr. Beckman and Mr. Donavan. I'll try and get back with you as soon as I can. Kiss Morgan goodnight for me."

"Whatever you say."

"Oh, and Zack..."

"Yeah. What is it?"

"She's just fine."

"That's good to know," Zack said. He took the phone away from his ear and hung it up. Handing it back to Morgan, he started the engine of the car up.

"So. Are we looking for a room or are we taking turns at the wheel," Morgan said as she opened up the glove box and placed the phone inside.

Zackery pulled away from the curb and spun a U-turn in the street. "First thing's first. Let's just get out of this town."

Tripp pounded the side of his fist against the motel room door. When Katelyn unhitched the locks and pulled it open Tripp stepped past her into the room. Katelyn shut the door again and resealed the quarters. She walked back over to one of the twin beds in the room and took a seat on top of the covers, placing her back against the headboard and kicking her feet up as she faced the television screen across the room. "Did you talk to Zack?" she asked him.

"Yes I did." He sat down on the second bed in the room and faced her outstretched body. He pulled open the top drawer of the nightstand and pulled out a small wad of rolled up bills. Katelyn picked up the remote for the television from the bed beside her and began surfing through the available channels while cutting an occasional eye over at Tripp as he counted himself out a sizable portion of cash.

"Any particular reason why you're going through my money?" Katelyn asked him as the channels continued to scroll by on the television screen.

"A few. One of them being I need money for cab fare into town. Another is that I tend to take offense to being thrown about at other people's discretion which usually leaves me with the burden of seeking out ways to alleviate my pain and suffering." He placed the money that he'd separated in his pocket and replaced the rest back in the drawer.

"Can I ask what it is that you're going into town for?"

Tripp flipped open the phonebook that was on top of the nightstand and picked up the phone receiver. "Can I ask how it is exactly that you survived a drop from a fourteen story window?" Katelyn remained silent with her eyes locked on the television. Tripp placed the phone to the side of his head and continued to flip through the phonebook. "I thought so."

Tripp sat the steaming paper cup that held his third round of liquefied coffee beans down on the desktop next to the computer. The drink was nowhere near the quality that he was used to tasting when he sampled from the stock that the Coffee House at the Wicker Basket kept on tap but it was enough to do the trick. Tripp took up the mouse again and continued his search for any information that he could find on Thomas Donovan and his blood ilk.

Although this photocopy shop remained open on a twenty four hour basis the exhilaration that he had experienced that day had left him more than a little ready for some R & R. Tripp didn't want to spend any more time in this place than was absolutely necessary. After pulling up the next page his eyelids opened wide and he realized that there was a very good chance that he wouldn't require much more time in this establishment, especially after what he had just stumbled across.

Afternoon the next day saw Morgan moving back and forth through the motel room that she shared with Zackery gathering up the Styrofoam containers and paper bags that were the remnants of her and Zackery's breakfast. The two of them had been packed up and ready to pull out for a couple of hours now and it was all she could do to keep herself busy while Zackery sat around and waited for Tripp's call.

He'd barely gotten much sleep the night before. His tossing and turning and endless pacing back and forth had threatened to deprive Morgan of what little sleep she was able to sneak away with during the restless time between now and the moment they had checked in.

When the cell phone finally did come ringing to life Zackery couldn't get it answered fast enough. "Yeah. Where are you?"

Tripp had stepped outside of the roadside diner that he and Katelyn had stopped at in order to utilize a phone booth across the parking lot to make this call. "I couldn't tell you specifically, but I can tell you where we're headed."

"Guess that's as good as anything," Zackery said, pulling the cap off of a ballpoint pen with his teeth and pulling up a blank pad of paper.

"I did some checking up on your boy Thomas Donavan. Turns out that the apartment that we visited yesterday that got ripped to shreds with us inside of it belongs to the late Thomas A. Donavan."

"Late?" Zackery asked.

"Yeah. For about five years now. But get this. Katelyn Breanne Donovan has been dead for the past seven years."

"What? But that doesn't make any sense."

Tripp rifled through a few small slips of paper that he had retrieved from his back pocket. Some were newspaper clippings. Others were scraps of plain white paper that he'd been scribbling on. "Tell me about it. The paper said it was some kind of car accident. Go figure."

"What about this Beckman guy? Did you find anything out on him?"

"Nada. But there was a name mentioned on that tape we saw back at the apartment. A Mercer. Frank Mercer."

"Anything we should be interested in?" Zackery asked him.

"It seems that Thomas Donovan was this big shot data processor at this company called Verticom. He worked there for about fifteen years as one of their chief engineers until he was transferred out. Doesn't say where exactly, and he wasn't alone. Guy named Mercer, Franklin J. took the move with him. From the looks of things I'd say the two of them were pretty tight. I managed to dig up a last known address."

"Where is it?" Zackery said, posing his pen to write again.

"A town called Wilmington. It's in Colorado. And let's just hope this guy's home."

"What about you guys?" Zackery said as he wrote. "Where are we going to meet up?"

"There's a truck stop on the south end of town. Shouldn't be too hard to find considering the size of the town we're talking about. Anyway. You might want to let Morgan hold the map just in case."

Zackery stayed behind the wheel for the entire duration of the afternoon. As wound up as he was he didn't think he could stomach Morgan's foot on the gas pedal in place of his. He barely gave any thought to the posted speed limits as he guided the car down the highway toward the destination that Tripp had designated. On the way he filled Morgan in on Tripp's findings, specifically where they concerned both Thomas Donovan's and Katelyn's status among the not so recently deceased. She was as perplexed as he was.

"Does Katelyn know about this?" she asked him.

"No. As far as I know she's still in the dark about all of this. Until we had something a little more solid Tripp didn't think there was any reason to alarm her about the rumors of her demise. All things considered, I'm inclined to agree with him. For now at least."

He couldn't imagine what it would do to Katelyn after all she'd had to contend with in the past few days given the knowledge that she'd recently uncovered about herself if she also had to be burdened with the information that she was presumed dead. At first glance Katelyn appeared to be taking all of this with a grain of her typical stoicism but there were moments when Zackery was able to catch a quick glance past the hardnosed veneer that she maintained where he witnessed something quiet and poignant taking shape. It was probably best that it was stoked as little as possible.

They found the truck stop with no problem. Tripp had called in to his cell phone to guide them in through the home stretch although Morgan was having little to no trouble following the directions on the map she had. They reached the truck stop just before sunset and Zackery pulled up to the front of the diner just as Tripp was walking out to greet them. Zackery and Morgan got out of the car.

"My baby," Tripp said. "Glad to see you took good care of her."

Morgan stepped up on the sidewalk and Tripp embraced her in a bear hug. "Were you referring to me or the car?" she said to him.

"My car of course," he said, letting go of her. "But I'm glad to see you two in one piece."

"Speaking of which," Zackery interjected, "how'd you manage to make it this far without your ride?"

"The open road can be quite a welcoming place to the average hitchhiker. And it's not too shy around the seasoned car thief either. By the way, thanks for leaving me back there."

"Wasn't like it was something we planned," Morgan spoke up. "Despite the resulting peace and quiet that came of it."

Just then Katelyn came walking out of the diner. She stopped at the sight of them all and stood there staring for a moment. "Katelyn," Zackery greeted her, his true elation in seeing her standing there after all this time masked behind the blandness in his voice. Katelyn responded with a simple lifting of her chin in his direction.

"Well," Tripp said, breaking up the awkward silence. "Now that the gang's all together again what say we get this show back on the road? It's getting late and we'd better not keep Mr. Mercer waiting."

The orange sun began to sink low over the thick tree line that surrounded the road that Tripp navigated his car along. This Franklin Mercer looked as if he enjoyed his privacy almost as much as Mr. Beckman had come off as doing so; only instead of acre upon acre of unkempt farmland Mr. Mercer's home was entrenched upon by miles of forestry that didn't appear to have any end in sight. Tripp located the beginning portion of a driveway and followed it up the winding path along the small hill that lead up to a three story brown wooden home.

"You sure this is the place?" Zackery asked after Tripp stopped the car and the four of them stepped out. He looked all around the grounds that the home rested on for any sign of life and though he found plenty none of it resembled anything human.

"It better be," Tripp said. "Otherwise I'm fresh out of stops on this tour."

The quartet moved up to the front door and when they got there Zackery did the knocking. He didn't have to wait long for an answer. *"Who's there?"* a distant voice cried out from the other side of the door. Considering the last two addresses they'd visited that sound alone was a very good sign of some major progress.

"Uh..." Zackery struggled to find the appropriate response. "It's nobody you would know...sir. If you wouldn't mind we would just like a moment of your time to speak with you."

"What?" The voice was closer now. The locks were undone and the door swung open swiftly. A bit astounded by the quick motion of the door, the four of them were left standing there with a surprised air about them as they stared into the gently textured salt and pepper toned beard and mustache covered face of the man standing before them. He straightened the glasses on his face. "Who are you? What's the meaning behind..." His eyes fell on Katelyn and his expression paled over into something ghastly. He sucked in a deep breath and let it out. "Chaos?" he said as he exhaled.

"Who?" Tripp said, alternating a glance between Katelyn, who was standing behind him, and the man in front of them.

Now the man's eyes were bouncing back and forth between each one of them. "Who...who are you people!?!" he said frantically. "Who sent you!?!"

"Nobody sent us," Morgan said. "We..."

"Well then who are you?" he cut her off, nearly yelling at them now. "What are you doing here?"

Katelyn stepped up to the front of the pack. "You knew my father. Thomas Donavan."

"Right. Right. Thomas. Right." His voice was jittery now and his nerves were twitchy to the point that it seemed he might break out into a running stride at any moment just to get away from them.

"Then you know me too. I'm Katelyn. Katelyn Bree. I'm his daughter."

Her words widened his eyes to their absolute limit. He was in a complete state of bewilderment. "Oh my God," he breathed out softly.

"They're here because of me," Katelyn told him.

"Yes. Yes. Of course." The once pinkish hue of his face was now a pasty shade of fear mixed with mind numbing confusion. He stepped back inside of his house and pushed the door open wider. "Hurry. Come inside. Quick! You have to hurry." His eyes were no longer on them now. Instead they scanned the horizon all around for any sign of...anything. Once they all complied he checked the area out in front of the house once more before slamming the door closed and bolting it up tight.

"Mr. Mercer, I presume," Zackery said as he stepped into the open area of the front room and turned around to face their skittish host. Tripp took a seat on one of the couches in the room and Morgan sat down on the one facing him. Katelyn, along with Zackery, had remained standing. The man had stepped over to the window next to the door and slid aside the thick fabric of the curtain to get another peek outside. "You are Franklin Mercer, right?"

He turned to face them again looking almost surprised to find them still there. He put his eyes on Zack. "Of course," he growled angrily, trying to keep his voice low as he spoke.

As pleased as Zackery had been to find this man here in the flesh he had to admit that he didn't care for his attitude very much. He tried to take into account that this man must not have been accustomed to receiving many visitors all the way out here if in fact he ever entertained any at all, but this guy was seriously pushing his way past the line of grossly intolerable. "Fine. Great. Well would you mind terribly if we skipped all the pleasantries and just got right to you telling us how exactly it is that you know Katelyn."

"Katelyn?" Mr. Mercer cracked a slight grin. "Katelyn? Right. Katelyn." He walked past where she had been standing by the fireplace on his way to a cupboard that he opened and alleviated of a large crystal container of brandy and a small glass.

"You are aware..." Zackery continued but was immediately silenced by Mr. Mercer's overlapping voice.

"Look! Now I don't know what you're doing here or how you found me but what I do know is that Katelyn

Donavan is dead. And unless you people are harboring some deep admiration to join both her and her father in the hereafter then you'll forget what it is that you think that you know and head back to wherever it is that you came from."

Watching the man steady his hand enough to place the glass down on a nearby table and pour him a drink, Tripp shared a puzzled look with Morgan who was sitting on the couch across from him before saying, "Well if that's true then do you mind explaining to us the true identity of our most annoying traveling companion here. Because I have to tell you I, for one, am a little confused."

"I don't need him to tell me what I already know," Katelyn said with a look on her face that conveyed her outright aggravation at where the nature of this discussion was headed to. After coming all this way and being forced to dodge the many treacherous obstacles that she'd encountered between this point and the start of this journey she was in no mood to stand here and debate her own mortality with a virtual stranger.

Mr. Mercer downed the double shot in one quick gulp and poured himself another. "Is that so?" he said, lifting his glass and peeling away a finger to point at her. "Do you want me to tell you who you are? You're a testament to a foolish old man's pride. You're a grieving father's stubborn refusal to...to just let go," he said in a much softer voice as he looked Katelyn in her eyes. "And as long as you're here you're a death sentence to anyone near you." He swallowed the liquor in his glass. "Why did you come here?"

"It's like this," Tripp said. "Our girl the late great Katelyn here's been suffering from one major case of amnesia. Seems she can't remember a single thing past the last four years and we've spent the past few days trying to backtrack through the minefield that she calls her life which eventually led us right to your doorstep. So feel free to plug in any missing pieces at your leisure."

Mr. Mercer listened to Tripp speak with a perplexed look on his face while alternating his eyes between him and Katelyn. Once Tripp was done and he was able to fully absorb the meaning behind the words coming out of his mouth Mr. Mercer found himself having the hardest time trying to conceal the grin that had began to grow on his face. "Is that so?" he said nearly in laughter as he moved back over to the small round glass table to his right and took up the bottle of brandy again.

He poured himself another shot, drank it down, and then poured up another; this time to the sound of a soft bout of his own laughter. He stepped backwards until he came to a rest in a recliner next to the fireplace. "Four years? Really?" His laughter continued much to all of their surprise. "And it's a bout of amnesia that we have to thank for all of this, now is it?"

Zackery let his eyes float around the room that was now filled with one man's quiet chuckling. "Uh, right. Excuse me, but I fail to see the humor in all of this. Now if you have anything even remotely interesting that you could tell us about Katelyn, Mr. Donovan, Mr. Beckman, or this Tobias McPhearson person then tell us." Franklin Mercer's laughter stopped cold. "If not could you please stop wasting our time."

"McPhearson?" Franklin Mercer rose from his seat again. "Did you say McPhearson?"

"Yeah. You know the guy? He's been gunning for Katelyn, in the literal sense, for almost the past week now."

Mr. Mercer walked back over to the table and poured himself another drink. "Oh he's been gunning for her, as you put it, for a hell of a lot longer than that. And he's not going to stop either. Not until she's his."

"Then I take it that you know who he is too?" Zackery said, breathing out a frustrated sigh.

"I don't get it," Morgan said. "What's all this about?"

"What's all this about? You want to know what this is all about?" Franklin said. "It's about Thomas Donavan. He was the best and brightest scientist that Verticom had on staff. Perhaps too substantial for his own good."

"Is that why he was transferred?" Tripp asked.

Franklin shot him a look. "Yes. We were both transferred over to a covert company to head up work on a Project Chaos."

"Wait a minute," Tripp said, interrupting him. He thought for a second. "Chaos? As in K...A...O...S...S."

"Yes," Mr. Mercer answered him. "They said the work we would be doing was cutting edge, state of the art technology, unlimited funding." He took a drink of his brandy. "Top secret research, they said. There were rumors that the project was being funded by a black ops government branch but no one ever took it seriously."

"What the hell was Project KAOSS?" Tripp asked.

"The majority of our work consisted of the construction of multipurpose micro data processing units. The system functions were all basic at first just like the animatronics they were being applied to."

"Hold on," Morgan said. "Animatronics?"

"They were rudimentary contraptions at best. Mobile multi-wheeled units. The occasional humanistic dummies. We made them go of course. Move back and forth. Walk and talk," Mr. Mercer said with a faint grin on his face that soon faded. "After a while the applications began to grow more...complex along with the subjects. Simply walking and talking wasn't enough anymore. Much more precise movements were required of them and the proper annunciation of their words were as important as their vocal production."

"So what, you guys were building robots for the government?" Morgan asked.

"None of us knew exactly what it was that we were working on but it damn sure wasn't some automated collection of wires and steel pipes. Each division of the project worked independently of each other. None of it really bothered Thomas at first. He went about his work diligently, no questions asked. And after Katelyn passed," he said, cutting his eyes over to her and taking another drink from his glass. "He went about his work hardly speaking a word at all. He buried himself in the project. So deep not even I could reach him anymore. And then... One day... The trial runs were over. That's when we received the prototype."

"Prototype of what?" Zackery asked.

Franklin finished off the contents of his glass. "KAOSS. I'd never seen anything like it before in my life. The alloy that the skeletal structure was composed of was practically indestructible. The muscle fibers and mockup circulatory and digestive systems. And the casing. Even then, as taken in as I was by the advancements...it was the shape that the shell had taken on that had alarmed me the most." He raised his eyes and turned them in Katelyn's direction. Folding her arms in front of her chest, she leaned over against the mantel above the fireplace and returned his look with a set of iced over, unmoved eyes.

Tripp looked over at Katelyn. "By shape, you don't mean..."

"Clearly Thomas had had a hand in its design. His grieving had obviously reached a level even beyond my perception. It wasn't until the new order of upgrades and applications began to come in that I was finally able to snap him out of his obsession."

"What are you talking about?" Zackery asked. "What... applications?"

Franklin walked back over to the table and refilled his glass. "The archetype was already on the cutting edge of technology that had yet to even be discovered, but with each passing workup the advances continued to pour in. One after the other. Each one more disturbing than the next. The level of artificial intelligence embedded in the CPU aside. Sonar graphics. Motion detectors. Infrared and electromagnetic radiation ocular modules. The project was becoming increasingly more militarized with each week that passed. We were near forty percent completion and the thing was already well beyond combat ready. Our test simulations could barely keep up with it. Thomas, along with a few others, had started to get suspicious. They wanted to know exactly what it was that we were working on. They were stonewalled, naturally. But Thomas refused to let that stop him. Despite my ever present protests." He took another drink. "Needless to say, Thomas would have none of it. Started taking the whole thing entirely too personally. He wouldn't let anything stop him in his endless pursuit to find out the truth; the endgame behind Project KAOSS."

"Well did he find out what it was?" Morgan asked him.

"I'm not sure, but whatever it was that he found sent him completely over the edge. He all but lost it after that. Got together with a few of the other scientists and cooked up this outlandish plot to try and steal back the unit. Actually wanted me to help him!" Franklin said gruffly. "Oh course I refused him. Unfortunately I wasn't able to convince him to forget about all of this ridiculousness. His campaign turned out to be more successful than initially perceived. With the help of the small assembly Thomas was able to hijack the truck carrying the unit away from the base for its first field test and have it misplaced along with a considerable amount of equipment pertaining to the project."

"I'm guessing the people at Project KAOSS didn't take too kindly to this turn of events," Tripp replied.

"Tobias McPhearson headed up the investigation and rounded up everyone involved in the incident for interrogation. It didn't require much prying in order to get them to admit to what it was they had done. But it was Thomas alone who new the location of the unit. He past away while in their custody and the hidden whereabouts of the unit passed with him. They questioned me about the incident and after determining that I had nothing to do with it they left me with the option of quietly resigning."

"What about Beckman?" Tripp asked.

"Who?" Mercer said with an expression of confusion on his face behind his glasses.

"Beckman," Tripp continued. "That guy had to have had *something* to do with all of this."

"I'm sorry but I'm afraid I have no idea who you're talking about," Franklin said. "I don't know any Beckman."

"There is no Beckman," Zackery spoke.

Morgan's eyes opened wider and she moved her body to the edge of her seat on the couch. "Right! Because Thomas Donovan was Beckman."

"Which means that the KAOSS unit is..." Tripp slowly rose from the couch while holding his eyes on Katelyn. The look on his face was a combination of fear and shock. "Katelyn? Are you trying to tell us that she's..." He lifted a finger and pointed it in Katelyn's direction. "That she's one of those animatronics, android, robotic things that you guys were working on?"

"But the amnesia," Morgan spoke up.

Franklin Mercer's face crumpled up into a frustrated mass. "Oh, there was never any amnesia! That's impossible. Wherever Thomas was keeping her stored she would have most likely remained in her dormant state while he monitored the vitals of her system with the equipment that he'd confiscated. Once Tobias took Thomas into custody there would have been no one there to keep an eye on the equipment. After that all it would have taken was an extended severed link between KAOSS and the monitoring support system for the unit's own auxiliary power to switch on."

"So then the reason she can't remember anything past the last four years is because..."

"There was no memory," Franklin said, cutting Morgan off. "The unit would have just been switched on."

"Right," Katelyn spoke up. "Because I'm just this mechanized automaton that you and your fellow pedigree pieced together out the spare parts dished out to you by the gentlemen kindly enough to see to it that you stayed busy."

"Katelyn..." Zackery said, sensing her uneasiness brought on by the words being spoken here.

"Don't," she responded, turning a glare in his direction. He was instantly silenced.

"She would have had nothing but the default settings of her programming to guide her," Franklin said, interjecting through the swell of tension that had began to fill the room. Katelyn gave him her eyes again. "Being abandoned out in the open with no specific set of orders issued to it, the unit would have been remanded to seeking out viable cover and maintaining a low profile until a proper retrieval could be successfully conducted."

"This is ridiculous," Katelyn said.

"The subject is withdrawn," Franklin continued. "More or less unresponsive to suggestion, any immediate need pertaining to its survival not withstanding." Tripp, Morgan, and Zack took turns alternating glances between the three of them. "Adaptation. Indoctrination into a societal mainstream to avoid suspicion." Franklin looked at her with an eerie sense of disdain in his gaze. "All combat systems active. Self preservation status initiated," he said firmly as he went about his tirade, taking special attention to keep his eyes in line with hers. "Defensive protocol activated. Aggressors are to be subdued as long as the probability of the outcome continues to result in the existing functionality of the subject. Any hostility acquired beyond that to be met by any level of lethality deemed necessary to ensure said survival. The implanted psychoanalytical personality programming adaptors and modifiers would have taken care of the rest. Does any of this ring any of the tens of thousands of bells that were surgically implanted in that complexly organized, strategically analyzed and compiled, mathematically defined, fiber optically coiled brain of yours?"

"Just stop it!" Katelyn replied.

Tripp looked back over at Morgan. "The power *was* out at the farm when we got there."

Katelyn unfolded her arms and reached out across the top of the fireplace mantel for a small gold container resting there. She thought back to the noise of the rumbling clouds that were hovering overhead that morning when she'd first woken up in the basement of that barn and the smell of the moist air that she had breathed in upon taking her first step outdoors. "You're all insane," she said, flipping open the lid and taking out a cigarette. Placing it between her lips, she removed a matchstick from a box next to the container and struck it to flame on the bricks above the fireplace.

No sooner than she'd taken her first drag Mr. Mercer had made his way over to her and snatched the smoke from between her fingers. "Will you cut that out," he said, smashing the cigarette out into an ashtray on the mantel. He tossed the butt into the fireplace. "God knows what you've been doing to your atmospheric analytical nodes."

Katelyn stared at him with an unrelenting fury in her eyes. "Whatever," she said, stepping around him and heading toward the other side of the room. When she got there she shoved open a door that was obstructing her path and continued on her way.

13

Zackery stepped off of the patio and continued on through the backyard toward the tree line just beyond. He walked through the woodland area under the dimming twilight using the continuous sound of small solid objects coming into contact with water to guide him on his way. Stepping out into a small clearing, he made his way toward the shoreline of a lake where he found Katelyn standing near the water tossing small stones out into the rolling waves. She turned her head and looked back at him for a moment, jostling around a fistful of rocks. Swiveling her head back around she tossed the next stone.

"You okay?" he asked her, moving up beside her.

"Not sure," Katelyn replied, tossing another rock. "Do you think there's any chance that he was telling the truth?"

"I don't know. I'd be lying if I said that there wasn't something freakishly off about you." Katelyn jerked her head around in his direction. "In a good way, mind you. More than a few that I'm completely crazy about, but if you're asking me, that explanation back there went a little too far off the deep end for me. I don't know. Maybe we should keep looking. There might still be some stone out there that we haven't turned over yet."

Katelyn put her eyes back on the water once more. "One that won't have a paramilitary unit under it looking to take me in?"

"Doubtful," Zack said with a bit of laughter in his voice. "So...is this your way of saying you believe him?"

Katelyn turned to look at him again. She jiggled the rocks that she held in her hand around and tossed one up in the air. After catching it she turned her attention to the wooded area on the other side of the lake. Katelyn drew back her arm and brought it forward swiftly, releasing the rock as she did.

The small object streaked through the air across the water. When it reached the shore it continued on into the woods smashing its way through the trunk of a small tree in its path as it moved. "No. But it would explain a thing or two, now wouldn't it?" Katelyn dropped the rest of the rocks she held and moved back away from the water.

"So would steroids. That's some pitching arm."

Katelyn leaned back against a tree and craned her neck to the side to get a view of the lake. Zackery walked over to her. "Do you have any idea what it's like to wake up day after day and stare into the mirror at a person that you don't even recognize?"

"Do you? Sleep, I mean?" Katelyn flashed him her eyes. "Because if you did I was just thinking that it might lend some credibility to the contrary." His eyes dropped down to the ground at her feet and came back up to hers with a coy smile. "If you were interested in such a thing."

"Of course I sleep," she said to him sternly.

"I was just saying."

"When I'm tired and there's time for it I sleep." Her irritableness was starting to show in her voice.

"No need to get pissed at me. I'm on your side."

Katelyn was silent for a moment as she looked around at the trees and shrubbery. "It's just that when I do...it's kind of the same as when I'm awake."

"I see," Zackery said with a slight tilt of his head.

"I mean I'm lying there. My eyes are closed but I'm still aware of everything. I can hear and...still see for some reason. Damn it!" she said through gritted teeth as she shut her eyelids tight and slammed an elbow into the tree at her back. Katelyn pushed off of the tree and walked out past Zackery.

"Alright," Zackery said, moving over to the tree she had just abandoned and turned to face her. "Say it's true. Worse case scenario it for me."

"I don't know." Katelyn tilted her head back and looked up at the night sky that could be seen past the leaf covered branches. "Inside of me. Inside my head. I've got all of these voices and each one of them right now can list dozens of ways for me to cut out of here and head to the nearest town." She dropped her eyes back down and turned to Zackery. "They're all different depending on the probability for success given the severity of various scenarios. All of them. Telling me what I should do. What I could do. None of them can tell me why."

"Does that mean you're in a hurry to get out of here? Because I was thinking that once we got back to Chicago and we put all of this craziness behind us that maybe you could see your way around to giving me another shot at dinner." Katelyn shut her eyes and stretched her lips out into a smile before letting her head drop down in front of her chest. "Don't worry. The public forum requirement is still intact."

"Have you even heard a single word that I've said?" Katelyn asked him, lifting her head and placing her eyes on his.

"I haven't heard your answer yet."

Katelyn turned her back to him. "I can't do this," she said, taking a step away from him.

"What do you want from me? You want me to take you by the hand and tell you don't worry about it, that that guy's full of shit? If I thought it'd make any difference I would. But you'd probably just break my fingers anyway so what's the difference?" All Zackery could do was stand there and take in the image of the long black strands of hair draped down along her back. He opened his mouth and sounds came out but he had no idea what sort of effect, if any at all, they were having on her.

Under the circumstances the fact that she was even suffering the mediocre oratory sounds emoting from him was something of a feat within itself. He had no idea what he was expected to offer up in the way of comfort or advice, or if that was even what she required of him at the moment. What he did know was that he was here for her and that he would continue to be as long as conditions would allow.

"And supposing this Mercer guy's on the level," Zack said to her. "What does that mean? Does that mean you can't eat?" Katelyn turned around and glared at him. "I know you can eat. I've seen you eat."

"You're unbelievable," Katelyn said to him.

"No. You are. And to top it all off you still haven't answered my question."

Katelyn took a step in his direction and fixed her mouth to speak to him but no sound made it past her lips. Her interest had been diverted toward the area to her right. Katelyn stared out into the darkness just beyond the trees, her expression lost in a trance-like state. "Look," she said, giving him her eyes again. "The last thing I want you to do is to walk away from all of this thinking that I didn't appreciate all that you've done for me. It took a lot to do what you did and I doubt that I would have made it this far if not for you."

Zackery continued to look back and forth between Katelyn and the darkness that she had been staring into. "What? I don't understand. What are you talking about?"

"But I have to go the rest of the way alone."

"The rest of the way?"

A strong breeze began to kick up the foliage that lay scattered about the ground and shook the branches of the trees over their heads at a steadily increasing rate.

Soon the tree branches everywhere began to tremble violently under the weight of the gust that was blowing. A blinding white light that was bright enough to force Zackery's left arm up in the air to shield his face pierced the thick of the forest and scoured the oncoming night with a most unnerving illumination.

Zackery jerked his head back around. "We have to..." Katelyn pulled him forward and into her lips, silencing him immediately.

"I really hope that you can find a way to understand," Katelyn said after pulling back away from him.

"Understand wha..."

All it had taken was one right hook from her to render him unconscious. Katelyn caught his body before it dropped to the ground and gently lowered him down, leaning him back against the tree behind him. Katelyn placed another kiss to the corner of his mouth and stroked her fingers down the side of his face. Afterwards she stood up and moved through the thicket of trees toward the light in the distance.

"For heaven's sake, get away from the windows!" Franklin cried out

Tripp had been peering through the curtains at the sight of the helicopters coming in over the horizon as well as the numerous men repelling down from them. "Anybody care to chime in with any suggestions now's the time," he said as he stepped back from the window toward the center of the front room.

"Zack and Katelyn are still out there," Morgan replied.

"There's nothing we can do for them now. But if we hurry there's a shelter in the basement. It should be able to withstand any offensive that they're prepared to mount against it."

"Well are there any weapons down there?" Tripp asked. "Because I'm not just going to leave them out there and hope for the best."

Katelyn walked around the side of the house to the front of the home to the sight of several downed helicopters and the few that still remained airborne. Everywhere across the front of the lawn were armed men preparing for an assault on the small villa that currently housed Tripp Manning, Morgan Paleto, and Franklin Mercer. When Katelyn appeared every sight of every weapon present as well as the eyes training them turned on her. She allowed none of it to so much as slow the steady pace at which she walked. Her approach remained constant as she continued to move toward the center of the gathering.

"Hold your fire," she heard someone call out from the crowd. She recognized the vocal pattern in mere seconds. Moments later she saw the body that it belonged to making its way out of the background and moving towards her. "Nobody move a muscle."

The two of them continued to walk until they stood face to face with one another. "One condition," Katelyn said. Tobias remained silent. "I want to know the truth."

His sinister eyes bore into hers and the face that remained a block of stone before her finally fixed the pair of lips that were adorned on its visage to say, "As you wish." His voice was as devoid of empathy as the expression that he wore.

Turing his body to the side, Tobias allowed her to pass and watched as she was promptly escorted aboard one of the helicopters present on the ground. As pleased as he was with the ultimate capture of his long sought after quarry he couldn't help but to feel the effects of this anticlimactic conclusion of this enduring pursuit. Given the inherent vitality of this particular game, he was starting to feel especially cheated. Nevertheless, she was in his custody and that's where she would remain until he got her back to headquarters.

Tobias boarded the helicopter and sandwiched Katelyn in between himself and another soldier. When the helicopter lifted off she was able to get one last glimpse of the home that her former fellow Wicker Basket employees were currently hold up in. The soldiers left the structure unmolested as they boarded their vehicles with their prize, giving no more thought to the rest of the civilians still occupying the grounds.

She watched the front of the helicopter pass over the woodland area in back of the home where she had left Zackery. The thought of the very definite possibility that she may very well never see him again crept into her mind and played havoc with the entirety of her sensibilities as she actually pondered over the ramifications of such a thing. No doubt his initial response would be one of a depressant, ire stirring nature, the effects of which would surly fade with time.

But what would *her* reaction be? She had no idea where Tobias was ushering her off to or what exactly would happen to her when she got there. She did, however, know that upon her arrival the chances of her returning to the life that she had once inhabited were almost nonexistent at best.

Whether or not Franklin Mercer was telling the truth would soon prove irrelevant. Whatever she was set to discover while in the company of Tobias McPhearson was sure to be something that would steer her life on a course that would force her to come to terms with the illusion that she had previously been living. There would be no more Wicker Basket. No more Jordan Carthright. No Morgan. No Tripp. No Zackery. And quite possibly no more Katelyn Bree. How did she feel about that? What was someone supposed to feel about something like this? A normal someone? Katelyn was still mulling over all the factors of this scenario as she watched the scenery set against the dark purple sky pass by the front window of the helicopter cockpit.

Tripp tossed a cold beer fresh from the refrigerator over to Zackery who was seated in the recliner next to the fireplace in the front room of Mr. Franklin Mercer's home. Upon catching it, Zackery immediately placed the bottle against the side of his face. "How's the head? Looks like she clocked you pretty good."

"I'm fine," Zackery uttered, the fury that swelled inside of him hardly allowing any unclenching of his jaws. "What I haven't heard is what we're doing about getting Katelyn back."

"What do you mean, what are we doing?" Tripp said. "You heard the guy, man. There is no Katelyn. Katelyn Bree is dead."

Zackery pulled the freezing wet bottle away from his head and twisted off the cap. "Oh, screw you, Tripp!" He drank deep from the open glass container.

"Oh yeah?" Tripp said to him as he moved away from the chair and paced out into the center of the room near the glass coffee table. "What do you want us to do, Zack? Huh? It was one thing altogether just trying to keep away from these guys. Alright? Now that they've got her...what do you really expect us to do about it?" Zackery stood up from the chair and slammed his bottle down on the table next to it before moving toward Tripp. "Come on, man. The game's over," he said, attempting to reason with the unbridled anger that he was reading in his friend's face. "It's time to face facts. We were in over our heads even before this whole thing began. And now it's high time we got back to our normal lives...while they're still there waiting for us to get back to them."

Zackery took in a deep breath and let it out slowly, trying to calm himself. "I'm not going anywhere without Katelyn. Do you understand me?" Tripp turned and walked away from him throwing his hands up in the air beside him as he did. "There is no life to go back to without her."

"Tripp's right, Zack," Morgan said from the couch where she was sitting. "They've got her. What exactly do you expect us to do?"

Zackery spun around and looked behind him. His eyes quickly zoomed in on the area in front of the fireplace where Franklin Mercer was standing nursing the drink that he had resting on top of the mantel. "You," Zackery said, making sure that he knew who he was referring to.

"Me? What do you want from me?" Franklin took a drink from his glass.

"Where would they take her?"

He thought for a few seconds. "Most likely they'd head directly back to headquarters, but I fail to see how that's of any relevance here."

"And where's headquarter?"

"Zack, you've got to be kidding me," Tripp called out to the ceiling.

"Where?"

"It's in Nevada," Franklin said. "What difference does it make?"

"I'll tell you why," Zackery said. "Because you're about to finally make good on a favor to an old friend."

14

The convoy of helicopters were flying low as they glided though the air above the desert floor. The fleet had managed to come up heavy a few more aircraft as they traveled along their route, almost quadrupling the size of the initial fleet that had picked up Katelyn. She stared ahead out of the window from her seat near the rear of the helicopter and watched patiently and silently as the desert cliffs and ridges rolled by them. Occasionally she glanced over in Tobias' direction but eventually found that taking more than one look was a complete waste of time. Not a single thing about his demeanor or mien had changed since the first instance that she had turned her eyes to inspect him.

Katelyn looked out at the night cloaked area of land in front of the helicopter and saw the ground beneath them suddenly come to an end, dropping off to reveal a very deep valley just beyond the cliff. Embedded within the floor of the gorge was a settlement of small buildings lit up against the night that nearly spanned the length of a mile from its western most tip to the east.

The pilot put the helicopter down in one of the landing fields near the center of the base and Tobias stood from his seat as he prepared to take his leave of the vehicle. The lamps that lit up the entire area faded out the stars that had previously lit up the pitch black night sky and painted the concrete platform as well as all of the nearby buildings a ghostly shade of pale white.

Katelyn stood up and exited after him, stepping off of the helicopter to the sight of a multitude of armed men rushing out to greet them. She stopped dead in her tracks and listened to the sound of their scuffling boots and cocking firearms compete with the dull roar of the helicopter engine behind her. After Tobias quelled their tension he turned back to face Katelyn.

"Welcome home, Kaoss. I believe that you'll find that you're eagerly awaited."

She resumed walking in his direction. "My name is Katelyn."

"I'm sorry. As I recall, hearing the truth was a condition specifically laid out by you."

Tobias turned back around and began walking. Katelyn started after him and noticed that the two of them weren't alone in their march. There was an armed escort that accompanied them with troops remaining both in front of Tobias and behind her.

She kept in stride with the Colonel, staying one step behind him just over his left shoulder. "My father endowed me with that moniker. Had he wanted me to answer to anything else then it's presumable that he would have made it so."

"Father?" Tobias said, taking a quick look back over his shoulder. "I gather that you're referring to the individual who crafted your outermost casing; programmed your default oratory audio output; wrote the base programming for your central data processing network? Your creator? Mr. Thomas Donavan? Yes. I suppose he bestowed upon you a great many favors, including his flare for nostalgia."

Katelyn swiveled her head from left to right as they walked and let her eyes scan over everything in sight. Everywhere she looked she saw and heard the faint noise of helicopters touching down on landing pads along with numerous land roving vehicles that were pulling into fuel dumps and motor pools; all emptying of their payload of troops who were quickly being gathered into formation and marched off toward parts unknown.

She couldn't see a building present that stretched over more than three stories high, leading Katelyn to believe that the surface of this base of operations did nothing to compliment the expanse that rested just beneath her feet.

She followed Tobias into a building through a set of automatic sliding glass doors. She had barely made it past the threshold before the soldiers in front of Tobias stopped moving and did an about face. Tobias mimicked their motion and Katelyn's feet came to a halt on the linoleum covered floor. Two men dressed in lab coats wheeled out a metallic seating contraption and positioned the shiny silver apparatus behind her. "What's this?" Katelyn asked, turning her attention back to Tobias.

"If you don't mind," he said, extending his arm, his hand palm up, out to her. "We'll be accommodating your mobility for the duration of this expedition."

"No thank you. I should be able to manage on my own."

The guns in front of her raised and took aim. "I'm afraid I'm going to have to insist," Tobias said to her. "As adept as you are in the trade of tactful evasiveness, I remain overly confident in the fact that the forces present here, both near and far, possess the capabilities to forcefully subdue you if need be. But taking into account the passivity with which you turned yourself over, I'd be willing to forego such action in lieu of your further cooperation. The ball's in your court, Kaoss."

If it was a fight she was looking for then she was certainly in the right place, but if that was all she'd wanted she could have gotten that back at Franklin Mercer's place. No. She wanted answers. She wanted at least one something, any twisted mixed up something in the abnormality that was her world to make sense, and though she felt that Tobias' faith in the success of the forces mounted against her was sorely misplaced, this fortress undoubtedly held what it was that she sought the most.

Katelyn took a step back and slowly lowered herself down into the seat. She placed her feet one at a time on top of the footrests and gently eased her back against the seatback. Touching her elbows on top of the armrests, Katelyn interlocked her fingers over her abdomen and leaned back in the seat, her eyes glued to Tobias.

One of the lab coats walked around from behind her and headed over to Tobias. He pulled a small handheld console out of his pocket and handed the device over to the Colonel. Tobias held the flat gray rectangle up beside his head. Katelyn's eyelids lowered and her brow crinkled at the smirk that appeared on his face. He pressed something with his thumb and Katelyn's body stiffened. Her outermost extremities twitched rapidly as a high voltage of electricity passed through her.

When Tobias lifted his thumb away from the console every artificial muscle fiber in her body that had been jolted into action suddenly fell limp and Katelyn slouched down in the seat. Lifting her chin up from her chest, she raised her scowling eyes to Tobias again and tried to find her footing as she prepared to rise from the seat. He hit the button again and sent another current of energy through her that drained the remainder of the fight right out of her.

He couldn't have been more disappointed. This girl. This...thing could have easily disarmed the cadre that lorded over her and either sought out whatever it was that she wanted from this place or taken her leave of it. Whichever was her choosing. If she lived up to even half of what was regarded to be true about her then her abilities balanced against the numerous troops and weaponry present on this base, however overwhelming, still allowed for a chance of success on her part, however large or small that may have been.

But no.

Despite the multitude of capabilities that she had been bequeathed she'd floundered and went belly up without so much as a harsh word in her defense. Watching the soldiers take up her flaccid limbs and place her upright in the seat, he had half a mind to hit her with another jolt just for good measure. It was pathetic. A waste of a lot of precious money, time, and energy, had anyone bothered to ask him.

The soldiers stepped away from her and Tobias put his thumb back to work on the remote he held. He didn't send more voltage through her as he so desired. Instead, the controls that he worked now closed a clamp around each one of her wrists and both of her ankles. The material for the restraints sprang forth out of each armrest and leg stand and bound her to the seat.

Tobias walked over to her. He grabbed her chin up with his thumb and forefinger and turned her head from right to left, examining her face. "You had quite the day yesterday," he said to her. "Coming out of that window the way you did." He let go of her chin and lifted up the sleeve covering her left forearm. "The tact van. That chopper." He rubbed his hand up her arm and stroked his thumb back and forth across some of the healing scars he found. "Yes. That was quite some show. And I see that the visible damage to your outer shell is already well into remission." He lowered his face down closer to the side of her head. "You see, it's your circulatory system and all of that junk that you must've been stuffing your face with on the outside. That fluid coursing its way throughout your entire body," he said right next to her ear, "is jammed packed with billions and billions of these itty bitty teeny little nanobot techno droids that run the entire gamut of this physique of yours repairing all the wear and tear that comes with the mileage that you've seen fit to put on yourself. They simply take what chemicals they need from the food you eat and put them to work where they're needed." Tobias stood back upright and turned his back to her. "That's the short version anyhow. Just think of yourself as similar to one of those self cleaning toaster ovens," he said, walking away from her. "Only a hell of a lot more expensive."

Katelyn lifted her weary eyelids and stared at the back of his pressed uniform. She saw him raise the hand he held the small console in up over his left shoulder. His thumb hit another button and Katelyn felt a slight jerk as the chair she was sitting in suddenly began to roll across the floor after the Colonel. He continued on down the corridor until he reached a large cargo elevator at the end of the hall.

The soldiers that moved across the linoleum path in front of him hit the button to call the car and then stood along either side of the entrance portal with a stature that could rival any stone gargoyle positioned along the outer architecture of a cathedral. Once the elevator doors opened Tobias paid them no more attention as he boarded, still standing with his back to Katelyn.

The chair she was bound to soon boarded and came to a stop in the car on his right flank. He didn't so much as bother to even look down at her. After three soldiers boarded the elevator behind her the doors shut tight and they began their descent.

When the doors opened up in front of her Tobias was the first one off of the elevator and, courtesy of the remote in his hand, Katelyn was carted off directly after him. As they moved down the corridor Katelyn saw the military presence that filled the upper level of the structure they were in replaced by one that appeared to be of a more medically oriented criterion.

Black tactical uniforms were replaced by blue and green scrubs. Semiautomatic machine guns were now stethoscopes and clipboards. With every turn that Tobias McPhearson guided her around, the facilities seemed to take on more of a hospital's feel than that of a military stronghold.

"Right now we're moving into Diagnostics," Tobias spoke. Though he failed to make any kind of eye contact, Katelyn could only assume that he was speaking to her. Her body was numb all over. She squirmed around in the seat a bit in a vain attempt to free herself but found it all too exhaustive and futile, thus she ceased her motion. "I'm not sure whether or not you can recognize anything around you but I can assure you that you'll have ample time to catch up with the technicians and staff assigned here. I'm sure they can't wait to get you up on the rack and check out all your hoses and gaskets."

They moved down a windowless corridor to the sound of the rubber soles of boots colliding with polished tile. The chair that Katelyn was in made almost no sound as it trailed behind Tobias. "Donovan," she breathed out weakly.

"What was that?" Tobias said.

Katelyn straightened her body up in the chair. "Thomas Donovan. What happened to him?"

A soft chuckle escaped Tobias' lips. "Still obsessing over old ghosts, are we? Alright then. I'll indulge you in a saunter down memory lane. Thomas Donavan was as brilliant as he was passionate. His contributions in the field of technological research and development were quickly becoming unrivaled. It was practically criminal what they bought out his contract with Verticom for. Everyone thought he'd make such a wonderful addition here. And they were right, for all intents and purposes. As it turns out he was a bit too intellectually advanced for his own good."

"The KAOSS project," Katelyn whispered. "Tried to stop you."

Tobias spun his head back and looked at her for the duration of a few steps. "You've been apprised of quite a bit of ancient history. I see that a good aged cognac still does the trick when it comes to loosening Mr. Mercer's lips. Yes. It's true. Donovan went poking around well above his security clearance. What a mess that all turned out to be. If you're asking me whether or not his untimely passing was a purposeful repercussion then the answer is no. Or so my clearance has lead me to believe."

"KAOSS," Katelyn said. "Final protocol."

The rate at which Tobias walked slowed until he stopped altogether. Katelyn's chair came to a synchronized stop with the boots he wore. He spun around to face her and a sinister grin took over his visage as he eyed her suspiciously. "So that's what this is about. Like creator, like creature, is it?" Katelyn's eyes returned the stern look that he gave her and remained unrelenting in their hold on him just as his had done with her. "Alright then. I'll show you."

Her neck was still a bit stiff from the jolts of corporal punishment that Tobias had administered to her earlier. As she craned her neck from side to side to get a look at the scenery that passed by on either side of her she could hardly feel the effects anymore. Her chair continued to wheel along behind the Colonel and she struggled against the restraints only to find that she was unable to free herself from the hold that they had on her.

Wherever this tour ended she was in for the duration of the ride. As time slowly ticked by her thoughts of whether or not that was entirely a bad thing lingered in ambivalence. In the end, where else did she belong if not here? She certainly hadn't been designed for the sole purpose of aiding the pedestrians who happened to wander in to Jordan Carthright's Wicker Basket from off of the street.

Thomas Donovan had stolen her away from this place once upon a time. What exactly it was that he had planned on doing with her after the fact, whether it be carting her off to some inaccessible region of the world where she was to masquerade as the daughter he'd once lost while the two of them attempted to carve out something resembling a normal life, or if he merely meant to keep her stored away for safe keeping, was as of now inconsequential. He was gone and she was back here, trapped beneath the ground in the corridors that he had once been so desperate to liberate her from. And now Katelyn was going to find out why.

Tobias halted her chair behind him and stepped over to an electronic pad on the wall beside a pair of large gray metal doors with the letters **K A O S S** painted across them in large print. Tobias had brought them down seven more stories below the surface in order to reach this level. He pulled a small plastic card out of one of the cargo pockets in the pants he wore and slid it down through the slot on the security panel.

Katelyn watched the **O** imprinted on the door split down the center as the two halves parted. Tobias remained where he stood as he pressed the button on the console he held, setting the chair Katelyn was confined to into motion once more, sending her inside the room.

Katelyn's eyes slowly moved from one side of the large bay room to the other. Everywhere her eyes fell they found people. There were people everywhere. Some were up and moving. Others were seated behind terminals. Some spoke into wireless headsets. Others conversed with their fellow lab coat adorned colleagues. The floor of this room swarmed with human traffic and the walls and every aisle in between were alive with technology.

Katelyn could hear them all; every whirl and bleep of the machines present, every keystroke being entered, every vocalized conversation being carried on between man and man as well as man and machine. The average onlooker might have looked on this scene and been under the impression that this army of lab coats were preparing to send something designed by the National Aeronautics and Space Administration up into the far reaches of space but Katelyn could see that their intentions were nowhere near that docile.

The entire wall at the far end of the room across from her was covered in monitors that varied in size from large to enormous. All of them were covered with satellite images of the planet depicting various ranges of magnifications in an excessive arrangement of displays. Weather patterns were being tracked. Magnetic fields around the equator and the north and south poles were on display. Geothermal scans. Current positions and predicted shifting patterns of the major fault lines covering the surface of the entire planet.

Above the entire exhibit, stretching from one end of the wall to the other were the letters again. **K. A. O. S. S.** With her head tilted over towards her right shoulder Katelyn let her eyelids fall shut until a shroud of darkness concealed her vision. She'd seen enough.

The sound of Tobias' footsteps as he closed in behind her was somehow able to distinguish themselves from the parade of noises that bombarded her ears right then. "I imagine you can feel it now, can't you? Assuming that you couldn't before. Can you? Buried right there amidst that nest of fiber optic wiring and processor chips. That's it, little lady. That's you." He placed both of his hands down on her shoulders. "Guess they figured that your applications in the arena of espionage along with your abilities in the field as an infantry unit continued to leave something to be desired on the battlefield of tomorrow. Perhaps being the sole proprietors of a state of the art delivery system for a fully armored combat operative with the added feature of being fortified with the capability of dispatching thousands, tens of thousands, maybe even millions of enemy combatants at a time would be enough to place the purveyors of such a force in favor with the Gods of modern day warfare for quite some time. Wouldn't you agree?"

Tobias lifted his right index finger and stroked it across her cheek. Katelyn jerked her head away. "Don't touch me," she breathed.

He laughed a quiet little laugh. "Oh come now, Kaoss. As I recall, we used to get along much better than this." He lifted his hand from her shoulder and stroked his fingers through her hair just above her right ear. All Katelyn could do was lean her head to the side. "Do you have any idea the tedium that has engulfed this entire facility ever since your departure? I mean, this particular room alone. The endless surveillance of enemy correspondence, although it was highly unlikely that Donovan would have made an attempt to cash in on you on the black market, but the higher ups thought it naive not to make sure. The constant monitoring of every seism and minor tremor that this bright blue rock saw fit to shake with." Tobias' hand dropped back down to her shoulder. "The Kinetic Auxiliary of the Orbiting Seismic System. Stolen right out from under us. Can you imagine that? All this time, floating around up there in the great black beyond was this multibillion dollar piece of junk satellite with the capability of generating seismic waves powerful enough to topple cities and flood entire coastlines and the trigger for the damn thing has been shacked up in some rat infested hovel somewhere in the downtown area of Chicago, Illinois for God knows how long." Another bout of low baritone laughter slipped from his lips. "Yes. It was quite the vexation." Tobias moved around to her side and knelt down, leveling his face with the side of hers. "But all of that's over. You're home now."

15

"Do either of you mind if I take this opportunity to explain to you once more just how monumentally bad this idea, in all actuality, truly is?" Tripp said as he walked across the sand and gravel underneath the early morning sun.

Zackery walked along side of him on his right. "I mind," he said to him.

"I second it," Morgan spoke up from the area on Tripp's left.

The trio shuffled their feet across the desert floor as they cautiously approached the edge of the cliff in front of them. Slowly, each one of them came to a stop as the expanse of the valley that lie below came into view along with the miniature city that dwelled within it.

"Right," Tripp said. "What was I thinking? Everything I said about turning around and heading back to Chicago before we wind up doing something stupid and getting ourselves killed...Forget it. This is as good as cake."

The three of them turned and headed back to the jeep that Morgan had parked some thirty yards back from the cliff's edge. Once they were there she reclaimed her position behind the steering wheel and started the vehicle up once more. The jeep was a rental. They secured it no sooner than they had gotten off of the redeye that had brought them out here a few hours ago.

The facility that provided them with their current mode of transport came highly recommended by Mr. Franklin Mercer. Along with that helpful bit of travel aid and footing the bill for their flight out, Franklin Mercer, thanks to Zackery's aggressive persuasiveness, was going to continue to prove invaluable to this excursion.

Morgan navigated the jeep over the off-road terrain as she wound her way down through the cliffs toward the valley that housed the black ops military base. Among other things most beneficial, Mr. Mercer had sent them on this mission armed with his knowledge of the most accessible route that would bring them nearest to the most viable entry point on the base while at the same time allowing them to avoid as much activity as possible. Activity that was being conducted by the perimeter guards.

She applied the brakes and the tires slid to a stop on a narrow gravel path at the bottom of a hill between two small walls of dirt. "Tell me again that you guys are ready for this," Morgan said to them.

Tripp inserted a small plastic devise into his left ear canal and slung a knapsack over his shoulder. "For the last time the answer is that we are one hundred percent absolutely positively and without a solitary doubt not in any single way imaginable ready for anything that is about to transpire here today. So without further ado," he said, standing and hopping with both feet over the side of the jeep. When he landed squarely on the dusty ground he turned back to face them and said, "What are we waiting for?"

Zackery reached behind him and grabbed up the rolled up maps and schematics that were on the floorboard behind Morgan's seat. He placed them in her lap before picking up the satchel at his feet and opening up his door. "Wish us luck," he said as he climbed out of the seat.

"We're going to need more than luck," Tripp commented.

"Just...just come back, okay? Both of you."

"Don't worry about us," Zackery said. "You just make sure you're here to pick us up. All three of us."

Morgan put the jeep in reverse and pulled away from them, leaving Zackery and Tripp standing there alone. "Come on," Tripp said to him. "Let's get this over with. Not that I'm worried that it's going to last for very long."

The two of them struck out for the edge of the dirt wall. When they got there Zackery put his chest to the dirt and carefully peeked around the corner. There was nothing there. Nothing but barren earth and a perimeter fence some two hundred yards out. Just beyond that Zackery could see a tower and though he couldn't make out any human silhouettes through the glass structures near the top he knew that there was no question about whether or not it was manned.

They would have to be quick about their business. Slipping unnoticed passed the watchful eyes beyond the perimeter fence might have been a challenge in itself, but a roving patrol that was sure to make its way passed this portion of the valley would be sure to shorten this game up considerably before it had a chance to truly get underway.

"Let's go," he said softly over his shoulder, and with that he shuffled his feet out across the sand and pebbles as he struck out across the field toward a small creek bed. Tripp stayed right on his heels and soon the both of them were hopping down the short slope toward the flowing stream that awaited. "There," Zack said, jutting out his arm and pointing his finger.

They hurried over to the mouth of a large gaping metal pipe that was sticking out of the wall of the creek bed and leaking a flow of water out into the stream below it. Zackery unslung his knapsack and handed it over to Tripp. He gripped his fingers around the bottom lip of the pipe and hoisted himself up into the shaft as the waterfall poured over him. Once he was inside Tripp tossed him both bags and then climbed in himself.

Zackery passed him his pack and they both unzipped them in unison. There was enough room for them to stand upright but they still had to stoop over some to keep from hitting their head against the top of the pipe. After digging around inside of the packs for a few moments Zackery and Tripp located two small devises that they switched on and clipped onto the collar of their shirts.

"Morgan?" Zackery said as he placed a small plastic insert into his ear canal. "Morgan, can you hear me?"

"You're coming in loud and clear," Morgan said into the handheld radio that she had raised up to the side of her face. "How's Tripp doing?"

"As to be expected," Tripp radioed in.

A phone call had been placed the night before to Chicago and Mr. Jordan Carthright had picked up on the other end. Morgan had been left with the responsibility of sitting down and trying to find a way to bring the bookstore proprietor up to speed on what it was that they had found out about the young amnesiac that he had taken into his care so many years ago. It was a hard sell to say the least.

Morgan had to sit through several lingering moments of silence at a time and even after she'd hung up with him Morgan couldn't really say that he fully believed any part of the yarn she had spun for him. Thankfully before he'd hung up with her to ponder over the insanity that she had just spieled Morgan had convinced him to overnight them a small cache of some of the devises that he constantly tinkered with up in his apartment. Devises that the three of them would find invaluable if they hoped to even stand a chance at retrieving Katelyn from the people that were currently holding her.

"Okay," Zackery said to Morgan through the transmitter attached to his shirt. "We're in your hands now. So try and remember your right from your left."

"Got it," she said, staring down at the blueprints in front of her. "Now keep on ahead until you meet your first intersection."

"Status report, gentlemen, and do try and be quick about it." General Selinski said as he shuffled around some papers on his desk. "I've got a meeting with the Board of Directors and I'm already late."

Tobias started to open his mouth to address the General when the lab coat standing next to him blurted out ever so cheerfully, "We've just moved her up to medical, sir, but as far as we can tell there's been no irreparable damage imposed on the unit. And according to the Colonel here she had in fact been put through quite the endurance run." The bubbly air of humor in this man's voice was unmistakable. "Once we get her down to Diagnostic we should be able to get a more accurate reading of her internal systems."

"Sir, once they do have the unit in Diagnostic it is my recommendation that they go ahead and proceed with the memory wipe."

"What?" the lab coat uttered as he turned to look at Tobias with a frightened look on his face.

"Is that going to be a problem for you, Dr. Caleb?" Selinski said, lifting his eyes and looking up at him.

"In more ways than one," he said, alternating his glances between Tobias and the seated gentleman in front of him. "Sir, aside from the extremely important fact that this unit has indeed been active in the field for an indeterminate amount of time, it's been battle tested to an extent that we have yet to even begin to explore. The data for all of which is still currently stored in her memory cells. A complete wipe now would cost us priceless information."

"There's that," Tobias said. "Or we wipe her clean, along with the rest of the time that we've already wasted, and pick this project up from exactly where we left off."

"As much as I can understand and appreciate your stratagem, Colonel," Selinski said, "I don't see why we should have to walk away from this debacle with nothing at all to show for it. You've got twenty four hours, Doctor. Make them count. The both of you are dismissed." The two men turned and started their departure from his office. "Colonel," the General called after his subordinate before he made it across the threshold of his office doorway. Tobias craned his neck back in his direction. "I just realized that I never formerly commended you on your successful recapturing of the KAOSS unit. Congratulation."

Tobias stood in silence for a short duration just staring back at his superior officer. "Thank you, sir," he said in a flat and stale tone that displayed no elation at all to the honor being laid at his feet. "Will that be all?"

"You're dismissed, Colonel."

Tobias stepped through the doorway and out into the hallway just beyond it. What sort of pride could possibly be gained by receiving any accolades from this man? Tobias wondered as he continued on his way. Sitting there behind his desk all day pushing pencils and conferencing with various financial entities while at the same time continuing to retain the authority to make tactical decisions where he was concerned. He would let it go for now. He had much more important things to worry about at this juncture than politics and bureaucratic red tape.

Tripp crawled through the air vent on his hands and knees. There was a grate embedded in the floor of the vent just ahead that was of particular interest to him. He tried to remain as quiet as possible as he moved through the tunnel toward his destination while being guided by Morgan from her position well outside of the perimeter of the base.

When Tripp reached the vent he rolled down onto his side and pulled the knapsack off of his shoulder. After rummaging through it he came out with a black tube about as long as a ballpoint pen. He extended it out six more inches and bent the tip over at an angle before sliding the end through a slit in the grate.

"You should be in the ceiling area of some kind of medical facility," Morgan said as she trailed her finger across the schematic that she had lying in her lap.

Tripp placed his eye over the top of the instrument and peered through the lens there while slowly rotating the pintsized periscope. "So it would seem," Tripp said to her.

"Well?" Morgan asked.

"What do you want me to say? Number four on Franklin Mercer's top ten places where they would most likely be holding her looks like a bust." Tripp panned the periscope he held around some more. The lens eventually fell on a row of hospital beds that each contained human sized covered up lumps. "Hold it a sec. I got a few bodies on the beds in here."

"Well is either one of them Katelyn?"

"How should I know? They're all covered up. But it looks like they're alone in there. I'm going in to check it out. Cross your fingers."

Tripp retracted the periscope and replaced it in the knapsack. This time he pulled out a small socket wrench and used it to undo the bolts on the vent cover. After slowly removing the grate he lowered himself down onto the counter top below.

The room with its white walls and green floors smelled strongly of ammonia and other deodorizing and sanitizing agents. Once he was on the floor he hurried over to the first bed and pulled back the sheets covering the lump, revealing the practice mannequin that was resting beneath it. He checked the other two beds that gave on the appearance of being occupied and found that they were heavy with the same type of cargo.

There were voices in the hallway. Voices that were getting closer. They were soon accompanied by the sound of footsteps and Tripp quickly turned his eyes back to the hole in the ceiling that he had used to climb down into this room. Unless the chatting individuals who were moving through the hallway decided to pass this room up and continue on their way then there was no way that he would make it back up on the counter and through that vent before they stepped through the door and spotted him. Morgan's voice was loud in his ear.

"How are we doing, Tripp?"

"Tripp?"

Someone outside in the hallway twisted the doorknob.

"What's going on?" Zackery chimed in over the radio Morgan held.

"I don't know," she answered him. I can't get Tripp to answer his mic."

"What's wrong? Is he in trouble?"

"I'm not sure. I just told you he won't answer. Where are you?"

Zack had his back pressed hard against the wall of the air vent behind him. He pressed his feet up against the opposite wall with enough force to keep his body from slipping and falling straight down through the shaft that he was attempting to shimmy his way down. "Still heading down towards Maintenance as far as I know."

"Let me know when you touch down. I'm going to keep trying to raise Tripp."

The lab tech walked into the medical bay and went over to a set of cabinets on the wall leaving his colleague standing in the doorway. Pulling it open and removing a few small jars of pills, he found himself distracted by a noise emanating from the row of beds against the wall just off to his right. "Yeah, yeah. Hold your horses," he said to the mumbling guy still standing in the doorway awaiting his return. He turned his attention away from the three covered bodies and shut the cabinet door.

Walking back over towards the door, he was suddenly stopped by the twitch he felt creeping up his spine again and this time he walked over to the bed to the annoyed protests of his fellow technician. He jerked back the sheets and revealed the practice dummy that was lying on top of the mattress. The other two were uncovered and once the technician was satisfied with the results he moved back over to the door and silenced his partner before they both found their way back into the hallway.

Tripp lifted the sheet up and slid across the floor out from under the bed. "I'm right here," he spoke to the voice in his ear as he hurried back over to the counter below the exposed vent on the ceiling. "Don't worry about it. I'll tell you later." He climbed up on the counter and hopped up into the ventilation shaft. "Just get me out of here."

Zackery's feet touched down lightly on the floor of the vent beneath him as he gently lowered himself down out of the shaft he had just finished traversing. Upon landing he was immediately greeted by a multitude of voices that seemed to be coming from everywhere. "Alright, Morgan. What's it look like?"

Morgan unrolled a fresh set of schematics over the map she already had lying across her lap. She raised the radio up to her lips. "Look to your right. Is there a passageway leading away from you?"

Zackery took hold of his collar where he had the transmitter attached and tried to stretch the piece of fabric closer to his mouth. "I'm standing in a four way intersection," he told her.

"Okay. Then that most likely puts you somewhere over Diagnostics."

"Diagnostics? You said I was heading down to Maintenance."

"Will you give me a break," Morgan said into his ear, raising her voice a bit. "It's not like I built the place."

"Hang on," Zack said to her.

He started off down one of the corridors being guided by the many voices that he heard making his way up into the vents from the room beneath him. When he spied a vent covering in the floor down one of the adjacent pathways he made a beeline for it. Once there he lowered himself down and peered through the grate at the floor of the room beneath him. When he saw a white lab coat step across the area directly underneath the vent he tried to slide himself back out of sight. It was then that he noticed the body strapped down to a metal table a little further across the floor from where the man had just walked by.

Black pants.

Black shirt.

Raven hair.

"Morgan, get Tripp over here as quick as you can."

"Is this for a good cause or should I be worried?"

"I'm not sure. I'll tell you when he gets here."

Zackery explored every area of ventilation in the ceiling that he could get to without risking the possibility of drawing any attention to himself before finally making it back to the vent that gave him the most accessible view of the bound woman. "I know you can hear me," he spoke in a voice that knew couldn't be detected by the ears of the men occupying the room beneath him. "And I know you don't need me to tell you that things aren't looking particularly good for our situation here."

He stared down through the vent at her motionless body and breathed out a sigh. Zackery hoisted his body up and sat sideways in the shaft. "It also shouldn't come as any big surprise that I'm going to need your help if there's going to be any chance of us pulling this off. Actually...I was kind of counting on you to do most of the heavy lifting. Unfortunately that's going to require you getting up off of your ass and lending a hand in us busting you out of here. So if it wouldn't be too much of a bother to you..." Zackery tilted his head down over his right shoulder and took a look down through the vent. The body lying on the silver table continued to show no signs of life. "Come on, Katelyn," he said, his frustration apparent in his voice. "Time's running out here."

"Kaoss," a faint feminine voice uttered softly, the sound of which wafted up through the vent to find Zack's ears.

A pair of scientists in the room turned around to face the supine figure that was lying there with its eyes closed. "Pardon?" one of the men said to her. Katelyn didn't respond.

"It's probably nothing," his colleague answered him. "They must have did more damage to her than they thought. I'll have Jameson take a look at her when he gets back up here."

She'd told him that she needed to make this journey alone. A journey that would bring her back to the source of the tumultuous well from which she sprang. Where she would once and for all find the answers that she sought. Perhaps she'd been a little too successful in her venture.

Whatever the case, somewhere along her journey to find herself Katelyn had done just the opposite. The nature of Katelyn Bree had somehow gotten lost in the translation of the origins of the KAOSS unit of which she had recently acquired a deeper understanding of. And now he was losing her. Zackery was losing Katelyn to KAOSS; to Tobias McPhearson; to everything this base stood for.

"No," he said from the position where he was perched high above her. "Your name is Katelyn. Do you understand me? You're Katelyn Breanne Donavan. The most rudely annoying, anal retentive employee that the Wicker Basket has ever allowed through its front entrance. You're an awful houseguest, and an even worse hostess. Your wardrobe is atrociously dismal, and your bedside manner leaves entirely too much to be desired. It's just too bad for me that you also happen to be the most ridiculously amazing woman that I've ever had the misfortune of meeting. Guess that would explain what it is that I'm doing sitting in a ventilation shaft on a black ops military base in the middle of nowhere talking to the worlds most stubborn bookstore clerk."

"Katelyn's gone," the weary body uttered out to the ceiling. "I was never Katelyn. She was never me. And I could never be what she was." Katelyn had had the entire night to lie there on her makeshift bed and rationalize her situation to herself. It was all Col. Tobias McPhearson had left her with; time to come to terms with what it was that Thomas Donovan had helped the rest of the personnel working here to create; with what in fact she truly was.

The auxiliary counterpart to an orbiting satellite system capable of generating a wide range of seismic activity on the surface below.

Katelyn Donovan, the real Katelyn Donovan, had an existing birth certificate that was now accompanied by documentation marking the record of her passing. The only thing that she'd had to validate her existence was a serial number and a string of letters that spelled out her designation in this base' s stockpile of armaments.

"It was Thomas Donovan who stole you away from this place, named you after someone he cherished more than anything else, and sacrificed everything just to make sure that you didn't end up right back in the position that you currently find yourself in. Now I never met the man personally, or his lovely daughter for that matter, but I'm still inclined to see the tragedy in letting all that was sacrificed, both intentionally and not, on their behalf fall to the wayside because you happen to be struggling with an identity crisis. Now get up!" he ordered her gruffly. He looked down through the vent again and saw that Katelyn had yet to make a move. His state of uneasiness was moving well beyond the stage of frustration. He was advancing straight into outright anger. "Do you still need a reason, Kate? Is that it? Are you still looking for a reason why? Okay then. Do it for me. Do it because I asked you to."

"Why would you?" she said.

Zackery paused for a moment and dropped his chin down to the front of his chest. "Come on. You're going to make me say this right now?" Zackery heard a quiet rustling that was being carried through the shaft with the aid of the acoustics. He leaned his body to the side and stared down the tunnel intersection in front of him only to find Tripp positioning himself near the vent at the other end. "Tell you what, you get up from that table and help us get you out of here and we can work this whole thing out over a nice cup of coffee. That or two shots of bourbon. Your choice."

Katelyn lie there in place with her wrists and ankles still shackled contemplating the outright foolishness of the words that Zackery was relaying to her. He must have been out of his mind. What in the world could he possibly want from her in the arena that he was hinting towards? What did he possibly expect from her in return assuming that she was even capable of such a thing? Who in the world could have known? But there was something that she was aware of in lieu of her capabilities and in regards to the sentiment that he had brought up concerning Mr. Thomas Donovan and his initial intentions for her. He'd given his life trying to put an end to Project KAOSS and all of its promise. Perhaps this final gesture by her would be enough to see his intentions take shape as well as redeem herself in the eyes of her creator for the original aim of her existence.

"Get out of here, Zack," she said. "You have to get out of here now."

One of the scientists present walked over and stood beside her. "We might want to think about getting somebody from Maintenance up here stat."

"Alright," Zackery said. "That's it." He maneuvered up out of his sitting position and put his feet underneath him. "We're coming down there on three." Tripp swung his head in the direction of his friend and stared at him in amazement. "And you're either going to help us get you out of there..."

"What the hell are you doing?" Tripp said, his words low and harsh as he stared down the shaft in Zackery's direction.

"...or you're going to watch them take us out trying."

"You're bluffing! Tell me you're bluffing!"

"One..."

"Jesus, Zack! You think that maybe we should plan this thing out a little bit before we go all kamikaze?"

"Two..."

Tripp positioned himself upright over the vent beneath him. "Fine. Guess today's as good a day to die as any."

"Three!"

Zackery raised his right foot and stomped down hard on the vent cover, knocking it loose. He dropped down nearly twenty feet to the linoleum floor below, startling every lab coat in the room. He tossed the knapsack he held at the man standing next to Katelyn and he threw his arms up in the air in a panic to block it.

One of the doctors ran at Zack from his left side and he shoved an elbow into his gut before turning and smashing his fist against the side of his face. By that time Tripp was on his way down from the ceiling on the other side of the room. Zackery rushed over to the technician standing next to Katelyn who was trying to regain his footing. He blocked a punch the lab coat attempted to throw his way and countered with a right hand to his face that sent him down to the canvas.

Zackery turned around to see Tripp thrusting his knee up into the midsection of one of the scientists that he had gotten hold of. Once he had him doubled over he grabbed the back of his lab coat and shoved him head first into the computer equipment lining the wall nearest to him.

The rest of the rabble, the ones that were still standing, turned tail and went for the exits. Zackery turned to Katelyn who was still lying splayed out on the table before him. "What happened?" he yelled to her. "Why didn't you help us?"

Katelyn rotated her head in his direction. "Because I'm stuck to this thing, you idiot," she said as she made another effort to struggle against the restraints that held her in place. "I can't break through these braces. There's a remote over there next to that console," she told him, motioning toward her feet with her chin.

"Right."

Zackery walked over to the elongated desk covered with electronic equipment and picked up the small devise. After looking it over he pointed it at Katelyn and hit a button. The table she was on collapsed down into the form of a chair; the mechanisms that composed the machine folding and retracting until Katelyn found herself in a seated position. The restraints clasped around her ankles and wrists released their hold on her and she slowly rose up from the contraption.

"I hate to be a killjoy," Tripp said, "but I'm pretty sure that those guys who just beat it out of here are probably going to be back any minute with a ton of people who most likely aren't going to be very happy to find us here. Anybody else up for us getting the hell out of here?"

"You shouldn't have come here," Katelyn said to Zack.

"That's a pretty pointless discussion now, wouldn't you agree?" Zackery retorted.

One of the technicians that walked the floor of the large control room seven floors down from the Diagnostics lab tucked the clipboard that he held underneath his arm as he walked over to one of the many seismographs present there. It was the unusually odd jerking motion of the needle on the machine that had caught his interest and drew him nearer to the machine. After getting a better look at the reading it was displaying he let the clipboard that he held onto drop to the floor. He snatched up the paper feed spewing out of the machine and brought the sheet up closer to the glasses on his face. The eyes behind the set of eyewear were wide with complete shock.

"And when you're done with that get Lieutenant..." Tobias let his sentence trail off without giving any further thought to either the words he spoke or the person that he was relaying them to. His eyes were focused on the lightly trembling coffee cup that rested on the desktop that he stood next to. The fluid inside of it began to ripple with the gentle motion with which the black porcelain mug shook. Then came the barely audible rattling noise that accompanied the containers slow slide toward the edge of the desk that was mere centimeters away.

When it fell over the side and shattered across the tile floor, the steaming fluids and pointy shards spilling over the shine of his boots, Tobias turned his eyes up toward the ceiling. His jaws clenched together as tight as a vice and the bottom row of his teeth grinded against the ones above them. "Kaoss," he grunted.

He shoved the subordinate that he was previously speaking to out of his way as he rounded the corner of the desk. "Move," he blurted out. Tobias picked up the phone receiver and punched in a number. "What the hell is going on up there!?!" he said. "I already know that! Initiate the override sequence!" He listened into the phone for a few seconds, his lack of patience for the yammering person on the other end of the line apparent on his face. "What do you mean you're locked out? Shut her down! Shut her down now!" His patience had officially been expended to its last drop. The technician's voice could still be heard spouting excuses as Tobias pulled the receiver away from the side of his head. He slammed it down on the base hard enough to smash the communications devise apart before he stormed out of the office room, shoving bodies out of his way as he moved.

16

Morgan looked over out of the side of the open window on her right and stared at the cliffside. A small cluster of rocks began to tumble down the side and startled her. Morgan's first thought was that her position had been uncovered and she was being approached by soldiers coming to either take her into custody or shoo her away, but she saw nothing present in the vicinity that could have possibly disturbed the earth enough to create that phenomenon. The sound of a low rumbling forced her to turn her head in every direction in search of the source of the noise. She lifted her radio to her lips. "Hey, there's something going on out here. Whatever you guys are going to do, do you mind doing it fast and getting the hell out of there? I'm really not liking this."

"Katelyn, can you get us out of here?" Zackery turned to her and asked.

The noise being produced by a cadre of shuffling boots found its way into Katelyn's head through her ear canal. "There's a small squadron of eight men making their way up the eastern stairwell." Suddenly her ears abandoned the clamor emanating from the stairwell and began filtering through the multitude of noises originating from elsewhere on this level. There were panicked voices everywhere. Shoes pattering against linoleum. Deep, panicked breaths being taken in and out. Doors were being shoved open and rushed through. Equipment was being knocked over in the shuffle. Katelyn could hear it all and when enough concentration was applied she could hear nothing except what she wanted.

"There are six men coming down in the cargo elevator, and the fourteen men suiting up in the barracks around the corner down the hall have an ETA of approximately twenty three seconds. There will eventually be plenty more where they came from." The sound of an alarm began to blare in a pattern of one drawn out noise that was constantly stopping and repeating again. "That I'm sure of. I can get you to the service elevator. From there you can take the car up to the surface. After that you're on your own."

"What are you talking about?" Zackery said to her. "What do you mean, we're on our own?"

Tripp looked toward the ceiling for a source of where the blaring siren was coming from. "We don't have time for this," he said, dropping his eyes back down to the couple.

Katelyn stepped away from Zack and moved toward the pair of glass double doors leading out of the room. Zackery followed her and Tripp trailed after him. Katelyn came to a stop just before reaching the doors and watched the hallway outside fill up with black fatigue wearing armed troops. They came to a sudden halt and took on an assortment of defensive positions, training all of their weapons in Katelyn's direction.

"You'd better get down," she said over her shoulder.

Zackery and Tripp ducked off to her left out of the line of fire and Katelyn continued on toward the doors. When she got close enough to the doors they parted automatically and the sound of cocking mechanisms reverberated throughout the hall.

"Lie down on the floor and place your arms out beside you!"

Katelyn stepped across the threshold out into the hallway and watched every soldier in her line of sight tense up and retrain the sights of their weapons on her. Katelyn took another step and pushed herself up off of the floor and through the ceiling tiles above her head. The barrel of every semiautomatic rifle in the hallway tried following her ascent and once she was gone they remained locked on the hole that Katelyn had made in the ceiling.

There was an audible call for silence amongst the muttering troops and every helmet covered ear present attempted to train their focus in order to detect the slightest sound. The area above them crackled and crunched and the barrels of rifles everywhere darted back and forth in the hopes of zeroing in on the target's position as every individual waited for one of their brethren to let loose with a hailstorm of the electrically charged rounds that their weapons were loaded with. They'd been provoked. Now all they needed was a visual.

The ceiling came crashing down near the center of the entire assault team and Katelyn dropped down to the floor.

The sudden sound of automatic fire drew a wince out of Zackery's body as he remained hidden behind the concrete wall next to the door. He made a move to go investigate and felt Tripp's fist grip hold of the fabric that was the front of his shirt. It prevented him from darting out through the doorway in the hopes of assessing Katelyn's status and possibly lending her a hand if need be.

"Are you crazy?" Tripp said to him.

Zackery shook loose his hold on him and turned to make another go at the door. He barely got the sole of his shoe back down on the floor after taking a single step before the body that came smashing through one of the panels of the glass doors, covering the both of them with a shower of glass shards, forced him back behind the wall again.

The firing stopped and Zack hurried around to what was left of the door. He looked out into the hallway and saw Katelyn standing over a mass of downed black uniforms. She held the flaccid form of one of the soldiers by the front of his uniform, her body turned sideways in the hallway with her right hand hanging down in front of her, the fingers of which were curled up around the material that covered his chest.

Katelyn turned her body towards Zack and swung her arm forward, tossing the unconscious man across the floor in his direction. Zackery just stood there watching as the body came sliding his way. When it stopped he raised his eyes to Katelyn.

"The uniform," she said to him.

Zackery and Tripp donned the fatigues and even went so far as to arm themselves each with one of the discarded rifles that were strewn about the floor everywhere. The three of them moved through the corridors to the sound of the earsplitting noise of the siren that continued to sound coupled with the ruckus being kept up by the fleeing personnel that fled out from every doorway that lined their path.

A soldier stepped out from around the corner in front of them and Katelyn instantly sprang into action. She was close enough to him to grab hold of the rifle in his possession and use it as leverage as she bent his arm up and rotated the barrel of the weapon down over his shoulder, training the sights at the area at his back. Two more armed men appeared from around the corner and Katelyn, still holding her initial quarry in place despite his protest, reached her right up and took hold of the trigger guard that the soldier still held on to. She placed her thumb on top of his trigger finger and squeezed off a succession of shots that sent his two compatriots into convulsions upon the rounds' impact. After they dropped to the ground Katelyn let go of the weapon and slammed her elbow into the back of the neck of the man she'd had a hold of.

His blackout set in rather quickly and Katelyn was already on her way down the hall when his body finally collapsed to the ground. Tripp and Zack stayed on her heels until she reached the service elevator. Zackery hit the button repeatedly. Nothing.

"Damn it!" he exclaimed.

"Don't bother," Katelyn told him. "They shut it down. We're going to have to take the stairs."

"As long as they go all the way up it's fine with me," Tripp replied.

Katelyn pushed open the doorway and the three of them all spilled out into the stairwell. She lead the pack as they started up. They didn't make it up three flights before the sight of the armed faction moving down the stairs a few floors above their heads stopped them in their tracks. Looking down they saw a significantly larger cadre of troops making their way up.

"Come on! This way!" Katelyn ushered them through the nearest door that took them out of the stairwell. "There's another way up just at the end of this corridor," she explained to them as she rounded the corner.

Zackery was busy examining the walls and ceiling of the concrete hallway that they moved through. There was a rumbling that continued to grow louder with every second and the floor, walls, and everything else around them began to shake and shift with the vibrations that appeared to accompany the noise. "What is that?" Zackery asked, making the corner behind Katelyn.

She'd stopped walking and caused Zackery to collide with her back. "Tobias," she said as Zackery regained his composure.

The three of them stood there looking at the dark figure that blocked their path at the other end of the corridor.

"Kaoss," the Colonel uttered at the sight of her. He lifted the weapon he had and pointed it down the hall at them. The instrument he held took on the distinctive impression of a very large machine gun rifle except for the fact that there was a small rocket projectile sticking out of the barrel of the weapon.

Katelyn broke out into a full on sprint down the corridor extending to her left. Tobias kept the sights locked in on her as he stared through the multitude of green tinted panes of glass mounted on the walls and throughout the offices that separated him and Katelyn. He flexed his right index finger and sent the miniature missile firing out of the barrel of the gun he held.

The angle of trajectory that the projectile moved along sent it crashing through every glass barrier in its path as it continued on a collision course to catch up with Katelyn.

She dove for the door in front of her just as the rocket shattered its way through the window just off to her right. When it hit the concrete wall on the opposite side an explosion was produced that reduced every last standing pane of glass to jagged pebbles. The blast even managed to knock Zackery and Tripp off of their feet.

When the debris began to settle Tobias started to make his way down the hallway in Zack and Tripp's direction. "You two," he called out to them. "Rendezvous with Alpha team on the north twenty and order them to ready the motorcade. Hurry! Go now!"

The two of them just looked at him in a complete state of trauma as Tobias rounded the corner and headed off toward the wreckage that had consumed Katelyn. It must have been the appearance of the uniforms that had thrown him. When he noticed their lack of any immediate motion at his command Tobias turned around to see what exactly the holdup was.

"Ye...yes, sir," Tripp spouted as he stumbled to his feet, helping Zack up to his. "Come on," he said to his friend as he escorted him down the corridor. Tobias turned and continued on his way.

"Katelyn," Zackery said as he composed himself enough to walk on his own.

He tried to turn and head back but Tripp stopped him. "Will you get serious," he said to him very brashly above the noise of the rumbling structure that filled the hallway with a dull roar. "Have a look around! This whole place is coming down! Now we have to get out of here! Katelyn can take care of herself!" With another tug on his arm Tripp had Zackery moving again and they headed for the door that Tobias must have used to gain access to this level.

Zackery tried the handle.

Locked.

"Now what?"

Tripp unslung the knapsack that he continued to tag along with him. "Never fear." He removed a small black box with a flat credit card sized object attached to it by a series of covered wires. He slid the card through the slot on the security console next to the door. Instead of pulling the card all the way through, he held it in place in the slot while staring at the small rectangular display screen on the box. A ten digit string of numbers counted down to nothing and Tripp slid the card the rest of the way through the slot. A buzzer sounded and the locking mechanism holding the door shut detached. Tripp pulled on the handle. The door came open and he reached down to collect the satchel. "Remind me to pick up Mr. Carthright a nice fruit basket when we get back home."

The two of them moved on through the doorway and as they headed up the staircase toward what they hoped was safety but seriously doubted that fact, Zackery couldn't help but turn all his thoughts back to Katelyn.

Tobias moved carefully through the smoke filled corridor, stepping over the scattered debris of glass and rock that covered the floor. He strained his eyes to see through the soot laced atmosphere as he searched tirelessly for any remains of Katelyn's body. "Kaoss!" he called out to her as he walked. "I see that we've been getting to know ourselves a bit more intimately in these past few hours. Now why don't you be a dear and shut your little toy off before someone gets hurt. Agreed?"

Tobias continued on through what was left of the doorway that he had last seen Katelyn heading for. The door lay crumpled up and mangled on the floor at his feet. Shoving a few clumps of rock out of his footpath with a single swipe of his foot, Tobias discharge his rifle at a noise that he heard emanating from across the room.

The rounds he fired definitely weren't the electrical charges that had been previously issued to those men who were in pursuit of her. These were the real deal, indicating that he had no intention whatsoever of taking her back in one piece.

He continued to drag his eyes from right to left as he peered through the thin fog that filled the room. "Come on out, Kaoss! After spending the last half decade hunting down your sorry micro technological ass you wouldn't believe how not in the mood I am for a game of hide and seek with you." Tobias let loose another flurry of rounds, sending them flying out at nothing in particular. "Do you hear me!?!" he cried out.

Katelyn tried to remain as still as possible. With the structure of the building now in a constant state of trembling unrest such a feat was that much more difficult to accomplish. She could hear Tobias' footsteps and the slight gasping noises that he made that either arose from his struggle to fill his lungs with fresh air despite the ash and cinder floating everywhere, or the sheer rage that he was engulfed in as he continued his search for her.

Katelyn tilted her head back and looked up. With her feet interlocked against one another and a metal bar hugged between her ankles, for Katelyn, looking up gave her a view of the area of the floor beneath her. Though the haze of dust and smoke in the room had yet to settle completely, Katelyn found that she not only had a clear view of Col. Tobias McPhearson as he slowly moved across the floor beneath her, that view came in a variety of spectrums. All it took was a small amount of concentration on her part and there he was. Clear as all get out. The infrared vision of his body heat glowed in a small array of bright reds, oranges, and yellows. An x-ray scan of the area showed her the image of a skeleton covered in a transparent uniform carrying a very large firearm moving around the toppled over desks and mechanical equipment in the room. Katelyn shut her eyes to try and make it all stop.

"What am I talking about?" Tobias said as he went on with his search, trying to maintain his balance as the ground shook violently beneath his feet for a moment. "Of course you can hear me. You can probably hear every square inch of damage that you're doing all over this facility. You can hear everything, can't you? And do you know why?" He made a slow three hundred and sixty degree turn as he walked. "Because that's the way they made you. Mr. Thomas Donovan and the rest of those techno freaks. A waste of time if you ask me."

Tobias craned his neck from side to side. From what he remembered, this room, the main irrigation and waterworks core, had only one exit and it was at his back. She could have very possibly slipped by him and made it out of there by now but he wasn't leaving this room until he knew for sure. Not even with the entire facility falling to pieces all around him.

"Do you want to know why that is?" He fired off a few more rounds at a moving shadow in one of the corners. "It's because you've got no heart. Sure, you've got that thing pounding away in your chest behind that breastplate of yours. But you're no soldier. Not by a long shot. No. Just a bunch of wires twisted together. A fancy light show. Lots of neat bells and whistles slammed together to impress a few top end investors. In the end, there's just no drive. No desire. There's no fight in you, Kaoss. So just come on out and I promise I'll make this quick."

Katelyn listened to the sound of destruction engulfing the many floors between her body and the surface and wondered just how right Tobias was. After all, he was a soldier and thus had a better inkling of what it took to forge such a thing than she had. Possibly even more knowledge of it than the man who had provided the greatest source of inspiration behind her.

Tobias was a soldier. She was, by all accounts, merely an arsenal by which soldiers resolved the conflicts they engaged in, and thus the only drive she possessed belonged to that of the hand that wielded her. It was an existence that she longed to put an end to, for the good of so many and possibly the dismay of others. Her life was in her own hands now and such an end was what she had desired for herself. It was what she wanted. It's what Thomas Donovan would have wanted. Wasn't it? She'd been created for destruction even though he'd crafted her in the image of his own daughter. A daughter that he had been prematurely deprived of, an act that had afforded him with the loss of something that he had once held so dear in his heart.

His heart.

Katelyn.

That's what she was to him. Not a soldier. Not a weapon. She was Katelyn Donovan. Katelyn Bree. His heart. Surly he would not have wished such a fate revisited on him once more. Perhaps that was why he'd chosen to keep her preserved rather than put an end to this project's promise when he'd had the chance. Either way, the task, as well as her fate, rested in her hands now.

17

Morgan removed the maps and schematics from her lap and placed them down in the passenger seat. The cliffs all around her were crumbling to pieces. The ground beneath the four tires of the jeep she was in shuddered and shook with an ever increasing fury. She started the engine and put the jeep into gear. As if driving across the rocky floor of the desert wasn't enough of a distraction for her, the constant jostling of her body in the seat brought on by the shaking earth made steering the vehicle nearly impossible.

Morgan rounded the corner and the military facility that housed all of her friends came into sight. The place was in a complete state of upheaval. People were fleeing everywhere and in all directions; on foot, in trucks, by helicopter. A few fires had broken out and it wasn't long before Morgan witnessed an explosion. Buildings everywhere shuddered and shed pieces at a time. The ridges and cliffs all around the base rained down the masses shaken loose from them onto the base perimeter in increasingly larger clumps.

Morgan fumbled around in the seat next to her with one hand until she came up with the radio. "Where are you guys? We have to get out of here now!"

Tripp ran down the corridor toward the single set of double doors he saw at the other end with Zackery right by his side. The two of them moved as fast as they could while trying to continue to avoid the ceiling tiles, light fixtures, and other objects that continued to drop down on them. "I have no idea," he yelled out. Lowering his shoulder, he rammed his way through the doors and made his way outside into the mayhem that had been brewing on the surface. Looking past the multitude of bodies that swarmed in front of his face he managed to make out a small gathering of helicopters not too far off in the distance. "North side. Lots of choppers. You think you can find a way to get in here and pick us up?"

"I'm already on my way," Morgan said.

Katelyn released the grip that her ankles had on the bar high above the floor. As her body dropped Tobias quickly spun around and caught sight of her. She brought he legs down beneath the rest of her body and Tobias was leveling off his rifle just as her feet were touching down. Katelyn lunged at him. He squeezed the trigger. Katelyn got hold of the smoking barrel and redirected it before any of the rounds being spat out of it were able to come into contact with any part of her body. With one hard jerk Katelyn removed the weapon from his clasp and tossed it behind her.

Tobias swung a punch at her and Katelyn grabbed his wrist, blocking it. Still holding onto his arm, she quickly threw her other hand forward and wrapped her fingers around his throat. She applied pressure to his windpipe while slowly lowering his body toward the ground.

"What are you going to do, Kaoss?" he said to her, his voice crackling and gurgling as he tried summoning enough oxygen to form his words. "Kill me?"

Katelyn applied more pressure to his throat. She squeezed until his air supply had been cut off completely. Then... She relaxed her fingers. Her hand was still gripped around his neck as Tobias coughed out and choked back wind. "My name's Katelyn," she said to him.

"Well, Katelyn," Tobias uttered with the use of his now more oxygen enriched lungs. "Then allow me to extend you the pleasure of witnessing your own termination in the face of the ineptitude that must have also been present during the time of your conception."

Tobias pulled his free hand out from behind his back and Katelyn dropped her eyes down to the grenade that he clutched in his palm. Tobias lifted his thumb and the spoon went flying. Her foot came off the ground and slammed against his hand, knocking the explosive devise from his grip and sending it across the room behind him.

It landed near the base of a large tank embedded in the wall and when it exploded a tidal wave of water was released from the container and began flooding the floor. Water poured into the room from valves that began exploding loose everywhere. The pipes running across the ceiling began to burst as well as the ones just behind the walls. Before they knew it both Katelyn and Tobias were submerged in waste deep water that began to rise at an exponential rate. It wasn't long before their feet were kicking back and forth in search of the floor that was quickly distancing itself from the soles of their footwear.

The ceiling was closing in fast. Katelyn did what she could to dodge the floating debris that was moving through the water everywhere. She backhanded a desk out of her way and caught sight of Tobias struggling to stay afloat not too far away from her. Katelyn turned her head around. The exit from this room was at her back approximately thirty five feet below the rising water. There was nearly five feet of breathable air between the water and the top of the room. Katelyn filled her lungs to capacity and dropped down beneath the surface of the water.

Tobias maneuvered his way around the pipes and beams in the upper area of the room. He could make a try for the door. There was a very good chance that he could make that distance even with the harsh currents moving all around him, but the hallway outside was surely flooded by now. That explosion had ruptured the core of the entire reservoir supplying this area of the base with its water supply.

With this entire floor going under and quite possibly many more on their way, there was little chance that he would escape this scenario with his life. His biggest regret aside from the inevitable loss of his own mortality was that it would come in lieu of his failure to dispatch the KAOSS unit once and for all. Perhaps his ultimate demise would hasten his release from the indignity of such a thing.

The water level reached the apex of the room and his head was forced under. Something took hold of him by the front of his shirt and suddenly he was being pulled down through the aquatic disaster area at an unusually rapid velocity. Reaching his hand up to the front of his chest, he felt her fist gripped around the fabric of his shirt.

She dove under, went around, and dodged the moving obstructions that cluttered the hallway between her and the door to the stairwell that she headed for.

Katelyn found the door she had searched so diligently for in the underwater maze. It had been obstructed by the displaced office furniture and the caved in ceiling above it. Making it to the elevator was her only option now, but Tobias undoubtedly lacked the oxygen supply that would be needed to see him through to the end of such a goal.

Katelyn rolled her body over and pulled the masculine figure that she kept in tow into hers. She smashed their lips together and expelled a large portion of the oxygen that she held trapped in her body into his. She certainly didn't need it. Katelyn couldn't imagine how upsetting this must have been for the Colonel, being sustained in such a manner. Unfortunately neither one of them had a choice in the matter; not if he was to survive.

Katelyn broke her lips away from his and took hold of the front of his shirt again. She drug him back through the sunken obstacle course until she found a pair of elevator doors. Letting go of Tobias, she focused all of her energy on prying the door apart. After they came open Tobias followed her into the shaft and started his ascent. Katelyn had already taken off ahead of him, offering no further aid as he found his way up the water filled channel until his head finally breached the water level's pinnacle.

Tobias sucked in a deep gasp of air. Shaking the water from his night black hair, he immediately began eyeing his surroundings and attempting to assess the situation that he now found himself in. The elevator car was submerged somewhere in the depths beneath them and six stories worth of the shaft still hovered above their heads. "Nowhere to go but up," he said. The two of them stared at each other as they treaded water in the cramped space. "Long as you know, if we both make it out of here, I feel obligated to tell you that nothing's going to change between us. I will find you, Kaoss. And when I do I'm bringing you right back where you belong." Katelyn did nothing but stare at him as the small crests of water continued to splash against their faces, forcing Tobias to spit his breathless words through the splashing water. "I'll tell you what. Seeing as how you're responsible for extending my life thus far, you're free to consider the time you have now a head start."

Katelyn took hold of the elevator cable and began pulling herself up, not uttering a single word to him as she went about her expedient ascent.

Morgan aimed the front end of the jeep she drove toward the lowered post that barred entrance through the perimeter gate past the checkpoint booth set up there. With the huge score of traffic pouring out through that particular port one would have thought that the guard who continued to try and maintain a futile sense of order over the commotion running rampant in the area wouldn't have had neither the time nor the inclination to bother with the only vehicle that happened to be headed into the base instead of seeking shelter far from this disaster zone. Still, Morgan found herself facing off against an armed guard who found it necessary to place his body between her jeep and the barricade barring her entrance.

She stepped on the gas. When the guard raised his rifle Morgan crouched down in the seat and pressed down on the pedal harder. Her nemesis eventually abandoned his post without firing a shot. Morgan crashed through the lowered beam and continued on into the wreckage that was being made of the base.

The explosion that sounded not too far away knocked Tripp off of his feet. While lying down on the trembling concrete he watched, his wide eyes filled with fear, as a nearby building buckled and came crashing down to the ground. The dust cloud that was swept up began to spread far beyond the area of the building's foundation. Zackery helped Tripp back up to his feet. "How in the hell did you talk me into this, Zack?"

"Never mind that. Come on. I think I see our ride."

Morgan swerved around the fleeing pedestrians and flaming debris as she headed towards what was left of a helicopter landing pad. When she spotted two men dressed in black fatigues attempting to flag her down she had been tempted to simply avoid them and continue her sweep of the area for any visible sign of Zackery and Tripp. It wasn't until she got close enough to the two figures and got a good look at their soot covered faces that she realized who exactly it was attempting to grab her attention.

Morgan stopped the jeep and stared at the two of them with an unbelievable look of surprise and confusion on her face. "Ask questions later," Tripp said as he climbed up into the passenger seat. He turned his head and saw that Zack was hesitant in getting up into the vehicle. "Hey, what's the hold up, friend?" Tripp called out over the roaring chaos that ensued. "We stay here any longer and they'll be marking our gravesites here. Now let's go."

"I can't," Zackery replied. "I can't leave here without her."

"How do you know she hasn't made it out of here already?" Tripp said to him. "Come on. You've seen the girl in action." He watched the ambivalence take hold of his friend's demeanor. "Only way you're going to find out is if you make it out of here in one piece."

Tripp extended his hand out over the top of the door. Zack did a quick left and right with his head as he tried to get one more look at the demolished landscape in the hopes of catching a glimpse of her. Nothing. Perhaps Tripp was right. He'd seen her resilience first hand and was well aware of the boundaries that it was capable of transpiring. But when he'd last seen Katelyn he got the distinct feeling that that factor alone wouldn't be the deciding factor in whether or not she made it out of here alive.

Morgan cranked the gearshift into first and pulled off as fast as she could while still remaining able to exude some control over the vehicle. She didn't have a chance to make much progress in solidifying their escape when Zackery stood up from where he had been previously seated in the backseat and demanded that she stop. The tires left black streaks across the pavement as Morgan stomped her foot down on the brake.

Zackery stared at her in disbelief as Katelyn emerged from the shadowy depths of the building. She stopped walking the moment that she spotted them and soon started up again in their direction. Her walking motion soon sped up into a gentle jog. When Katelyn reached the jeep she hopped in over the side and sat down in the seat behind Tripp, her eyes locked on Zackery the entire time. Neither of them said a word to each other as Morgan lifted her foot off of the brake and reapplied pressure to the gas pedal.

The ground beneath the tires of the vehicle shook less with each mile that Morgan put between them and the military base. By the time they hit the highway and began to make some serious time the tremors could barely be felt at all. Katelyn had yet to put a stop to the activity that the orbiting satellite, for which she had an uplink to, was inflicting on the desert base. She wanted to make sure that the personnel charged with manning that station would be displaced for quite some time. She had no idea how long it would take for them to regroup, or how long it would take for them to come after her again once they had done so. Tobias had promised her that that would surely be the case. Katelyn didn't even know if he had survived the whole ordeal or not. For the most part she didn't care.

Katelyn was free of the hold that Colonel Tobias McPhearson and the other technicians in charge of researching the KAOSS project had on her. In the physical sense anyway, and if she had her way it was going to stay that way for a long time.

Oddly enough she had Tobias to thank for it all. If it wasn't for him she would have never had the opportunity to gain the perspective that allowed her to recreate a second escape from those that would have her bound and subjected to their will. Tobias McPhearson had scolded her for lacking the true capacity for what it took to be a real soldier; all the while mocking the very nature of her creation. Thomas Donovan had in fact aided and abetted in the creation of a piece of military hardware, but that wasn't what he had stolen from them so many years ago.

Thomas Donovan may have created a mock soldier for his superiors, but it was the purity of the memories of his daughter, the heart and soul that he had put into his work that he had once liberated from that facility. Katelyn had been obliged to follow in his footsteps. It's what he would have wanted.

But according to Tobias their actions were all in vain because despite all of Thomas Donovan's hard work she had no heart, or soul for that matter, to speak of. Thomas Donovan's daughter was gone. The weapon that he had been commission to create was indeed just that and would never be anything more.

Maybe he was right. Who was to say? Katelyn was so twisted up inside that she didn't really know what to believe anymore. But she did save Tobias' life when she could have rightly left him to his fate. Perhaps that said something about her as well. In either event, maybe it would be left up to time to decide the true nature of her purpose. Meanwhile she would do what she could to make an attempt at realizing Thomas Donovan's vision for her potential, all the while making a go at denying those of Col. Tobias McPhearson.

The journey to find out exactly where the line between the humanity instilled in her and the protocol of her inherent programming would begin here. She would use the heart that her creator...her father had forged for her to seek out the nature of that which he sought so desperately to preserve.

For that task Katelyn would require a significant amount of help.

Her hand was resting on the seat cushion beside her. Suddenly she felt the warmth of Zackery's palm cover the back of her knuckles. Her first instinct was to pull away but after turning her head and taking a look at his profile as he continued to stare forward, Katelyn decided against it. Turning her eyes back to the front, she even took the liberty to stroke his fingers with her thumb a time or two.

The sun was beginning to set when Morgan pulled the jeep off of the main road. The quartet had taken up lodging in a motel nestled against the outskirts of a small wooded area and were planning on staying for the duration of the night. Zackery was on his way back to his room after stepping out for a moment to hit up the soda machine when he found Katelyn standing against the wall next to his door. Zackery stopped walking and they stood there for a moment in silence just looking at each other.

"Some day, huh?" Zack said, breaking the silence.

"Some life," Katelyn replied.

"Don't worry. We'll have you back at the Wicker Basket before you know it. Guess you'll be needing a place to stay for a while. You can always crash with me. You know... Just until you get back on your feet."

"Don't push it," Katelyn said to him. Zackery hunched his shoulders and sighed quietly. "I am inclined to take you up on that offer to dinner though."

"Public forum rule still apply?"

Katelyn produced a slight smile. "Up to you."

Zackery stepped around her and opened the door to his room. "Come on in. I'll order a pizza."

SoulSeeker: Rise to Chaos

About the Author

So here we are again. All back of the book and whatnot. The part where I'm supposed to make an attempt at trying to offer you something in the way of a slight glimpse into the twisted batch of firing neurons that pieced together the words on the pages you've just finished flipping through. You did remember to actually read the book, didn't you? Or did you just skip ahead to this page hoping to find Graves of the same ole sorts?

If so, color him both flattered and disappointed. If not, feel free to draw him in whatever shade of gray you find fit to color such a literary gallivant. I doubt he'd mind much either way. Most likely he's busy crafting his next piece of soon to be defunct artistry. Graves. Man. Myth. Purveyor of miraculous farcicality.

In any event, if you haven't already read the book feel free to do so now. I'm sure this page will be here when you return. If it's gone don't panic. It's all just part of the show.

Thank you.

Printed in the United States
67674LVS00004B/76-90